Flying *Too* High

Iain Cameron

Copyright © 2024 Iain Cameron
ISBN: 9798880253005

The right of Iain Cameron to be identified as the author of this work has been asserted by him in accordance with the Copyright, Designs and Patents Act 1988.

All rights reserved. No part of this publication may be reproduced, stored in a retrieval system, or transmitted, in any form or by any means, electronic, mechanical, photocopying, recording or otherwise, without the prior permission in writing of the copyright owner.

All characters and events in this publication, other than those clearly in the public domain, are fictitious and any resemblance to real persons, living or dead is purely coincidental.

All rights reserved.

To find out more about the author, visit the website: www.iain-cameron.com

DEDICATION

For my proofreader, accountant, tax advisor, mother of my children and arbiter of good taste; this one is for you.

ONE

He rolled his large fleshy body off the lithe figure of Claudette and lay on his back panting. A few minutes later, Roger Maitland reached over to the bedside table, picked up a pack of cigarettes and sparked one. Nothing could beat the first one in the morning, or the one straight after sex with a good-looking woman.

'Aren't you going to give me one?'
'I thought I did that already.'
'You're so funny.'
'Fill your boots.'

She leaned over to grab the pack, her large, pneumatic breasts pushing into his chest and chin, but he'd had enough of them for the moment. She lay back for a minute or two taking a couple of deep draws, while tapping something on her phone. Presumably ordering her transport home.

Shutting off the phone's screen, she got out of bed and started to dress. If there was business to be had, Claudette didn't want to miss it. He looked at his watch: one thirty in the morning. He didn't imagine much would be doing in Brighton at this early hour, but he was a businessman and she was a tart; what did he know?

Claudette went to the dresser and scooped up the pile of twenties left for her in a deft, practiced movement.

'See you next time, handsome,' she said.

'Count on it.'

She bent over the bed and kissed him.

'I'll let myself out.'

He listened to the *clump-clump* of heels as she went down the wooden staircase, a key feature of the house when first stepping into the hallway. The other day he'd spotted little indentations in the steps. Perhaps when they got together next time, he would give her arse a good hard spanking, or force her to play the sex game she hated. The door slammed shut, increasing his annoyance.

He lived in a house in North Chailey with a long driveway behind metal gates and set in five acres. When he first bought the house, it had been neglected for decades, so it had been gutted and modernised at great expense. The front door moved on well-oiled hinges, allowing it to close with the merest of touches. Hadn't he told her about it before? He would have to spank her harder for that.

He doused the cigarette and stared at the ceiling, bathed only in the light from the moon through the open blinds. This was when he did his best thinking, after sex with Claudette, or Marcella, or Gabrielle, although he couldn't say this to any of the directors at his company, Vixen Aviation. They were more strait-laced than he, and no doubt would think less of him if they found out where he got his inspiration.

The company was on the brink of greatness. Their latest drone, Avalon, had impressed the Ministry of Defence team the previous week at yet another demonstration. He didn't believe in wasting taxpayers' money, so why did they need to see the machine in action so many times before making a decision?

His man at the Ministry of Defence (MOD) had assured him not only was a verdict imminent, a large order would be on its way very soon. His heart had swelled at the news. A large order from the UK military was excellent in itself, but where it would lead was what really interested him. With MOD reassurance behind it, the European Union countries would soon follow suit, and before long Vixen would have the big one in their sights: a contract with the US military.

His main goal was to expand the company in the US. In time, he believed it would become bigger than the European operation, allowing him to relocate there. His daughter lived in Boston, and unlike her mother, a person he never wanted to see again, he missed her. He also hoped another important prize would be forthcoming. A CBE was all very well, but how he coveted the top one: a knighthood.

He must have dozed off, as the next time he looked at the clock it was 2:15. He was bursting for a pee. He'd been out on a date in Brighton with a girl he met on a dating site, and they had drunk way too much. At the end of the evening she went off in search of her bed, which was disappointing, but Claudette would always respond to his call.

He pulled on a pair of shorts. He never wore more than this to bed as the sophisticated heating system was designed to keep the house at a steady temperature no matter the weather outside.

He headed into the bathroom, but didn't switch on the main light. He was a bad sleeper, had been since his teenage years, and read just about every book on the subject. A bright light would increase his serotonin levels and ruin any chance of sleeping tonight. In any case, his electric toothbrush was on charge, plugged into the socket behind him. It emitted a pulse of LED light every couple of seconds, enough for him to find the toilet bowl without making an unsightly mess on the floor or down his leg.

The pee was a long one and while standing and waiting to finish he realised how tired he felt; it almost had him sleeping on the job. At last, he was done. He pulled up his shorts and pressed the flush button. Then turned.

In the pulsing light, he saw a figure enter the bathroom. It wasn't Claudette, she was smaller and thinner. The light pulsed again and he spotted something shiny in the black-clad figure's hand. Before he could react, it shot towards his bare stomach.

He moved his hands to protect himself, but felt the knife go in once, twice, three times. He dropped to his knees. Seconds later, he fell face-first on the cool tiles of the bathroom floor.

TWO

The gentle sway of the yacht changed as it rocked from side to side. It woke a dozing Angus Henderson and it took some seconds before he realised what had caused it: a speedboat passing close by. He lay still for a few minutes, enjoying the soporific effect of the waves lapping against the hull, and thought nothing could touch it for giving him a good night's sleep.

It helped having Kelly beside him, her eyes closed and her chest moving with monotonous regularity. They hadn't gone far, only along the south coast to Selsey. He couldn't go any further on account of being on-call. He got up and wandered into the 'head', one of the nautical terms he'd been teaching Kelly.

A half hour later, he served breakfast inside the cabin of *Mingary*, Henderson's thirty-one-foot Moody yacht. With warmer weather, they would have moved to the rear deck with their plates on their knees and enjoyed the view. However, at this early hour on a May morning, the thermometer barely reached ten degrees.

'I could get used to this, it looks delicious,' Kelly said, admiring Henderson's version of a full English.

'If something can be made more or less in one pan, it can be cooked on a small boat like this.'

'In the *galley*.'

'Good, you're getting it.'

'There's only another four hundred years of sailing terminology to catch up on. I might get the hang of it by the time I'm eighty or ninety.'

'How would you rate your first sleepover on a boat?'

'I didn't notice. I only had eyes for you, my handsome captain.'

'There's a seafarer's tale if ever I've heard one.'

'Delightful, if you must know. I thought seasickness would be a problem, as it had been the last time I was on a boat, but no, it felt great. I mean, the weather yesterday was calm with a blue sky, what's not to like?'

'The forecast is for a little more breeze today, which is good as we need help getting back to Brighton.'

They finished breakfast and tidied up. It was an essential job, not only in case they hit bad weather, when loose plates and cups would become an injury hazard, but also because it was a small boat. It was easier moving around and doing jobs when everything was back in its proper place.

With the domestic duties out of the way, they set sail for home. Henderson needed to get back but not desperately; if anything kicked off, he could pull into a number of ports along the way and have one of his team pick him up. Kelly needed to return as well. She was a guest speaker at an Offender Symposium in Chicago in a couple of weeks, and she wanted to do some research away from her day job at Sussex University, where she taught Criminal Psychology.

When clear of the port and out on the open sea, he switched off the engine and unfurled the main sail. Soon, *Mingary* picked up speed as the big sail filled with wind, forcing the yacht over to one side. He called Kelly over and asked her to take over the helm as he wanted to make coffee.

'Aim the bow at that large white building with all the balconies, do you see it?'

'Yes. What is it?'

'One of the big apartment blocks along Brighton seafront.'

'Why are we heading towards it?'

He gave her a quizzical look. 'Where did we depart from, and where my car is parked?'

'Brighton Marina.'

'So, where are we headed?'

'Back to Brighton Marina, but–'

'Aim for the apartment block for now. When we're a bit closer, we'll change and head towards the marina. Unlike a car, everything happens at a much slower pace on a boat.'

'So I'm starting to appreciate.'

'How does it feel to have the lives of two people in the palm of your hand?'

'Am I the captain now?'

'Why?'

'I want to order you about, as you did to me on the way out.'

'Whatever floats your boat, but no, you're only the helmsman. A hired hand, no less.'

'Trust you to spoil the illusion.'

They entered the inner sanctum of Brighton Marina around lunchtime. He and Kelly were discussing where they would eat lunch when his phone rang.

'DI Angus Henderson.'

'Good afternoon, Inspector. This is Lewes Control. We've received reports of a fatal stabbing at a house in North Chailey. Can you attend?'

'I can. Let me have the details.'

Henderson repeated the instructions out loud for Kelly to jot down. He could steer the boat into the marina, akin to a city centre car park, and talk on the phone, but doing a third activity at the same time? No chance.

He finished the call and manoeuvred *Mingary* towards the berth he had vacated the day before. He imagined the cool weather had discouraged many owners from taking their boats out.

'I guess it puts lunch on the back burner, Kelly. I'm sorry.'

'Some other time. I do understand. The big question I'd like answered now is, as we both came down here in your car, how do I get home?'

THREE

Henderson drove through the open gates of Oakwood House and parked. The house looked large, not sprawling with many outhouses and extensions, but self-contained and imposing. The parking area was equally large, with not only an open area where a couple of pool cars, the pathologist's car, and a SOCO van were parked, but also with a timber garage containing what he assumed was the victim's car, a red Bentley convertible.

Climbing out of the car, he saw what looked like a large grassy expanse at the back of the house, bordered by trees on three sides, making the property more or less private. This meant whoever killed the house's occupant could stake out the house without being disturbed and had a means of escape no one would see.

He checked in with the cop manning the clipboard in the hall. While donning an over-suit and boots, he flicked through the letters lying on the hall table. They were addressed to Roger Maitland CBE. He repeated the name in his head. It rang a small bell, but he couldn't place him.

Following the copper's directions, he headed upstairs. It looked like a conventional house from the outside: red tiled roof, leaded windows, and a beautiful oak door, but inside, as modern as anything displayed in the Sunday colour supplements. Even the wooden staircase made a statement. It didn't just convey him to the upper floor, it swept him round and upwards, making him feel he was about to enter something elegant like an art gallery or a major fashion house. An art gallery wasn't a bad metaphor as paintings lined the walls. Most of it was modern art, plenty of curly squiggles and distorted faces in various shades. They weren't to the DI's taste, but somehow they added to the house's ambience.

'Afternoon, gov,' Detective Sergeant Carol Walters said, walking towards him. 'How was your trip?'

'Lucky we were almost berthed when the call came. Any earlier and it would've taken a while before I could get here. Who found the body?'

'The vic's personal trainer. She's downstairs with the FLO. Came round to give him a workout.'

'It's some place this, don't you think?'

'From what I've seen, the words *modernised* and *remodelled* don't cut it. He must have taken the house back to its shell and kitted it out with no expense spared.'

'Where's the body?'

'Through here,' she said, as they walked along the hallway.

'Why does the name Roger Maitland ring a bell?'

'Maybe because he's chief exec of a major defence contractor in Uckfield called Vixen Aviation.'

Henderson shook his head. 'Good to know, but no, I think it's something else.'

He walked into the bedroom. The room and bed looked big enough to host a children's party, and with the blinds open, huge sheets of glass gave panoramic views of the trees and fields at the back of the garden.

To Henderson's surprise, the body that pathologist Grafton Rawlings was bending over was of a portly man, aged around mid- to late-fifties. Henderson imagined anyone with a personal trainer, and no doubt with a home gym to match, would have looked a bit fitter.

'Afternoon Grafton.'

'Ah,' he said, looking up. 'Hello Angus. Someone's been sailing, even if Carol hadn't told me.'

'What's the giveaway? Is it the healthy, ruddy complexion and salt-incrusted hair on which a wire brush couldn't make much of an impression, or the time I took to get here?'

'All of the above. It's a look that takes me four or five whiskies to emulate.'

'This is Mr Roger Maitland CBE, I take it?'

'Yes, it is, and I'm afraid to say he's been brutally stabbed.'

'Define *brutally*.'

'Well, he has three wounds to his stomach, which would have been sufficient to kill him, but when he fell on his knees, or perhaps turned around, he received two more wounds in the back.'

'That's brutal right enough.'

'And all done with a large knife, so I suspect there will be extensive internal damage.'

'I see what you mean.'

It didn't look like the small, neat incisions of a stiletto or a paring knife taken from the kitchen, but the wide thrusts and ragged lacerations from something like a hunting knife, one with indentations on the back of the blade. His uniform colleagues were seeing the result of using knives like this more often. They were bought from a range of on-line stores and adventure outlets. They were formidable weapons and even looked threatening.

'Do you know when he was killed?'

'Rigor mortis is beginning to ease, so I would say around twelve hours ago, but I will be more precise when I get him back to the mortuary.'

'Understood. Thanks Grafton.'

Henderson stood and took a look around the bathroom and the bedroom before walking over to Walters in the hall. 'Do we have any idea how the killer got into the house?'

'Maybe. There are no signs of a break-in, but when Jess Green, his PT arrived for their afternoon session, she walked in through an unlocked front door.'

He looked at her, a horrified expression on his face. 'What? A house with all this stuff inside and he doesn't lock the front door at night?'

'What can I say? I'm just following the evidence.'

'Let's go talk to Jess.'

FOUR

She turned to face the band and counted out with her raised hand, 'One, two, three, and four.' They began playing her new song, *It's Time to Stop.*

Sonia Walsh walked to the microphone and waited until Jed, the guitarist, finished playing his short introduction piece. She pulled the microphone towards her in two hands and counted in her head, one-two-three, before taking a deep breath and singing:

> *'We had it all,*
> *You said so yourself.'*

Her face contorted in exasperation. 'No, no, no,' she shouted. 'Stop. Stop!'

The band stopped playing.

'What's the problem this time?' Jed asked.

'I said before, at the start of each verse I don't want standard drumbeats, I want half beats for a bar, single beats for the next bar, and half beats for the next bar.'

'I thought you said you didn't like it?' Terry, the drummer, asked. 'I played it that way three or four versions back.'

'Play it again,' she said.

He did.

'Yes, that's it, but when you reach the fourth bar, go back to the regular pattern, no half beats.'

'Got it.'

'Let's go again.'

'Sonia,' Jed said in an exasperated tone, 'why are we rehearsing a new song so close to playing a gig? We're on stage for real in...' he looked at his watch, 'six hours.'

'I've said it before and I will say it again: I think our show is getting stale. We need to recover the spontaneity we had two, maybe three, years, ago.'

'I don't think it's stale at all,' Chas, the bassist said.

'It's not up for discussion,' Sonia said, raising her voice to show her irritation. 'Just bloody do it.'

The faces suggested they didn't like it, but she didn't care. *Left Field* was her band. She had put it together, she wrote all the songs, and with her former-husband's help, got themselves a record deal. She liked the band members as they were a counterbalance to her feisty temperament and her inability to tolerate fools, but at the end of the day, they were musicians. She could get rid of one, or sack them all, and by tomorrow a queue of wannabes would be outside her door ready and waiting to take their place.

'Right,' Sonia said 'From the top. One, two, three, and four.'

Five minutes later, the song ended.

'Excellent,' she said, 'that's just what I wanted. Whatd'ya all think?'

'It's really good,' their keyboard player, Rick said.

'I bloody well like it,' Jed said. 'Where do you want to put it in the playlist? I think after *Freefall*.'

'I'm thinking after *Returned your Love*. At that point, the mood will be slow as we'll have done a couple of slow numbers. This will pep things up before we move into *Freefall*.'

It took a few minutes of discussion, but they all agreed with her; of course they did, because she thought about issues like this long and hard, and they didn't. She had arranged the new song to be upbeat on purpose. She had always felt the move from a ballad like *Returned your Love* to a rocky number like *Freefall* didn't give the listener time to adjust to the change in mood.

The sound engineer was loving this and had a big smile on his craggy face; the band rehearsing with a real song. All too often it was like pulling teeth asking Terry and Chas to play anything which would allow him to adjust the sound levels. On the other hand, if he asked Rick or Jed to play something, he would be subjected to a long dose of Mussorgsky or Shostakovich in Rick's case, while Jed would happily play a long guitar solo from Pink Floyd or Led Zeppelin.

They finished the sound check a few minutes later and trooped out to the minibus to take them back to their hotel. Sonia lived in Brighton, a house in Sussex Square, but they were on a UK tour and for the sake of unity she would stay in the hotel with the rest of their entourage.

Outside the Ocean Hotel, a boutique hotel in Hove, a small crowd had gathered. When the band started out ten years ago, autographs and signing programmes was the norm, now it was selfies. This, she liked. In an age of scanners, Photoshop, and scammers, she had always been uncomfortable with putting her signature on seemingly innocuous bits of paper. That said, people could do some amazing things with only a photograph.

Like most famous people, she sometimes found the business of being recognised a pain in the arse, in particular when in a restaurant with friends, or out walking with her young nieces. However, she would miss the attention if it disappeared.

They made their way into the hotel where she spotted the band's manager, Vince Jesmond, standing near the reception desk with a selection of hotel keycards in his hand.

'Good afternoon, Sonia. Fellas. How did the soundcheck go?'

'Excellent,' she said. 'I've always loved the acoustics of the Dome.'

'Fantastic. Here are your room keys, folks,' he said, handing them out.

'I want a sea view,' Jed said. 'Have I got one?'

'Think of it like a birthday present,' she said. 'Wait until you see what you've got.'

'I hate birthdays,' Terry said. 'So much disappointment as a kid.'

'The pickup will be at six,' Jesmond said, 'so make sure you're all scrubbed, rested, and smelling like new born babies. I'm looking at you, Terry.'

'Fuck off.'

'See you later, folks.'

Sonia glanced around as she headed for the stairs. She froze. He was there again. He had been in the hotel when they played Bath and Cardiff last year and it might have been him at Birmingham and Liverpool. She looked at him now: untidy sandy-coloured hair, stocky build, and a cocky stance; he noticed her too, as he stared right back.

FIVE

Henderson and Walters walked away from Roger Maitland's damaged body. It looked to be a brutal attack as Grafton had said, which felt at odds with the tranquil setting of the house. Ignoring the rattle and hum of SOCOs, the pathologist and the police officers downstairs, he heard the sound of many small birds twittering, the cawing of bigger birds, perhaps crows or woodpigeons, and the neighing of horses.

'It looks as though our vic has been killed by a vicious enemy,' Walters said.

'I have to agree with you, and I can't think the motive was burglary,' the DI replied. He'd looked into each of the rooms as he passed and nothing looked amiss. 'I'm no judge of art, but there's plenty of what looks like original paintings on the wall here and in the hallway, and I can't see a space where one has been lifted.'

'It's the same downstairs. Nothing looks to be missing.'

'If not a robbery, what?'

'Jealousy, perhaps?'

'What are you suggesting, someone is targeting rich people?'

Walters looked thoughtful for a second. 'Maybe.'

'Maybe it's a case of good old-fashioned jealousy, if Roger Maitland was in the habit of banging the wife or girlfriend of a violent criminal?'

'Where did you get that from? Are you running through a list of common criminal motives straight out of the Detectives Handbook?'

'Nothing so formal. Looking at the victim's bed, both pillows are indented. This says to me two people had occupied it in the last day or two, sleeping or otherwise.'

'I missed that.'

They stopped at the top of the stairs. Henderson said, 'First, we need the area around the house searched: the driveway, the back of the house, out to the woods. Maybe the killer dropped something.'

'I'll sort it.'

'Next, it's essential we get a handle on Roger Maitland's life, and fast: his friends, colleagues, relatives, enemies.'

'I agree.'

'What does his company do?'

'Makes military drones.'

'What, one of those big things that fly for hours before hitting a house or car with a missile?'

'No. These are no larger than about a metre. They look similar to the ones you buy on Amazon with four rotors, but they're armoured and fitted with a weapon. Some have a machine gun, while others can drop bombs or fire small missiles. They will either attack designated targets or use its own sophisticated AI system. All the operator needs to do is input the details of the target and the drone will fly away, find it, and hit it all by itself.'

'Scary.'

'It sounds it, but the military love them.'

'I'll bet they do. Does this mean we'll be dealing with stiff military types who will tell us nothing because it's a breach of the Official Secrets Act?'

'Let's hope not.'

They made their way downstairs and into the lounge. Jess Green looked a great deal fitter than her former client, and not only because she wasn't dead. Her bright and tight-fitting gym clothes: yellow top, patterned leggings, and pink-embossed trainers, did everything to emphasise the lithe figure underneath.

Following introductions the DI asked, 'How often do you come to Oakwood House, Jess?'

'Twice a week, Wednesday and Sunday. The midweek one can vary due to Roger's work schedule, but the Sunday one is almost always on.'

'This afternoon you let yourself in through an unlocked front door, am I right?'

'It's not unusual. Roger will sometimes be in the gym warming up or sitting in the kitchen having a coffee. I often open the front door myself and go looking for him.'

'I understand, but as Roger wasn't in a position to unlock the door for you before you arrived, the house must have been unlocked all night. This is how we think the killer got in.'

'I don't know why it was unlocked, but I do know Roger likes a drink, at times more than is good for him. Maybe he conked out after drinking too much.'

'How do you know this?'

'I find out plenty about my clients, from the questions I ask about their nutrition, sleeping, and recreational habits, as well as the confidences they choose to share. You catch my drift?'

'I do.'

'To me it's the same as, maybe not a doctor, but an analyst or psychotherapist.'

'Okay.'

'I know a lot about Roger, but...now I think about it, I'm not sure I want to share it with you.'

'Why not?'

'He's a client of mine, like, and I respect his privacy.'

'Jess, your client is dead. He won't give a toss if you tell us something embarrassing about him or not.'

'I hear what you're saying, but what if I tell you stuff and his family find out? Like his daughter, Laura. She's a real piece of work. If she thought I was telling tales out of school she would rip my eyes out.'

'Let me say a couple of things in response. This is a murder investigation. What if you hold something back which might have led us to the killer and instead, this person kills again? How do you think that would make you feel?'

'I suppose.'

'Also, any information you tell us will be in complete confidence. Nothing will be attributed to you.'

'Yeah?'

Henderson didn't think the decision would be a difficult one for Jess. From her visible lack of emotion, and the dispassionate way she spoke about the dead man, the DI suspected the relationship between her and Roger Maitland hadn't been a particularly warm one.

'I've known Roger for five years, and except for one time when he fondled my bum, he's been the perfect gentleman.'

'What did you do or say when he did that?'

'I told him if it happened again, I would walk and never come back. I also told him that wouldn't be the end of it. I would put the incident up on social media where I'm followed by thousands, including a number of PTs, so he would have trouble finding another personal trainer.'

'Tell me about him. What was he like?'

'With me?'

'In general.'

She paused, thinking. 'He's head of a pretty large company, yeah?'

'Okay.'

'His work involved him meeting with military types on a regular basis, and he went to demonstrations of guns, tanks, and things. What he's like is how I imagine many of those generals and colonels are like: he's loud, used to people following his orders, doesn't tolerate fools, and tramples over any opposition.'

'Is that what you've heard?'

'No, straight from the horse's mouth. He'd tell me stories of when he went to this place or how he dealt with this guy.'

'I see.'

'He also told me about his sex life.'

'He did?'

'Yeah, I remember one time we were talking about older men and he admitted he still had the same sexual desire as guys half his age.'

'Impressive.'

'Maybe. He's separated from his second wife, Sonia, who's the lead singer with *Left Field*, a pretty popular indie band. She left him about a year back but they still talk regularly. According to Sonia, during the marriage he made unusual sexual demands. Roger didn't tell me that, I read it in Sonia's autobiography. With no woman living in the house, he brings in prostitutes.'

'What?'

'He calls them escort girls, and gets them from an agency in Brighton, called something like *Blue Horizon* or *Blue Sea*, but to me they're no different from prostitutes.'

'What about family? You mentioned his second wife, and a daughter.'

'His first wife is called Cynthia. Roger and her had two kids: Laura, an actress, and Katy, a doctor living in America. Roger is closest to Katy, but he said he wouldn't stay in the same room as Cynthia.'

'Why would anyone, in your opinion, want to kill Roger?'

'There's a list. There are people who hate his company, the women, who, in my opinion, he's mistreated, and the business people he's trampled underfoot to reach the top. Take your pick.'

SIX

Henderson drove to his office at Malling House in Lewes. Walters turned up minutes later. Late Sunday afternoon and the car park looked quieter than normal. This reflected the makeup of the huge number of staff who worked at the Sussex Police HQ complex, including many civilians: some working shifts, others nine-to-five, and contractors only coming in when required.

He walked into his office to await the arrival of the murder team members. Some were about to sit down to Sunday lunch, enjoy a football match on television, or getting ready to take the kids to the park. He didn't like doing it, but if the death they were investigating involved one of their loved ones, they would expect a rapid response from the police. If one of them felt reluctant to come into work at this unsociable hour, they had to ask themselves if they were cut out to be a detective.

He woke his computer and looked up Vixen Aviation. On their website, he found Roger Maitland's picture along with five other directors. A short bio described how he and another student from Imperial College came up with the idea for an intelligent drone. Roger had been the engineering genius who created the machines, while Jerome Potter, the programming guru, wrote the AI code upon which the drones operated.

He looked at the product pages and they reinforced the view he had formed of the drones when Carol Walters first mentioned them at Oakwood House. They looked to be a scaled-up version of a household drone, but clad in light, highly protective armour, armed with a weapon, and equipped with a long-range propulsion system. This meant they could loiter for hours waiting for a target, or cross many kilometres of terrain before attacking one.

He went back to Google and scrolled down the other entries to see if they triggered his earlier recollection of Roger Maitland's name. He soon got sidetracked by an article in *The Guardian* describing protests outside their building in Uckfield. They were, in the main, anti-war protestors, but the journalist also came across anarchists and members of various well-known environmental groups.

He finished the information searches then dealt with his emails, before walking over to the corner of the Detectives' Room where the murder team were gathered. The whiteboards behind him were almost blank, and over the coming days and weeks the team would add information, photographs, and connections. For the first few days, at least, it was akin to firing a shotgun at a wall and seeing what patterns it created, hence the reason for having such a large team, with around ten detectives and a similar number of uniforms. Other specialists would be drafted in as required.

'Been sailing, gov?' DC Phil Bentley asked, as Henderson perched on the edge of a desk and took a sip from his mug of coffee.

'Not you as well.'

He looked around; a sea of familiar faces with no significant absentees. Good. He decided to make a start. He stood. 'First let me thank you all for coming in on what for many of you had been a scheduled day off.'

'I didn't fancy Brighton's chances for this afternoon's match with Arsenal,' DC Seb Young said, 'so at least I saved some money.'

Henderson turned to the board behind him containing only a name and picture. 'This is Roger Maitland CBE,' he said, tapping the photograph. 'He's Chief Executive Officer of Vixen Aviation, a drone manufacturing company based in Uckfield. He was found dead, with multiple stab wounds, in the bathroom of his home in North Chailey this morning. According to the pathologist, he was killed late last night, early this morning. It's clear from these other pictures,' he said, lifting the small pile off the desk and sticking them on the board one-by-one, 'this was a vicious attack. He's been stabbed three times in the stomach and two in the back.'

'Gruesome,' DC Sally Graham said. 'It definitely doesn't look like mistaken identity. Somebody wanted him dead.'

'I had the same reaction,' Walters said.

'Robbery doesn't appear to be the motive,' Henderson continued. 'The house contains original pictures on the walls, a decent amount of electronic gadgetry, and a Bentley convertible in the driveway, but nothing appears to be missing.'

Before a range of common hypotheses could be postulated, Henderson said, 'We have so far identified three threads that need to be examined. His personal relationships, his apparently colourful sex life,' which brought a murmur of interest, 'and his business life. Vicky,' he said to DS Vicky Neal, 'I want you to take on the task of investigating his personal life and relationships.'

'Okay.'

'He's been divorced once with another pending, and wife number two, Sonia, is the lead singer with *Left Field*, a popular indie band.'

'I like them,' Phil Bentley said.

'Maybe if you're nice to Vicky, she'll let you tag along,' Walters said.

'They're due to play Brighton Dome tonight,' Sally Graham said. 'I wonder if anyone has told Sonia about his death.'

'In which case, Vicky, if you are planning to talk to her soon, it might be easier to talk to her before she moves on to the next gig, but perhaps wait until after the concert.'

She nodded.

'Roger and Sonia still speak, according to Maitland's PT, so their split didn't sound too hostile,' Henderson continued. 'However, with wife number one, Cynthia, and the mother of his children, he couldn't bear to be in the same room.'

'Got it.'

'Talking of his two children, there's Laura, an actress you might have heard of, and Katy, a doctor living in America.'

'Right.'

'Harry,' Henderson said, turning to DS Harry Wallop. 'According to Jess Green, his PT, Roger often resorted to the services of prostitutes.'

In response, the room resounded to a hubbub of excited voices.

'You don't expect to hear that sort of thing about a prominent businessman,' Wallop said. 'I wonder if his fellow directors at Vixen were aware.'

'He didn't pick them up in the street, from what Jess said, but used an escort agency in Brighton. She thought its name was something like *Blue Horizon* or *Blue Sea*, but wasn't sure. I don't imagine it will be difficult to narrow it down.'

'I shouldn't think so.'

'Find out, if they'll tell you, how often he used the service. If not, try and question some of the girls. I also want to know if he had any favourites.'

'Are you thinking one of them might have killed him?'

'The ferociousness of the attack suggests otherwise, but this sort of work attracts a range of nefarious characters: drug dealers, drug users, and pimps. Our killer might be one of them.'

'Got it.'

'Also, indentations in his bed suggest someone else had been there, either the night of his death or a day or two before. Forensics found several long, black hairs not belonging to the victim. Find out if his companion was one of those escorts.'

'Will do, gov.'

'DS Walters and I will investigate Vixen Aviation. Being a military supplier, they, and the companies they deal with, are staffed with a number of military types. Such people have the skills to confront and attack someone like Roger Maitland.'

'For sure.'

'We have to get to the bottom of this case as fast as possible, because if it's connected to their military work or network of contacts, other directors and employees could also be in danger.'

SEVEN

Sonia made her way out of the stage door at the Brighton Dome and headed towards the tour bus. A small crowd had gathered on the pavement and she happily posed for selfies.

She imagined the after-concert crowds at a Harry Styles or Ariana Grande concert would be much more boisterous. Her band's music had a cerebral quality which attracted students and thirty-somethings who worried about social issues and read *The Guardian*, not pubescent girls more interested in the hair and clothes of the star than any music they were playing.

She had built a break into the tour schedule so she could spend the next two days in Brighton. She not only lived in the town, but also had been brought up in the area and still had many friends there. Not to mention, her estranged husband, Roger Maitland, owned a house in a village nearby, and had told her he wanted to discuss something with her.

Roger wasn't the sort of man who dealt in fripperies, or the type to arrange a meeting when a phone call would do, so it had to be something important. His daughter, Laura, had become a perennial thorn in his side, as Roger liked order and punctuality while Laura's life seemed a continual see-saw between the disorganised and the chaotic. It was probably something to do with her, and Sonia could get through to her while discussions between her and her father often ended in an argument.

Once they'd left Brighton, they would play seven gigs in quick succession, at various points north of Watford, before wrapping up the tour with two shows in London. She liked it that way.

When playing a number of shows one after the other, muscle memory kicked in, and everyone could play the song list in their sleep. This gave the band the freedom, on occasion, to go off-piste with an improvised piano or guitar solo, and still return to the sheet music without missing a beat.

'What a show!' she said as she took a seat on the bus where the rest of the band were already waiting. 'You guys were amazing and the crowd's reaction was fantastic.'

'The new song is a real winner,' Jed said. 'I watched the audience as we played. They sometimes go quiet when we play something new, but loads of them were up dancing. A triumph, the local rag will be forced to concede.'

The bus set off on a short hop to the Ocean Hotel. The guys found it hard to sleep straight after a gig and would spend hours drinking in the bar. She was the opposite; if she hit the sack after a successful show, she would be out like a light. If it had been a disaster, as had happened the previous year in Bristol when the sound was awful, several pieces of equipment failed, and the audience was more pissed than they were used to, she would toss and turn for hours, or go downstairs to join the boys in the bar.

No matter how secret they kept their hotel location, some fans would still find it. Those fans tended to be more determined than those at the stage door; not content with a selfie, but keen to engage in conversation. It was bad enough having to talk to music journalists, but they at least would pose thoughtful questions. All fans wanted to talk about was their top-selling second album, when the current shows were showcasing their fourth, or the deep messages allegedly buried in the lyrics.

Vince Jesmond, their elusive band manager, hated touring and couldn't wait to return to his nice office in Earl's Court. Hence he didn't magically appear for a second time. Once was probably enough. She walked to the front desk and asked if there were any messages.

'Here you are madam,' the receptionist said, handing her a single envelope. It was from Vince, as she recognised his spidery scrawl on the front. 'Also, two police officers are over there, close to the bar,' he said, with a subtle nod of the head, 'and they would like a word with you.'

Sonia turned and noticed it wasn't a grisly old guy in a dirty raincoat and his aggressive sidekick itching to dig his teeth into a suspect, but a young woman and a handsome young man. Perhaps she would speak to them after all, instead of indulging her first reaction, and slinking off upstairs.

'Did they say what they wanted?'

'No, I'm afraid not.'

She walked towards them.

'Sonia Walsh?' the woman asked.

'Yes. What's this about?'

'I'm Detective Sergeant Neal and this is Detective Constable Bentley. We're from Sussex Police Major Crimes Unit. It's a personal matter. Is there a quiet place where we can talk?'

'How about the corner over there,' she said, pointing at the far side of the bar, 'or I suppose there's always my suite upstairs.'

'The corner of the bar looks suitable enough.'

Making their way in that direction, Bentley asked, 'How did the concert go tonight?'

The banality of the question took her by surprise, as her head had filled with all manner of bad things the police might want to talk to her about. *Left Field* didn't have a reputation as a particularly rowdy or druggy band, although Terry the drummer liked to smoke the occasional spliff. In any case, she wouldn't tolerate any hard drug users within her sphere of influence. The music business was a hard place to make a living, and they all needed their wits about them if they didn't want to fall prey to one of its notorious pitfalls. Not to mention, a drug conviction could scupper any chances they had of touring the USA or performing at lucrative gigs in the Middle and Far East.

'I loved it. We'd been trying to fine-tune a new song in rehearsals, and I'm pleased to say it came off note-perfect tonight. I love playing Brighton as the crowd always gives us a brilliant reception.'

'I wish I'd been there. I had a ticket, but as you can see, I had to work.'

They arrived at the far side of the bar. She and Bentley occupied the banquette in the corner while DS Neal sat on a chair facing them.

'Would you like a drink before we start, Sonia?' Neal asked. 'I appreciate you've been singing for the last couple of hours and you might be dying of thirst.'

'That's kind of you. A soda water and lime. Have something yourselves, put it on Room 34's tab.'

'I'm sure police budgets can stretch to a drink.'

'No, I insist. It's not often I speak to anyone outside the music business.'

Neal walked to the bar and Bentley asked, 'How's the tour going?'

'Better than I thought. We released our fourth album, *All Our Sins*, at the beginning of this year. When we started the tour, I worried the material would start to sound a bit stale by now, as we've played it so many times in shows, but judging by the reaction of fans so far, it hasn't.'

'Good to hear, as I think it's a brilliant album.'

'Thank you.'

Neal came back to the table with the drinks, and after distributing them and retaking her seat, she said, 'I'm sorry we've had to meet like this, Sonia, but I'm the bearer of some bad news.'

'Oh?'

'Your husband, Roger Maitland, was found murdered earlier today.'

'What? Roger? Oh, my God.' Tears welled in her eyes and she pulled out a handkerchief. 'I apologise, Detectives, it's come as quite a shock.'

'No need to apologise. Take as long as you need.'

'I'm surprised by my reaction,' Sonia said, a minute or so later. 'When we separated a year back, after only three years of marriage, I felt certain I was over him.'

'Can you think of anyone who might have wanted to harm him?'

'Roger? I'm sure he's made a number of enemies over the years, but enough to kill him? I don't think so.'

'Why did you split up?'

'You can read all about it on the internet or in my memoir, *When the Music Stops*, which came out about nine months back.'

'Humour me.'

'I spiced it up a bit for my publisher, you know how they like a saucy soundbite, but not too much. In essence, Roger liked rough sex and I did not.'

'Define rough.'

'Slaps, punches, nips, heavy grabbing. I decided the time was right for me to leave him when he wrapped a scarf around my neck. He nearly choked me to death.'

EIGHT

On Monday, Henderson and Walters drove towards Vixen Aviation in the Bell Lane Industrial Estate in Uckfield. The building looked to be the largest unit in the area, making it hard to miss. It was L-shaped, a long section on two floors with few windows suggesting a manufacturing unit, while the short section on four floors had plenty of windows, the shining lights indicating activity, and most likely offices.

Fifteen minutes later, they were sitting in the large top floor office of the development director, Adrian Chapman. According to the company's website, Roger Maitland had been fifty-nine, Chapman, five years younger, but in pictures they'd seen, Maitland looked old for his age, despite the attentions of a personal trainer, while Chapman looked younger.

The neat navy-blue suit hugged his slim figure, and a fitted white shirt, no tie, contrasted with his dark skin. His black hair wasn't just short, but cropped close to the skull. Surprisingly for his age, the DI couldn't spot any bald or grey patches, perhaps hidden by the sheer hair style.

After introductions, Chapman gave them a potted overview of the company. 'Roger Maitland and Jerome Potter, who died some five years back, started Vixen over thirty years ago. They met as students at

Imperial College, London, where Roger was a brilliant mechanical engineer, and Jerome a chemical engineer, and a genius at writing computer code.'

'A good combination.'

'Yes, they were. The business began by making spare parts for civilian aircraft, but drones soon became their main interest. Now, it's all we do. People tend to think of drones as being a modern invention, and you can now pick one up from a hobby shop for about twenty pounds, but they were first developed in the 1930s.'

'I wasn't aware.'

'Inventors and aeronautical engineers have long been fascinated by pilotless aircraft. It has come to the fore in the last few years due to the astronomical cost of developing new fighter aircraft. They can cost over eighty million, and a pilot about three million to train. A drone can be deployed at a fraction of the price with no risk to the pilot whatsoever.'

'Fascinating. What encouraged Roger and Jerome to work for the military?'

'Ah, that's a good question, Inspector. Most people assume in order to win military contracts you need to be a former soldier and have contacts in the Ministry of Defence.'

'Yes.'

'They pitched their idea for an intelligent, self-targeting drone to one of the lecturers at the university both men had attended. He liked it so much he put them in touch with a friend of his who worked at the MOD in procurement. Roger, the great salesman, only needed this introduction before he was up and running.'

'What did Roger do in the company?'

'As CEO, he ran the business and dealt with the myriad of issues that cropped up with monotonous regularity every day in a place like this. In addition, as I alluded to a moment ago, he was the MOD's main point of contact. We have a sales team, of course, but when negotiations start to become bogged down, or we find ourselves in a situation where we have to make a special effort, such as now with our new Avalon drone, Roger would become involved.'

'Was he friendly on a social level with anyone here?'

'Yes, Roger and Lester Grange, our Distribution Director were the best of friends. They attended many client meetings together and often went out drinking after work. One of Lester's great strengths is he is ex-army. I'm sure you'll recognise what a great advantage this is when it comes to meeting the folks from the MOD.'

'I can.' Henderson made a note. Grange would be next on their interview list.

'We couldn't help but notice.' Walters said, 'the placards and discarded posters outside.'

He sighed. 'Yes, they're from yesterday's demonstration. I've told the maintenance staff to clear it away, I guess they haven't got around to it yet.'

'How often do they take place?'

'At least once a week. Now and again, perhaps about every five or six weeks, there will be a social media push to do something big and everyone with an axe to grind will get in on the act. It can mean up to fifty demonstrators outside.'

'That many?'

'With social media these sorts of things are much easier to organise.'

The hot drinks were brought in and all discussion halted as the cups were handed around. When they first arrived at Vixen, the detectives weren't taken straight to the office area, but were given a guided tour of the manufacturing facility. Henderson had expected to see many workers, but instead robots were doing much of the heavy lifting and a large number of assembly tasks. Watching them work was mesmerising, each repetitive task an exact replica of the one done minutes before.

Vixen looked to be a well-run and successful company, not only evidenced by a sizable investment in manufacturing technology, but also the range of expensive metal in the car park.

'Do the demonstrations ever turn violent, Mr Chapman?' Henderson asked, as he sipped a rather fine cup of coffee.

'A few years back, some people broke into the offices and did a lot of damage, smashing computers and prototype drones. Thankfully, entrance to the manufacturing area is through a thick security door, so they couldn't get in there.'

'That's awful,' Walters said. 'Did you do anything about it?'

'The police caught the culprits but they were found not guilty at the subsequent trial. This left us no choice, we had to take out an injunction. If any of the protestors attempt to do the same again, they will go to jail.'

'So, what do they do nowadays?'

'We can't stop free speech and free association, so they can protest out there as often as they like. The aggressive shouting, the jostling, the occasional bit of spitting doesn't bother me too much. However, I know some people are often spooked by it, and we've had people on sick leave as a result of it. In terms of violence, it hasn't come to blows yet, but their behaviour is the closest you can come without assaulting anyone.'

'If I can turn to Mr Maitland, are you aware if he had any enemies?'

Henderson had identified two areas where enemies might lurk: demonstrators whose sole aim, he assumed, was to stop Vixen making drones; and with Vixen being such a successful company, who had Maitland trampled to get there?

'I thought you might ask, as it's the first thing that came into my mind when I first heard he had been murdered.' He ran a hand over the stubble on his head. A nervous gesture, Henderson thought.

'Where do I start? About five years ago, we fought an acrimonious battle with a US arms manufacturer over patent infringement. I encouraged Roger to settle as the case could have dragged on for years, but he stuck to his guns. After six months the other side capitulated although it cost us five million in legal fees.'

'A good result.'

'Yes, but Roger made a sworn enemy of Chas Wenstrom, their CEO. Then, about two years back, an aggressive venture capital outfit tried to buy us. It got very dirty, with Roger threatening writs. We had reports of people raking through our bins, and had to sweep the offices for bugs. As you can imagine, it was a very stressful time.'

He paused, as if lost in thought.

'Anything else you'd like to add?'

'No, I don't think so.'

'Thank you for your time, Mr Chapman.'

NINE

'I don't think I've ever interviewed a celebrity before,' DC Sally Graham said.

'It happens to me all the time,' DS Vicky Neal replied with a smile. 'On Sunday, it's the singer Sonia Walsh, and on Monday, it's the star of stage and screen, Laura Maitland. Tuesday, who knows?'

'Yeah, yeah.'

They were walking away from Notting Hill Gate tube station towards an apartment in Elgin Crescent where Laura Maitland lived. She had a reputation in the film and television industries as being 'difficult', the type to walk off the set or stage when a script or leading man wasn't to her liking, and to shout at directors when asked to do something she didn't want to do. Neal imagined all actors offered up a bit of petulance at some time or other, but given the DS had seen several references on a few different websites, perhaps Laura was a special case.

Unlike her memories of visiting the Royal Crescent in Bath, which looked fantastic with all the houses painted white, the ones in this street were a variety of different colours. Neal counted the doors; Laura Maitland owned the gaudy purple one.

'Nothing like keeping a low profile,' Graham said.

'Yeah, she doesn't need a house number, she can just say it's the lurid purple one, halfway down the crescent.'

'Well, there's no mistaking it's Ms Maitland's,' Neal said, as they approached the front door, 'I can hear her shouting at the top of her voice.'

'We could be walking into a serious domestic,' Graham said, as they stood for a moment on the step listening.

'It's not a face-to-face argument, I'm only hearing one side of things. She must be on the phone.'

'I think it should be you knocking on the door, Vicky, as you're the senior officer.'

'Coward.'

Neal rang the bell. She gave it a few seconds and, after receiving no reply, leaned over to press it again. The door flew open.

'What the fuck do you want? No, I'm not talking to you, Walt,' she said into the phone. 'There's a couple of bozos at the door trying to sell me something.'

Neal pulled out her ID card and held it up to where Maitland could see it. Her facial expression didn't change, but she opened the door to allow them to enter. Through the open door on the right Neal spotted the lounge, so the two detectives made their way there. The door slammed shut and the irritated actress ambled in their wake.

'Look, Walt,' Maitland said into the phone, 'here's my idea for a compromise. Keep the fucking idiot director if you must, but I want rid of Chloe and Jeff. They're both a waste of space.'

She listened.

'No, I said I want the two of them out.'

She listened.

'Okay, okay have it your bloody way, but contract or no contract, if the first night bombs you'll be looking for a new lead.'

She finished the call and threw the phone across the lounge where it hit the back of the armchair. 'Bastard!' she spat. 'Just because the fucker puts up the money for the bloody show, he thinks he can decide the artistic direction. The bloody tosser! Aghhh,' she screeched.

A few moments later when the strop appeared to have blown itself out, she noticed the presence of the two detectives. 'What do you guys want? Has someone's house been trashed again?'

'You haven't seen the local news today or over the weekend?' Neal asked.

'Never watch it on TV or buy a newspaper, except *Variety*,' she said. 'Too depressing. It's either the bin men on strike, meaning rubbish will be on the street for weeks, or the country's being sucked into a war in some far-off place and our troops are being shipped out to fight.'

'In which case, you won't have seen or heard this piece of news. Late on Saturday night, early Sunday morning, someone entered your father's house in North Chailey. I'm sorry to say, Ms Maitland, your father was fatally stabbed.'

'What! Pop's dead?'

'Yes, I'm afraid so.'

Her face crumpled and she started to sob. Neal remembered seeing her 'do' a crying scene in one of her films, and it looked realistic, but this wasn't the product of a method acting class. Her upset appeared genuine.

Graham headed in to the kitchen to make a brew. By the time she walked back with a cup of tea for Laura, she had stopped crying.

'He supported my career right from the off,' she said, in between sniffles and sips of the tea. 'Not a lot of people know that side of him. He comes to all my opening nights and even flew to Hollywood when I had a dispute with the studio in the middle of filming *Searching for Two Brothers*. He sorted it out.'

'Can I ask, would you know if your father had any enemies?'

'You said the killer sneaked into the house. I take it we're talking about a burglary, right? Some of the rubbish passing for modern art on the walls of his house I would be happy to see gone, but I understand they're originals, so they must be worth something.'

'We don't believe burglary's the motive. Your father's wallet, phone, iPad, car, and the paintings, were left untouched.'

'If not a burglary, what then?'

'This is what we're trying to ascertain. Can I ask again, do you know if your father had any enemies?'

'Yeah, try the twenty-five fucking idiots who stand outside the factory most days waving their ridiculous placards.'

'We're aware of them. Is there anyone else?'

'Why the hell are you asking me? It's your bloody job to find out.'

'I realise these questions are not easy to answer, but it's the best way for us to uncover things about him. You know your father far better than we do.'

'In which case, take a close look at Pop's money-grabbing bitch of a wife, Sonia Walsh. She's a conniving cow, only interested in money and furthering her stupid music career.'

'Why would she kill Roger? What benefit would she derive?'

'What? Don't you guys see it! With him gone, she will inherit all his money. Pop changed his will when they married and left everything to her.'

'That may be, but when they eventually divorced, she would hardly walk away with nothing.'

'I don't know the legal niceties, but my money's on her.'

'Apart from Sonia, anyone else?'

'I don't know enough about what he's involved in business-wise. I do know they deal with the military, and God knows, I get my ear bashed about it when people discover we're related. But I tell you,' she said, shifting to the edge of her seat and pointing at Neal, 'if you don't find out who killed Pop, and soon, I'll use every platform I have access to and tell the world what fucking idiots you all are.'

TEN

At eight o'clock, Tuesday morning, Henderson walked into his office. He only had time to check his emails and grab a cup of coffee before heading into the Detectives Room for the morning update.

'Right,' he said to the assembled group, 'let's make a start. Based on Sunday's rough outline, we identified three key areas of interest: Vixen Aviation, Roger's private life, and his sexual interests. Vicky, if you could kick things off. I gather the visit to a genuine theatre and film star didn't go as expected.'

'She had a phone glued to her ear when we arrived, talking to a person I assumed to be the producer of her new play, and it put her in a foul mood. She claimed she never read or listened to the news, so we had to tell her what had happened to her father.'

'It's such a shame for her to find out that way.'

'I don't think any of the people I've seen so far have a motive for killing Roger. Sonia's and Laura's upset looked genuine. I think family jealousy is at the heart of Laura accusing Sonia of being behind it, and also a ruined friendship.'

'How do mean?'

'I looked her up and it turns out that she and Sonia had attended the same private school. Despite Sonia being a year and a half older, they became firm friends. Fast forward about ten years when Sonia started dating her father, that's when the friendship headed south.'

'I see, but don't you think Laura has a point?'

'Partly, as Laura mentioned his will had been changed when they married, leaving everything to Sonia. That said, Laura and Katy could contest the will if they believed they have been dealt a bad hand. According to a lawyer I spoke to, they would have a strong case.'

'Let's think about this issue for a second, as Roger appeared to be a rich man. There's the house and all its furnishings, the cars, and his paintings. In terms of shares in Vixen, forty percent is owned by stock market investors. Of the remaining sixty, forty-five belongs to Roger and the rest by his four directors.

'I think it would be useful to see the will,' Walters said. 'There might be a provision in the event of Roger's death to protect the integrity of the business. For example, by putting the shares in trust or distributing them to staff or directors.'

'If the directors are to benefit,' Harry Wallop said, 'we have a motive right there. Vixen must be worth millions.'

'It's a stock market listed company,' Henderson said. 'I checked yesterday and it's valued at eight hundred and twenty million.'

'Could we get access to the will?' Neal asked. 'Would his lawyers allow it?'

'I shouldn't think so,' Henderson said, 'but there's another way. In order for one of the directors to be motivated to kill Roger, they would have to be aware of the will's provisions.'

'True.'

'Which means someone like Adrian Chapman or one of the other directors might know.' The DI made a note on his pad. 'I'll follow this up.' He looked at Neal. 'Vicky, anything else?'

'I'm seeing Cynthia Leonard, Roger's first wife, tomorrow.'

'According to Jess, she won't be sad at his passing.'

'Yeah, it sounds like they didn't get on.'

'Do we know what's behind it?'

'No one's said, but I'll try to find out.'

'Okay, thanks Vicky. Harry, let's look at the sex angle.'

'I've tracked down the agency Roger used. It's called *Brighton Tide* and based in Brighton.'

'Jess Green sort of hit the crossbar with *Blue Horizon* or *Blue Sea*.'

'I've had a good look at the website. They talk about how the backgrounds of all their women are checked. Their service exists, they say, for the busy executive who doesn't have time to build relationships.'

'They don't mention sex?'

He laughed. 'Nothing so obvious, but it's implied. They're in a top-floor office in Black Lion Street. I said I wanted to ask about one of their clients, but made the mistake of telling them what I did, so they refused to speak to me. I don't think we've enough for a warrant, as we don't suspect the agency of doing anything wrong. I'll hang around at night and try to collar one of the employees.'

'Good idea.'

'If all else fails, I'll have to pose as a customer.'

'When you put the charges through expenses,' Seb Young said, 'the folks in Finance will have a good laugh deciding where to book it.'

'You may have to, Harry,' Henderson said, raising his voice to quell the ribald noises. 'Even if you manage to stop someone, they might not want to talk to a cop. I assume you're up for it?'

'No problem.'

'What about Hannah?'

'Oh, I'll think of something.'

'Keep pushing, as we know someone else was with him in that bed, either the night of his murder, or the one before. The bed looked ruffled, and as I mentioned on Sunday, forensics have found several black hairs on a pillow not belonging to the victim.'

'No problem.'

'Vixen Aviation,' Henderson said. 'Adrian Chapman told us about a patent infringement with a US arms manufacturer and a venture capital organisation, both of which turned nasty. Phil, you've been looking into them.'

'Yep. Gresham Armaments are well known in the industry for resorting to litigation at the first opportunity. Their ploy is to accuse others of patent infringement and hope for a settlement out of court. Vixen didn't, and made an enemy of their CEO. He died last year.'

'Ah, I suspect that's a dead end.'

'Me too. The venture capital company who wanted to buy Vixen are notorious for their aggressive tactics.

They're highly successful, but I don't believe it's personal, it's just their way of doing business.'

'Thanks Phil. When Chapman first talked about them, I thought at the time his killer wouldn't come from there. His murder feels more personal. One issue we need to get to the bottom of is the protest group who appear at regular intervals outside Vixen's building.'

'A lot of them are anti-war,' DC Lisa Newman said, 'and pissed off about Vixen producing drones for the military. I think it's a sort of Brighton-area phenomenon, as many of the other armament manufacturers don't get anywhere near the same amount of grief.'

'It's a good point,' Neal said, 'as you would think manufacturers of fighter planes, tanks, and ammunition would be more in the frame than Vixen.'

'What intel do we have on the groups?' the DI asked.

'The most prominent group, I would say,' Newman continued, 'is *Vixen Out*. They're peaceniks, all love not war. They're happy to wave placards and shout and such, but they're avowed non-violence. I doubt we'll find our murderer there.'

'I agree.'

'There's another outfit I think are a bit more interesting. They're called *Soldiers of Peace*. If it sounds like they're similar to the last lot, they aren't. They say they will use any means necessary to achieve their goal, which is to stop the UK fighting needless wars and spend the money saved on better health and education.'

'Laudable aims.'

'You would think so, but they've been involved in a list of violent incidents. They chained themselves across a motorway to halt an arms shipment, cut a fence and set fire to a military barracks, and closer to home, broke into the offices at Vixen and damaged a number of computers.'

'Adrian Chapman mentioned that. When did it happen?'

She looked at her notes. 'About two years back.'

'That's Lisa, and it's good to have you back. We've missed your valuable insights.'

'Thanks Gov, I'm glad to be back.'

Lisa was so good at her job, she'd been seconded to the Fraud Department who wanted her skills for a large internet fraud case they were investigating.

'I'll talk to Vixen about this,' Henderson said, 'and I think it would be a good idea to put someone inside *Soldiers of Peace*. We need to find out what they're about, and whether they were involved in Roger Maitland's killing.'

'Good idea,' Wallop said.

'I think so too,' Walters agreed.

'Who have we got? Who looks like a typical *Soldiers of Peace* member, able to slot unnoticed into their ranks?'

'It's predominately male,' Walters agreed, 'young, idealistic, not afraid to take action.'

'You've just described Phil Bentley,' Neal said.

ELEVEN

On Tuesday, Henderson and Walters were back at Vixen Aviation. This time protestors were outside. It looked as though they were packing up after hassling the workers as they'd made their way in this morning. Henderson parked the car in a place with a good view and the detectives sat for a few minutes watching.

'It's a big group,' Walters said.

'I count about twenty-five.'

'So, what do we have?' She paused, scanning the placards. 'I see *Vixen Out* and *Stop the War.*'

'Where?'

'See the guy with the red jacket holding up the large placard? That's *Vixen Out.*'

'Oh yeah, I see him. Lisa was right when she said yesterday about them being peaceniks. They look like the bead sellers at Gardner Street Market.'

'At the back, can you see a little knot of people, a few wearing green jackets with loads of badges?'

'Yes.'

'That's *Soldiers of Peace.*'

'A couple of them look real tough nuts, ex-army or nightclub bouncers.'

'Having second thoughts about deploying Phil?'

'No, we need to know more about them, but I'll double-up on my advice to him about being careful.'

'The other people who don't look affiliated to any group must be students from Sussex or Brighton unis.'

The detectives left the car and walked towards the protestors and the office block beyond. On approaching the group, the volume increased.

'*Stop all wars!*'
'*Turn guns into agricultural equipment!*'
'*Stop producing killer drones!*'
'*Get the fuck out of the Middle-East.*'

'If you work here,' a young man said, as he moved in front of them, 'you should leave now. Vixen are war-mongers, making money out of other people's misery.'

Henderson eased him aside, but before they got as far as the manicured lawn outside the office block, one of the *Soldiers of Peace* guys approached and held out a leaflet. Tall in height and broad in girth, he had meaty, scarred hands. The leaflet looked tiny in his large grip.

Henderson took the proffered piece of paper and looked the man in the eye.

'You two don't work here,' the guy said, 'you're cops.' He turned and headed back to his mates.

Henderson looked at the leaflet as they walked towards the building entrance. Not the generic type, printed by the thousand and thrust into his hand in Churchill Square or while walking in the North Laines, but an indictment aimed directly at Vixen. While waiting to be taken to their meeting, he scanned it. Flipping over to the reverse side, he saw a list headed: 'Vixen's Crimes'.

Upon reaching item number four on the list, he backhanded the leaflet in triumph. 'There it is!' he said.

'There's what?' Walters asked.

'Good morning, detectives,' a smiling and smartly-attired young man standing over them said. 'Mr Grange will see you now.'

They were led upstairs, the view from the windows and layout of the offices becoming more familiar. Glancing at a computer screen as he walked past, Henderson saw the three-dimensional image of a drone being rotated.

'You might have guessed,' their guide said, 'this is the design department. Once we spec out a new drone, either from requirements given to us by the buyer, who might be the MOD or a foreign government, or a design we ourselves have developed, this is where the product is created.'

'It must be a dream,' Walters said, 'for boys who grew up flying their own drones to work here.'

'We have a few of those for sure, but what we make is a world away from the flimsy plastic things you buy in hobby shops. Ours are made using metal composites such as titanium and magnesium, and incorporating a proprietary construction method pioneered by Roger, which can withstand the percussion wave of an explosion and enemy small-arms fire.'

'Impressive.'

The Distribution Director of Vixen, Lester Grange, was a big man in every sense. Taller than Henderson, and broad, the seams of his jacket straining as he reached over his desk to shake their hands. It looked a smart, handmade item and the DI felt sure the tailor had taken into account the stresses and strains his customer would put on the material.

'Thank you for seeing us, Mr Grange.'

'Call me Lester, don't be so formal. I understand you've already spoken to Adrian.'

'Yes, we have. He says you had a close relationship with Roger.'

'Aye, I have to agree with you there,' he said, a wistful look on his face. 'I hammered the vodka a little more than I intended the night I found out he'd been murdered.'

'How often did you get together outside work?'

'Once, maybe twice a week. Look, I'm no fool and I realise some people in this organisation say the friendship between me and Roger developed because I had been in the army and he hadn't. Nothing I can say is ever going to change their minds.'

'How long were you in?'

'Twelve years. Had my own platoon. Two tours in the Gulf and a couple of medals to show for it.'

'No cynicism?'

'That's for the birds. Life is for living, not looking back and regretting what you have or haven't done.'

'A refreshing attitude.'

'I think it was this, as well as my army experience, that initially brought me and Roger together, but from then on, it formed into a true friendship. We had plenty of nights when we discussed football, my favourite sport, rugby, his, women, drink, travel; anything but business.'

'How would you characterise Roger?'

'Him and me were two peas in a pod. We're both driven. Give us a goal and we'll achieve it.'

'You knew Roger well. Did he have any enemies?'

'Yeah, Adrian, trying to take his job.'

'Really?'

'No, I joke. Adrian's an ambitious guy and I don't have any problem with people who are, but he couldn't do what Roger does, or should I say, what Roger did. When Roger first comes across someone new from the Mod or military, you could ask him in a week or a month what the man's rank was and the job he held, and Roger could spit it out.'

'He must have had a good memory.'

'He did, but more than that. After the meeting, when Roger got back to the office, he made sure he understood what relationship the officer had to other officers he knew about.'

'What will happen to the company now Roger is no longer around?'

'It doesn't bear thinking about, but we must. I guess one of us directors will take over the post on an interim basis until we recruit a replacement with the relevant experience.'

'None of the current directors are ready to step into the frame?'

He shook his head. 'I wouldn't want it, and none of the other guys are up to it.'

'What about ownership of the business? I understand Roger's the main shareholder.'

'Now we're into the realms of inheritance. I know, although I often urged him to do otherwise, he left all his shares in Vixen to his wife, Sonia. He has two kids. Laura, a successful actress, and Katy, an A&E doctor at a hospital in Colorado. Katy will be well happy to receive the investments and money Roger has left her and won't quibble, but even though Laura will inherit the house and its contents, I'm certain, knowing how she approaches things, she'll contest the will.'

TWELVE

The cross-country drive from Lewes to Benenden in Kent had been straightforward with no holdups. Vicky Neal and Sally Graham's luck ran out when they reached the outskirts of the village. They had to wait as a large lorry carrying animal feed tried to turn into a farm. Neal couldn't see if the angle was too tight or the lorry driver had overshot the entrance, but it forced him to make a succession of small manoeuvres. All the while they and a few other cars in what passed for a traffic jam around this part of the country, waited.

Benenden looked to be a prosperous village, big houses bordering a sizable expanse of green which Neal presumed would be used to host visiting fairs and be a suitable venue for something like a national celebration or a summer fête. The house where Roger Maitland's first wife lived in Walkhurst Road looked as impressive as any they'd seen, and she wondered if the divorce settlement helped her and her partner buy it.

They turned into the long driveway with an open two-bay garage at the side. In one of the bays, a stunning blue-pearl coloured car, a McLaren. From the front it resembled a Ferrari or Maserati, but she knew better. She could also see the insignia on the bonnet.

'Do you have any idea how much a car like that costs?' she asked DC Sally Graham beside her.

'As someone who drives nothing more sporty than a VW Polo, no I don't.'

'Try upwards from about a quarter of a million.'

'You are joking?'

'No, I'm not.'

'So much money for a car. It's enough to buy a small flat in Brighton, or at least give you the deposit for something more salubrious.'

'It is expensive but cars like that are not for general motoring; you won't see too many of them in the Tesco car park. They're more for car nuts who will keep it like this in their garage and now and again take it out for a spin when the roads are quiet.'

'Listen to you, the Jeremy Clarkson of Malling House.'

'There are petrol-heads in Traffic who know way more about cars than I do. It's just a shame I don't earn enough to indulge my passion.'

Graham stepped out of the car. 'Gosh it's warm. This is the best weather we've had since October.'

'It's only May, but it feels like summer is coming.'

A sour-faced woman answered their knock on the door, but if she smiled, she would be considered good-looking. She had brown, shoulder-length hair, even white teeth, and a slim frame with prominent boobs.

'Yeah?'

'We're detectives from Sussex Police. We called yesterday.'

'Oh yeah, sorry. Such a lot has been going on, I forgot.'

Neal imagined her scattiness had something to do with her ex-husband's death, but she didn't want to raise the subject on the doorstep.

'Do come in. We'll sit in the lounge.'

If Neal thought the exterior impressive, this room beat it hands down. It contained minimal furniture making the room appear huge, but what there was looked high quality. Two settees were arranged in an L-shape with an Indian-style rug and heavy oak coffee table in the middle. At the far end of the room and overlooking the garden, a piano.

They took a seat on the settee while Mrs Leonard went into the kitchen to make some drinks.

'We'll soon be asking for iced tea and lemonade instead of coffee if this weather keeps up,' Graham said.

'I drink coffee whatever the weather. Nice room this. Do you play?' Neal asked, nodding at the piano.

'Reached grade 5 before an interest in sport took over.'

'I wanted to learn, but my folks couldn't afford the lessons.'

'You could start now.'

'You reckon I could still pick it up?'

'Here we are,' Mrs Leonard said, as she came into the room carrying a tray.

'I noticed the McLaren in the garage,' Neal said, as Mrs Leonard poured the drinks. 'Is it yours or your partner's?'

'God, I wouldn't be seen driving that thing. For starters, it's a horrible seating position for me as the seat belt crushes my chest. For another, stab the accelerator a bit too hard and before you know it, you're at the far end of the road. No, it's Stuart's. I shouldn't complain, he earns the money, so he's entitled to spend it how he pleases.'

'What does he do?'

'He runs his own air-conditioning business in London. They only deal with large commercial contracts, most of the time financial services companies based in the City of London and Docklands.'

'We are part of the team investigating the murder of Roger Maitland. I assume as you're nodding, you were aware of his death?'

'I read newspapers, don't I? Damn-all else to do in the back of beyond.'

Neal had spotted the well-thumbed newspaper too, hence she didn't have a problem wading in with the bad news.

'You don't like it here?'

'Not really. I never wanted to move. I liked living in Newick, close to where Roger worked in Uckfield. I had a wide circle of friends, good neighbours, but Stuart thought the area too busy. He said he needed peace and quiet after spending all day in the city.'

'When did you and Roger divorce?'

'Eleven years ago.'

'Have you taken an interest in what he's been doing since?'

'Have I hell. As soon as the ink dried on my decree nisi, I never thought about him again.'

'Why?'

'I don't mean to suggest he was a bad man; he just didn't feature much, even while we were married. When he made an appearance, and we were having dinner with the likes of Jerome Potter and his wife, after the meal Jerome and Roger would slink off to talk business. At least I got on with his wife, Stephanie, which wasn't so bad, but when it involved other people from Vixen or folks from the MOD I'd never seen before, I hated it. In the end, it was like being married to a stranger.'

'A witness said he couldn't be in the same room as you.'

She smiled and the attractive look returned to her face. 'Do they still say that? It wasn't because I would have a go at him, or attack him, because I wouldn't. It's because my presence would remind him of the one time in his life when he failed to get what he wanted. When we divorced, my lawyer did a better job than his. I got what I asked for, but he didn't and it cheesed him off big time.'

THIRTEEN

Henderson walked back to his office after Thursday's morning update. So far, Harry Wallop had registered with the *Brighton Tide* escort agency in Brighton. The DI had sounded out Phil Bentley about the role of infiltrating *Soldiers of Peace*. Vicky Neal had talked to Roger Maitland's close relatives, but despite them being a diverse bunch with differing interests, none of them expressed an inherent dislike of the man.

When Henderson had first heard Roger Maitland's name on arriving at Oakwood House in North Chailey, it had triggered a deeply hidden memory in his head, but he couldn't quite retrieve it. Yesterday, when he read through the *Soldiers of Peace* leaflet, the mystery was solved. He loaded Google and keyed in 'Vixen Drone Accident'.

He had to play around with the search words to move closer to what he wanted, but a few minutes later he clicked on a *Guardian* article, and there it was. One of Vixen's early drones, about twelve years back, 'went rogue' when deployed in Afghanistan and attacked a British army patrol.

It killed two soldiers and injured three others, two seriously. The surviving soldiers took cover, but despite hitting the drone several times with their own rifles, it kept firing at them. After about ten minutes, one of their bullets must have hit something vital as it started spinning out of control, before crashing into the mountain behind the rocks where the soldiers were sheltering.

The subsequent inquiry ruled the attack wasn't the fault of the drone. The army technician who had loaded it with the day's targets had not specified a parameter to stop the drone attacking friendly troops. This allowed the drone to prowl and loiter in hostile areas, before attacking anyone found to be carrying a weapon.

Vixen was exonerated, although Jerome Potter told the inquiry he would modify the software. This would ensure an operator couldn't deploy the drone until a short checklist had been accepted.

Henderson sat back in his chair and put his feet on the desk, thinking. A minute or so later, he leaned forward, lifted the phone, and asked Walters to come into his office.

'Hi gov,' Walters said when she breezed in. 'What's up?'

'Take a look at this.'

He turned his computer screen around to face her. She finished reading the article in a couple of minutes.

'I thought those drones were the bee's knees. How the hell did one manage to attack a British patrol?'

'The subsequent military inquiry found the product wasn't at fault, but blamed operator error.'

'What, the guy programming the thing before it goes out?'

'Yeah, but inquiries like this, be it government, military, or inside a prison, can be influenced by other factors.'

'Such as?'

'I'm not saying the MOD were so swayed by a love of Vixen's drones that it caused them to ignore any shortcomings and sweep them under the carpet. However, the soldiers who survived the attack might feel this way.'

'Ah, I understand what you're getting at, but if so, wouldn't their beef be with Jerome Potter? He's the designer of the drone's brain. As I understand it, the drone is a clever piece of engineering, but it's nothing without its smart AI program.'

'You're right, but Jerome is dead. I read something about him in another article. He'd been ousted from Vixen about eighteen months after the incident. The article didn't tie his departure to the attack on the army patrol, but I think it's too much of a coincidence to ignore.'

'So do I.'

'The company's statement announcing his death, which I read through a minute or so ago, focussed on his deteriorating health. He had testicular cancer. It had been treated, but came back and spread to his liver and lungs. Although he actually died from suicide.'

'Horrible.'

'I think we should take a second look at Jerome Potter's death in the light of this new information,' Henderson said, nodding at the computer screen.

'Why?'

'If the surviving members of the platoon have a grievance against Vixen, they may have killed Potter and made it look like suicide.'

She nodded in agreement. 'If so, the next in line would be Maitland.'

He nodded. 'There are two strands to this. First off, we need to talk to Potter's widow, hear her view on his death, see if she spotted any inconsistencies. Then, we need to track down the surviving members of this platoon.'

'When did the accident happen?'

'About twelve years ago.'

'So, the guys in the platoon are now, what, mid-thirties to mid-forties?'

'I guess.'

'Why would they wait this long for revenge?'

He thought for a moment. 'Maybe they're still serving and had been posted overseas, or they've been in jail.'

'It's possible.'

'Research members of the platoon, dig up their names and addresses. I'd like to talk to them. As we said before, military, or ex-military people have access to weapons similar to the one used to kill Roger Maitland. Plus, they also have the expertise to stake out his house, waiting until he was alone, and the skill and confidence to tackle him in a hand-to-hand combat situation.'

FOURTEEN

'I spoke to Phil last night,' Henderson said to Walters in the passenger seat beside him. 'He's made contact with *Soldiers of Peace* and they've invited him along to their next meeting.'

'Daniel into the lion's den'

'I didn't take you for the religious sort.'

'I'm from Wales, it comes with the territory.'

'I'm hoping it won't come to anything too dangerous. I've told him if they ask him to break the law by cutting fences or blocking roads, I'm okay with that. If it moves to something more serious, like breaking and entering, or assault, he's coming out.'

'That's always the problem using undercover cops to infiltrate criminal gangs. If they baulk at selling drugs or beating up a snitch, they'll blow their cover and endanger themselves.'

Henderson had his own misgivings. Phil had done undercover work before, but nothing long-term or involving an armed gang. They were not set up to manage such an operation, and while he harboured a hope the *Soldiers of Peace* outfit might include Roger Maitland's killer, another part of him hoped it didn't, so he wouldn't put one of his officers in jeopardy.

Henderson turned into Langdale Road in Hove. Driving away from the seafront, the houses retained the white, seaside look. Some were small hotels or

Airbnb lets, and others large, individual houses, some with small gardens. Stephanie Potter lived in one with two matching bay windows, either side of a first-floor balcony.

'What a lovely house,' Walters said, 'so clean and bright, and only a short walk to the seafront.'

'I don't imagine they come cheap.'

'Not the sort of place where we would expect to find retiring police officers,' Walters said, as Henderson parked the car. 'It looks more like an area for ousted company executives.'

'I'm sure he didn't leave the company empty-handed.'

A tall and slim woman with shoulder-length dark hair answered their knock on the door. If Jerome Potter had survived, he would be early-sixties now, and in Henderson's view, this put his wife around late-fifties. She had a serious resting face, the look of a woman who didn't tolerate the presence of fools.

'Ah, the Sussex detectives, do come in.'

Walters closed the door.

'I'm about to make coffee; would you like something?'

They both opted for coffee and were shown into the lounge. The furnishings were traditional with a large sofa and deep-cushioned chairs, a rug over a wooden floor, and a huge ornate mirror dominating the facing wall. Henderson looked at a few of the photographs dotted around the room. Jerome with his unruly hair and rugged face had the look of a serious academic, while their son had an easy smile.

'You never know what you're going to find in houses like this so close to the sea,' Walters said. 'Some go for a nautical theme, with washed floorboards taken from a ship, and pictures of sailboats and anchors. Others, bohemian or modern and out of keeping with the area; or something like this, that just seems to fit.'

'I take it your keen interest in houses and furnishings is because you've decided to redecorate once again?'

'Got it in one.'

'Here we are,' Mrs Potter said, placing a mug in front of him and another in front of Walters.

'Thank you,' Henderson said. 'You have some nice photographs.'

'Yes, it's good to remember Jerome back when he was healthy and strong. The young man you see, not so young now as he's in his thirties, is our son Lucas. He owns a security company in Crawley, and does a lot of work at the airport last time I heard, but I don't see much of him these days. He and Jerome were very close. His death hit him hard.'

'I hope you don't mind our visit, Mrs Potter, which is prompted by the killing of Roger Maitland. I appreciate it might open some old wounds.'

'I've been a GP for over thirty years, Inspector, and as a consequence I've developed a thick skin. Also, Jerome died five years ago. I've more or less come to terms with it now.'

'In the course of investigating Roger Maitland's death, we've uncovered a friendly fire shooting incident involving one of Vixen's drones.'

'You've hit the nail on the head, Inspector.'

'How so?'

'You know what Jerome did at Vixen?'

'Yes, he developed the AI used by the drones.'

'That's right. He was quite the brilliant programmer. Once he had a clear idea in his mind what he wanted it to do, he would bash out the code, even if it took him all night. I mean, the function of one drone is like another, so after the company had made and sold a few models, it allowed him to lift the code from an older version and update it.'

'I see.'

'Of course, developing the code for each new drone isn't one big job, it's compartmentalised. A section is for operating the weapon, another for controlling the engine, another for communicating with base, and so on. This is all coordinated by a management programme, the real brains of the thing, first developed by Jerome in his twenties.'

'Impressive.'

'I thought so too, but he felt sorrow that a product of his genius was being used to take lives and not save them.'

'Some would argue otherwise.'

'They will, and I've heard all their arguments. But, you were talking about the friendly fire incident?'

'Do you think the aftermath had anything to do with Jerome leaving the company?'

'Undoubtably. Despite the army's board of enquiry absolving Vixen of any responsibility for the shooting incident, Maitland used it as a rod to beat Jerome. He said the default settings for the drone should have been clearer.'

'Sounds reasonable.'

'Yes, but they were set up like this at the army's insistence. They wanted complete control of the thing, to make it work the way they desired. What they didn't bank on was the keys being handed over to an inexperienced soldier under the command of an equally green lieutenant.'

'An unfortunate sequence of events.'

'As incidents like this often are, but Maitland used it as an excuse to oust Jerome.'

'How?'

'The elements of a clause written into both their employment contracts. It stated that if it could be proved there had been a dereliction of a duty of care, or a clear occurrence of incompetence leading to a loss of life, they could be dismissed with immediate effect.'

'Jerome must have had a good case for unfair dismissal after the board of enquiry found in Vixen's favour,' Walters said.

'He did, Sergeant, you're quite right, but they sweetened the pill by giving Jerome a large payoff. His deteriorating relationship with Maitland and his failing health were what pushed him into submission. Roger Maitland, as you may have gathered from your enquiries, was a difficult man to like. He had all the traits of a school bully: arrogant, listened to nobody, and took pleasure in other people's discomfort.'

'I see.'

'He also appeared to me like a man with an insatiable sexual appetite. In social gatherings, I could see him sizing up all the women, and single or not, if spotted one he liked, he would zero-in. He touched me where he shouldn't on more than one occasion, and I heard the same from several of the wives of other directors.'

'Can I ask about Jerome's suicide? You mentioned his failing health.'

'Jerome had testicular cancer, and the anxiety he experienced due to Maitland's constant bickering and his subsequent attempts to kick him out, only made it worse. It didn't help with him being a smoker. About two and a half years after his sacking, a specialist told him he had no more than six months to live if he didn't stop smoking and start an exercise regime. He got depressed at the diagnosis, but he didn't do anything about it.'

'No?'

'God no. He loved smoking and hated exercise, and this from the husband of a doctor. One morning, Wednesday, 7th April five years ago, to be exact, he got out of bed before me. We didn't live in this house at the time, but one in Shirley Drive in Hove.

'Okay.'

'I came downstairs and noticed the smell of exhaust fumes coming from the integral garage. I opened the connecting door and found him slumped against the steering wheel, a hose from the exhaust pipe poking through the driver's window. I pulled him out, and started CPR. I had a defibrillator at home, for reasons I can't quite remember, and I gave him a few blasts of it, but it didn't make a difference. He was already dead.'

FIFTEEN

Lucas Potter left his house in Horley at seven-forty and drove to work. He hated working Saturdays. Despite owning his own business, and knowing many people in his position would be happy spending every waking hour at work, he wasn't. Rosie, his partner, made it easier as she worked for British Airways and had flown to Tampa the day before.

He climbed into his car, a new-this-week Jaguar iPace. His company leased the car, a sign they were doing something right. However, being a glass half-empty sort of guy, he knew his business, any business, was built on foundations of sand. An injudicious comment in the press, a remark or joke told to one of his staff, sharing a racist or misogynist post on social media, and it would all come tumbling down in the blink of an eye.

In his case, his business supplied security personnel to corporates. A little voice in his head piped up at frequent intervals to inform him he needed to reduce his reliance on his biggest customer, Gatwick Airport, and have his men guard more buildings, construction sites, and government installations. They did a bit of the other stuff, but the airport paid well and occupied a large number of his guys for long periods, both permanent and on contract hire.

When he'd arrived home the previous night, the car radio had been tuned to his favourite station, Planet Rock. While thumping guitar sounds wouldn't always suit his mood in the morning, they did today.

Four months ago, Potter Security moved into new offices. The old place was small and cramped, barely big enough to house him, his two lieutenants, and the admin team. He chose the new place as it had a series of rooms which he now used for training. One was set up for classroom-type learning where recent recruits, and even old hands, were trained in airport security protocols and procedures. In the other, a gym had been installed where the less than fit would be put through their paces, and in an ante-room, they would be taught the rudiments of hand-to-hand combat and self-defence.

For a small business, it was a big investment, and working with a number of contract staff he ran the risk they would take the training and move elsewhere. The firm's low turnover figures gave him the confidence this wouldn't happen. His guys appreciated the steady work provided and liked the fact that he, and his two mates, Tony Sherman and Al Cowan, were ex-services and could walk the talk.

The new offices were in London Road, Crawley, located in a red-brick building and supplying a level of kudos he wasn't sure they deserved. Their neighbours were financial advisors, media companies and web designers, and filled with earnest and well-dressed young people, their ears jammed with Apple earbuds.

By way of contrast, his guys were cynical, scruffy, tattooed, and not averse to telling a dirty joke. They were more interested in learning how to disarm a man with a knife than adding bells and whistles to a website or securing a new mortgage.

He keyed the code into the pad outside the offices of Potter Security and pushed the glass doors open. He headed into his office and put down his battered leather briefcase. It had once belonged to his father and at one time contained a paper copy of the AI central code used to control every drone made by Vixen Aviation; from Hyperion, their first, to Avalon, their latest.

He woke his computer and glanced at the screen while shrugging off his jacket and flicking through the morning's letters and junk mail. Few surprises would be in his email, the internal system they used, or in one of the letters. All security personnel were on a private WhatsApp group and a post would trigger an alert on his phone. All personnel were free to inform the group about any problems experienced, alarms raised, or rumours heard from airport management.

Every now and again, he would clamp down on jokey posts and funny videos circulating among the company's computers. He had seen all too often, in particular with reference to police officers and footballers, how a lax approach could degenerate into misogynist or racist behaviour, something he wouldn't tolerate.

'Morning boss,' Al Cowan said, breezing in before taking the seat opposite. 'We had some fun last night, did we not?'

'What time did you leave?'

'About two.'

'What were you doing until then? When I left around midnight it was starting to thin out.'

'Oh, let me think. I bumped into this group who were down at the coast for the weekend. I thought I'd been getting on great with this bird with wavy brown hair, Haley or Harriet or something, but after buying her a shedload of drinks, she blew me away.'

'Story of your life, mate.'

Lucas had been friends with Al since induction. They had bonded together from the off, and now they were like brothers. They were compatible. Lucas, the brains of the outfit, but often acting on impulse. Al wasn't too bright, but cool as a cucumber under pressure, and his peacekeeping skills had got Lucas out of a few scrapes, including some dangerous ones while they were serving.

'You asked me to find out all I could about this Roger Maitland murder case?'

'Yeah. How did you get on?'

'Give me the background again.'

'I'm telling you, mate, too much booze destroys brain cells.'

'Yeah, but they'll all come back this afternoon.'

'My dad started Vixen Aviation with a university friend called Roger Maitland.'

'I remember that much, at least.'

'Do you also remember they make military drones?'

His eyes looked skyward. 'I'm not ga-ga yet. We all saw the bloody things at work in Afghanistan, didn't we? Fucking amazing they were.'

'My dad wrote the computer code they use, and Roger did the engineering. About twelve years back, one of the drones, programmed by a private who didn't know his arse from his elbow, shot up a passing British patrol.'

'Yeah, right.'

'Maitland used the incident as an excuse to boot my dad out of the company.'

'So, your dad and Maitland owned this company together, fifty-fifty like?'

'Yep, but when Maitland booted him out, he took all the shares for himself.'

'The greedy bastard. How could he do that?'

'Their employment contracts stated it could be done, but only if Dad proved to be incompetent, which he wasn't. A military enquiry concluded the fault lay with the drone operator, and a young 2nd lieutenant, fresh out of Sandhurst.'

'One of them; it figures. So, this Maitland guy was a scheming, greedy bastard?'

'Right. He's also a greedy *rich* bastard as he floated the company not long after Dad left, something he would have opposed if he was still employed, making Maitland millions. Do you remember that bit?'

'Yeah, no worries. So, somebody topped him, saving you from doing the job.'

'Why would I wait all this time to do it? My dad died five years ago.'

'I dunno. Since we moved here, it's the calmest I've seen you.'

'Don't you repeat that comment if the cops come calling.'

'You know me mate, the soul of discretion.'

'And the source of all gossip. Now you're up to date, what did you come in for?'

'Oh yeah. I wanted to tell you about last night. I'm waiting for a taxi in East Street when I bump into that journalist I know from *The Argus*.'

'Mandy-something, the good-looking one who always blanks you whenever you ask her out?'

'She doesn't blank me. She talks to me.'

'However, she still refuses to go out with you.'

'She's got a contact at the cop shop and says a couple of detectives have been talking to your mother.'

'Have they?'

'Yep.'

He sat back in his chair, thinking. If they had a better relationship, any sort of relationship at all, she might have called to tell him. No, she wouldn't call him. She's a stoic woman, not given to outward displays of emotion, perhaps a requisite for being a GP, but not when caring for a sick man. Lucas didn't like the cold, pragmatic way she'd treated him. If he'd had the money, like now, he would have hired a twenty-four-hour carer or moved him into a home.

'In which case, they'll be here to talk to me soon.'

'Indeed, they will. You got your story straight?'

'Straight as a bullet, mate; straight as a bullet.'

SIXTEEN

Carol Walters arrived back at her apartment around five after spending most of Saturday in the office. She preferred it this way, being involved in a big investigation. It filled up her weekend with meaningful work, rather than the usual options: food shopping, tidying the flat, or taking a walk along the seafront.

She had a boyfriend, but the fresh and passionate relationship at the beginning had morphed into a friend-friend relationship without much petrol being left in the tank.

She had spent the last two days tracking down members of the unit attacked by the Vixen drone. While she believed this to be a positive lead, she also took note of Harry Wallop's work with the escort women. This was in part to offer some moral support while venturing into an uncomfortable area, same for Phil Bentley with the *Soldiers of Peace* protestors, but she had a vested interest in this subject. A former neighbour had done escort work, but had to give it up when she took a severe beating from an angry customer.

Her body had recovered from the ordeal, but in her mind, she was still scarred. The man she married subsequent to this knew nothing about her past and put her mental aberrations down to a difficult childhood. If her husband found out her escort name, the only name used in court, he would have no trouble finding the details of the case on the internet, as the perpetrator had been tried and jailed for five years. Walters, a Detective Constable at the time, had compiled most of the evidence against him.

The interior of her flat was as untidy as she'd left it: not a surprise as she lived alone, a plus point in her view, but by the same token, the dirty dishes in the sink still required washing. She ignored them as she made a cup of coffee and put a slice of bread in the toaster.

When ready, she carried her mug and plate into the lounge and sat at the table overlooking Queens Park in Brighton. She opened her laptop and munched on the toast, watching the activities in the park as the machine went through its boot-up routine.

The end of the first week in May, still in the grip of spring, and while some days were fine, the rest were wet, windy, or both. The evening felt warm but with little sunshine and a light breeze. This encouraged a few kids to be out in Queens Park throwing a ball for their dog, as others strolled along the path deep in conversation, one of the joys to be had at the end of a long winter.

She loaded Google and searched for escort agencies in the Brighton area. Many, she suspected, didn't need a website as they gained new clients by word-of-mouth recommendations, but some did. They were circumspect about what they offered, perhaps fearing the Vice Unit would close them down if they were more explicit.

Brighton Tide took a different approach. It read like a dating agency for short-term relationships, with no sex mentioned at all. They aimed the service, the blurb went on, at businessmen coming to town for a conference or a meeting, who required a companion for the evening. She imagined to the stupid or the drunk it might be confused with a normal dating agency and attract people wanting a short- or maybe a long-term relationship. She supposed the façade would fall when the visitor realised there was no carousel of faces for them to scroll through.

She went back into the kitchen and restarted the coffee machine. No, she thought, bugger it. She ignored the machine and instead reached into the fridge and pulled out a bottle of beer. She popped the cap and took a swig. It tasted good.

She switched on the oven to cook the curry she had bought earlier. She wasn't going out tonight. Tomorrow, Sunday, a full contingent of detectives would be in Malling House. Henderson, with his boss, Sean Houghton at his back, were demanding answers and they wanted them quickly.

At the start of this investigation, CI Houghton had expressed disbelief that a prominent businessman could be murdered in such a brutal manner. He believed the protestors outside Vixen were responsible. Henderson soon put him right about the darker side to Roger Maitland's personality, but it didn't stop those not party to this information pressuring them for a swift response.

She carried the beer into the lounge and sat down once again at her laptop. She cleared the open tabs and searched again for escorts in Brighton, using different terminology this time. She didn't want companies offering their services, but something about the escorts themselves.

She wanted to know the issues they faced. Did they experience prejudice or were their activities tolerated? With two universities and dozens of language schools, Brighton had a long history of supporting protests. Had protestors turned up outside the offices of those escort companies, or had there been a march in support of those girls, in the same way Brighton Pride supported the LGBTQ+ community?

She ignored the first few searches and only when she reached the bottom, an article written by an *Argus* reporter about missing escorts, did she find it interesting. The author, Louise Gatiss, had published the article over five years ago, and Walters doubted the woman still worked there.

Working as an Escort can be a Dangerous Business

The escort business has been active in Brighton for as long as anyone can remember. Some call it prostitution by another name, while others say they provide an important service, complementing the conference trade, allowing visiting business people to have a companion for the evening.

Enquiries made by this newspaper have revealed that over the last five years, a number of those women have gone missing. This is the nature of the work you might think: rootless women doing the work for only a short time to make some money. You would be right. But we think there could be a sinister side to this story.

We attempted to track down twelve of those women who had left the industry in the last five years. We succeeded in finding eight. Many are now happily married, their partner unaware of their colourful past. As for the other four, we can find no trace of them, despite using a reputable search agency who utilise a range of resources to locate missing people: social media, interviews with family and friends, employment agencies, local government records.

The four missing women are: Harriet Blackford, 38, born in Bromley. Lisa Daley, 34, born in Leeds. Barbara Hines, 32, born in Cheltenham. Ana Lomidze, 27, born in Tbilisi, Georgia.

The families of those four women are anxious for news of their whereabouts. If you have any information you think might help, please email me at the address below.

SEVENTEEN

He walked to the bar and ordered a pint of lager. The barman didn't want to engage in chat so he took his drink and returned to his seat. It wasn't at the back of the bar, but well away from others, easy to achieve when the place had few other patrons. Sunday night and collectively Brighton appeared to be exhausted after partying non-stop from Thursday to Saturday.

Harry Wallop felt nervous. He had no need to be, he had no intention of cheating on Hannah, and if he ever did, it wouldn't be with a prostitute. He likened the experience to dating after a divorce. Having been out of the loop for so long, his clothes might look out of place, he would say something offensive, not understand something she said, or dig a hole he couldn't get himself out of.

The Victory Bar, part of a 4-star hotel on Brighton seafront, didn't feel the sort of place Harry would ordinarily find himself, particularly given the 5-star bar prices. He and Hannah went out for a pub meal several times a month. It was more out of necessity than choice as even though she could cook, her repertoire was limited to a half a dozen dishes, while he couldn't boil an egg or make toast without making a mess of it.

He didn't think DI Henderson had given him the short straw in this investigation, but neither did he think Roger Maitland's killer would be found among the escort women. The vicious attack on Maitland didn't feel like the work of a female, not even one filled with hate and rage at Maitland's manhandling of her. In his opinion, they were looking for a man.

'Mr Wallop?'

He looked up from the newspaper he was having trouble concentrating on, to see the most beautiful woman he had ever been in the presence of. It may have been the result of expert makeup and hair styling, but the results looked stunning: wavy brown hair, dark eyes, prominent cheekbones and ruby-red lips.

'Ye-yes, I am.'

He stood and put out his hand for her to shake, but she leaned over and gave him a kiss on the cheek. 'Pleased to meet you,' she gushed into his ear.

When they parted, he asked, 'Can I offer you a drink?'

'That's kind of you. Vodka and orange, please.'

She took a seat as he walked to the bar.

'What can I get for you, sir?' the barman asked, a small, knowing smile playing on his lips.

He placed his order.

'Just down for the weekend, are we sir?' he continued, more interested this time around.

'Yes, here for a bit of business.'

'What industry are you in?'

'Office supplies.'

'I understand. If you wouldn't mind paying for the drink, sir, I'll bring it over to your table.'

'Okay.'

He proffered his credit card and his credit limit took another hit. He should have been more relaxed, knowing he could reclaim it all on expenses, but a negative thought niggled at the back of his brain: what if finance bounced it back? Hannah would find out for sure.

He returned to his seat and received a beautiful smile from Amber. She had been looking at his newspaper, at the place where he'd left it, an article about Roger Maitland.

'Your drink will be here in a minute. The barman will bring it over.'

'Yes, Alex is on tonight, he makes a point of taking care of me.'

He had been trying to trace her accent; not local, perhaps Surrey, but more neutral, the hard vowels and truncated consonants ironed out. She wore a black dress with crimson piping through it. It didn't look short when she first approached, but now, sitting down it had ridden up revealing a great deal of nylon-clad leg. She put the paper down and turned to face him.

'So, you're a businessman, Harry?'

'Yes, I come to Brighton, I suppose, a couple of times a month.'

'This is your first time using *Brighton Tide*?'

'Yes.'

'There's a first time for everything, even this,' she said, smiling.

'You're right.'

The barman arrived with Amber's drink on a tray.

'Here is your drink, madam.' He lifted it from the tray, and after moving a coaster closer to her, placed it down. 'If I can be so bold and say, madam, you look lovely tonight.'

'Thank you, Alex.'

He departed, his trademark smile playing on his lips, a man happy to have received the attentions of a beautiful woman.

'Amber, I'm going to be straight with you. I'm not a normal businessman, I'm here looking for answers.'

'Are you a journalist?'

'No, an investigator.'

He decided the word 'police' had too many negative connotations.

'Does that mean we're not going upstairs to your room?'

'No.'

She picked up her clutch bag, and sidled out from behind the table.

'Amber, wait. All I want is the answer to a few questions. Ten, fifteen minutes of your time, but you'll still get your money.'

'Will I? Show me.'

He reached into his pocket and pulled out an envelope. He opened it to display the money: a pile of twenties. Enough for a brief drink and conversation in the bar and sex in a room upstairs.

She retook her seat. 'If you mess me about, you'll have Alex to deal with.'

'I won't mess you about.'

'What do you want to know?'

He lifted the newspaper and tapped the open article. 'This is about a man killed in his house, Roger Maitland. I assume by the look on your face you know about it?'

'All the girls are talking about it.'

'Why, because he often used the services of *Brighton Tide*?'

'You're well informed. Are you a friend of his?'

He shrugged.

'As you say, he used the service a lot, but not with me. I don't go with older men. They have to be under fifty at the very least,' she said, smiling.

He smiled back. 'Who would go with him?'

'He had the reputation of not being an easy man to please. He liked bondage, sex toys, blindfolds. Most of the girls in the agency are fine with those, it sort of goes with the territory, but he also wanted rough sex: beating, slapping, punching, and not many are fine with that.'

'Despite this, are there girls who still wanted to be with him?'

She sighed. 'You will always find girls who will put up with whatever shit is going providing the money's good, and he paid over the odds.'

'Who were they?'

'Let me think. Marcella, Gabrielle, Claudette, and I think Cindy did it now and again.'

He noted the names down.

'That's it, I've answered enough of your questions.'

'Just one more thing. On the night Roger Maitland died, or maybe a day or two before, we know someone was with him in the house. Do you think it would be a girl from *Brighton Tide*?'

'I dunno.'

'C'mon Amber, this is important.'

'This isn't going to land her in a big heap of trouble, is it?'

'I shouldn't think so. All I want to do is find out his final movements.'

She paused for so long, Harry suspected she had clammed up, ready to grab the money and walk.

'One of our girls was with Roger last Saturday night.'

'How do you know for sure?'

'We talk, it's how we keep safe. She told me, but she's worried the police will come after her.'

He shook his head. 'She has nothing to worry about. The police are not looking for her as the murderer, only as a witness.'

'You are well informed.'

'It's my job. Can you tell me the woman's name?'

'I can, but it'll cost you.'

EIGHTEEN

Monday mornings didn't have the same fearful hold after spending the weekend working. Henderson didn't get that funny feeling in his stomach on a Sunday night, believing all the interesting and calming things he did over the weekend were about to be washed away. Instead, it was traded for a jaded sensation, a consequence of not having a breakthrough in this case in sight.

The team were seated as he made his way to the whiteboards at the corner of the Detectives' Room. One week after Roger Maitland's murder with still a number of leads to follow, he resisted any attempts to reduce the number of officers on the team. The boards were covered in photographs and lines connecting them, a weird jumble only making sense to him and the people in front of him.

'Let's make a start,' he said when they had quietened down. 'I'd like a status update from Vicky, Harry, and Carol. Vicky, why don't you go first?'

'No problem, gov. Myself and DC Graham have now met Roger Maitland's first and second wives, and Laura, his daughter.'

'What about Katy, the one in the US?'

'I called her, and she said Sonia had told her the bad news. She's hardly been at home in the last three weeks as there was an avalanche at one of the main ski resorts in Colorado. They've been dealing with the injured ever since.'

'Okay. What did you conclude from the interviews?'

'Not one member of the family expressed any rancour towards the dead man. Cynthia Leonard, his first wife, is happily remarried to a successful air-conditioning installer and says she doesn't think about Roger at all. Sonia, currently separated from Roger pending divorce, is, as we know, a pop star, and he helped her to secure a recording contract. Laura says he supported her acting career, going to all of her opening nights and flying to LA to watch her filming.'

'So, no one is offering a possible motive?'

'Not one I can find.'

'Can we close it as a lead?'

'Other than we need to keep an open mind about Sonia and Roger's will.'

'Because she will inherit Roger's shares in Vixen?'

'Yes. His forty-five percent share turns her into a multi-millionaire.'

'Okay,' Henderson said, after amending the details on the whiteboard. 'Harry, bring us up to date with your escort meeting yesterday evening.'

'First off I have to say, and without a word of a lie, the woman I met was drop-dead gorgeous. I'd imagined they would send me an old slapper who'd been around the block a few times, but this girl looked a real belter.'

'Worth every penny of taxpayers' money?'

'You bet. The news I have to impart is this. A woman was with Roger Maitland at Oakwood House on the Saturday night of his murder.'

This caused everyone to talk at once, forcing Henderson to call for quiet. 'Go on, Harry.'

'She's an escort from *Brighton Tide* and her name is Claudette, and yes, it shouldn't come as a surprise to anyone to know she has black hair.'

Henderson let the hubbub continue for a minute or so before calming it down.

'Amber said,' Wallop continued, 'when Claudette left the house in a taxi and went home about one-thirty in the morning, she left him very much alive.'

'Well, she would say that, wouldn't she?' Sally Graham said.

'Harry, try to track down the taxi she took. They should be able to give us an accurate time for the pick-up and also tell us about her demeanour. Did she appear anxious, did her dress have blood-stains, was she carrying a bloody knife? You know the drill.'

'No problem.'

'Are we thinking the escort killed him?' Phil Bentley asked.

'I don't think so,' Wallop said.

'I have to agree with Harry,' the DI said. 'You've all seen the P-M report. The victim received multiple stab wounds; the knife driven into his body with some force, right up to the hilt. To do that would have taken considerable effort.'

'And anger.'

Murmurs of agreement came from many. 'I won't shut my mind to believing it might have been a woman, but I do think it's unlikely.'

'I agree.'

'I do too.'

'Harry, how do we find this Claudette?' Henderson asked. 'Not her real name, I assume.'

'I asked Amber and she told me. It's Maggie Webster.'

'We need to locate her, Harry, soon as you can. Use any resources you need. The taxi company might help if she headed straight home. We need to speak to her, even if it's only for elimination purposes.'

'Will do.'

'When we started out on this investigation a week ago, we had three strands to the enquiry: Roger Maitland's personal life, his sex life, and his business life. We've dealt with the first two, but the last one has broadened into three more. The first concerns an incident a few years back when one of Vixen's drones targeted a British patrol in error, killing two and seriously injuring two.'

'I've managed to find contact details for several members of the patrol,' Walters said.

'Excellent,' Henderson said, noting it down. 'We'll talk to them soon. The second strand is Jerome Potter. He'd been sacked from the company and, as a result, lost his shareholding, his substantial salary, and any connection he had to a business he had been instrumental in establishing. His widow appeared sanguine about the whole thing, claiming a large pay-off calmed any discontent, but she has a son called

Lucas. He's ex-army and runs a security company based in Crawley. We haven't met him yet, but he now becomes a person of interest.'

'I would be well pissed off if my dad had been treated that way,' Seb Young said.

'Me too.'

'The third strand of the Vixen investigation is the protestors outside their building. Phil,' the DI said to Phil Bentley, 'tell us about your attempts to join *Soldiers of Peace.*'

'A number of protest groups make an appearance at Vixen about three or four times a month,' Bentley began.

'So often?' Sally Graham exclaimed. 'I'd hate to walk past something so nasty on my way into work.'

'I agree, it's not nice. The protest groups fall into three categories. The first is university students who are principled, but on the whole, peaceful. They come and go based on their study commitments. Another group, the largest contingent, *Vixen Out* and *Stop the War* are all about peaceful protest. They don't hassle the staff, and they're not the ones letting down car tyres and throwing paint bombs.'

'Not to mention,' Henderson said, 'breaking into Vixen and smashing computers.'

'Yes indeed. The third group is a more aggressive, action-orientated mob called the *Soldiers of Peace.* I've joined them, although it's nothing formal, but I gather when we reach the stage of swapping phone numbers and being invited to join their WhatsApp group, I'll be considered a true member.'

'How long do you think it will take?'

'According to a recent joiner who has been invited "in", they have to make sure your heart's in it, by seeing you turn up a few times to protests at Vixen and at an oil terminal in Shoreham. From what I've seen from the two meetings I've attended, they appear no different from any other protest group. I went to this scout hall in the North Laines and the leader, a guy called Simon Deacon, stood up and gave a speech about the evils of war and oil. Afterwards, we all had a coffee and started making placards for the next rally.'

'So far, so normal, but it's early days, Phil. You'll know more once you're invited in.'

'I guess so, unless I die of boredom first.'

NINETEEN

Adrian Chapman looked around at the august assembled group. It included five executive directors from Vixen Aviation, three non-executive directors, a representative from the MOD, and two others with a variety of industry experience.

'The last item on the agenda,' Chapman said, 'is the vacant chief executive position.' He paused a beat. 'Some might say it's too early for us to be talking about this, as the police haven't yet released Roger's body for burial, although they said it will be soon, but as we all know, business waits for no man. We have a demonstration arranged for the new Avalon drone and I'm sure Jack will agree with me when I say, this date is difficult to change with so many senior army and MOD people expected to be present.'

'You're quite right, Adrian,' Jack Hawthorn said. 'It's either the agreed date, or some other eight or nine months in the future.'

Hawthorn had been a lieutenant colonel in the artillery before joining the MOD in the procurement department. He was a good man to know as he had visibility of what the MOD had on the stocks now, and what would be coming down the pipe in the next five to ten years.

'Does anybody disagree with the motion,' Chapman continued, 'for me to take over the reins of the company as interim chief executive, until our recruitment committee makes a more permanent appointment? For reference, the committee comprises: Vixen HR Manager, Clair Scott; Daniel Hill,' he said, nodding at Daniel, Manufacturing Director of Vixen further down the boardroom table, 'and you, Graham,' indicating Graham Halliday, one of the non-executive directors.

The meeting broke up ten minutes later with Chapman confirmed as interim chief executive. He knew he could do large parts of the job well: manage meetings, ensure deadlines were met, talk to suppliers and customers, and handle a variety of personnel issues. What he couldn't do was walk into a room filled with army and MOD people and walk out with a fat order under his arm.

One reason was the colour of his skin. His grandfather came from Ghana and became one of the first black councillors in the town where he grew up in Yorkshire, but in doing so, he suffered a mountain of racial abuse. Race relations had moved on a great deal in the intervening decades, but in a meeting of the type he had just envisioned, he would be the only non-white guy in the room. Even if they were not openly racist, unconscious bias would be working against him.

On another level, he had never served in the military; not even in the Reserve or as a cadet at school. Roger hadn't either, but the not-so-subtle difference between him and his former chief executive was Roger behaved as if he had, and more to the point, other people believed it. He had stacks of credibility in the eyes of the military, more than Adrian despite his own glass brimming over with self-confidence.

At some stage, he would approach the recruitment committee and suggest he should remain in post, and for them to start looking for a superb defence-centric salesperson. He wanted then to find a former army captain or lieutenant colonel, a person whose principal goal would be to sell Vixen products to their previous employer. In support, Chapman would create for them a small department, with the primary function of maintaining the relationship between Vixen and the brass hats.

'These are big boots to fill,' Hawthorn said as he approached, a plate filled with a selection from the buffet in one hand, and a glass of orange in the other. For a former army man, Chapman found it strange that Hawthorn didn't drink. Perhaps early in his career he became involved in excessive imbibing that had taken its toll and left him with a dodgy liver.

'Yes, you're right. Roger was a big character in so many ways; larger than life.'

'One of those few people who could come into a meeting, and within a matter of minutes, dominate it. I watched him do it several times, and I still don't know how it's done.'

'He could be a force of nature, right enough. He will be missed around this place.'

'Is Vixen's direction likely to change?'

He needed to tread carefully here as Hawthorn wasn't making polite conversation, the post-board meeting chinwag over a table buffet and a glass of fine wine. Roger had told him that when the ex-L-C returned to Whitehall, he would chair his own meeting where he would discuss the meeting he had attended and the developments taking place. Roger always took this as a compliment: it left the former Vixen chief in no doubt what the drone programme meant to them.

Now with the interim chief executive's hat on, Chapman could now engage with the Maitland widow, Sonia. By everyone's reckoning, in particular Lester Grange who knew Roger as well as anyone, she was now the largest single shareholder in the business. If she had opinions about how Vixen should be run, he needed to listen.

'I can say with as much conviction as I can muster, it will not. Since the start of Vixen, Roger had been the engineering brains behind the company, but he'd done nothing in that department for the last three or four years. We have a brilliant in-house development and manufacturing team and they will continue to apply the high standards he set.'

'I'm pleased to hear it. How's the Avalon programme going?'

Chapman had given the board a summary of Avalon's current status, but it did no harm to say it again and uncover anything specific vexing Hawthorn, something he didn't want to share with other board members.

His fears were unfounded, as nothing seemed to be bothering the MOD man, and Chapman left the buffet a half hour later. He saw all the non-executives off the premises and headed in the direction of his office.

For a retired senior executive, a non-executive role in a different company looked like a good gig. He knew several, not only at Vixen, who had four or five such appointments in their diary. If each company paid the same as they did, fifteen thousand pounds a year, it was a fine way to keep busy and avoid dipping into retirement capital or a pension. He had many years to go before he reached the end point, but when the time came, he would be sure to put his own list of appointments in place.

While acting as Roger's replacement for the last week or so, he had worked in his own office. Now, he had moved into the big man's place. He walked in and breathed the air, but despite Roger being a keen wearer of Calvin Klein after-shave, he could find no trace of it. Roger also suffered from excess bowel wind, a result of his love of beer and curry, but thankfully, Chapman could find no sign of that either.

He decided to look through Roger's desk and cabinets and throw out anything which appeared no longer relevant. After all, he had to make room for his own things. He would, of course, err on the side of caution as he wasn't party to every issue Roger involved himself in, so he wouldn't chuck out the unfamiliar or anything that looked to be top-secret.

As development director, Chapman had responsibility for research and development. Research was tasked with designing new drones, either based on an internal idea or a request received from a military organisation. Development was staffed by engineers who would take the design from the research team and create a finished prototype for testing and demonstrations. If customers liked what they saw and wanted to buy it, all the information would be passed to manufacturing.

Chapman decided to retain his old duties while acting as chief executive, but would instruct his R&D heads to step up to the plate and assume more responsibility.

He opened the bottom desk drawer with a key found in the pen tray and hauled out all the papers and files. Roger could be a canny operator with balls of steel, and Chapman realised the more he searched, the more embarrassing things he would uncover. It took him twenty minutes to understand Roger had access to a secret fund of money which he used to entertain and glad-hand anyone who needed it. It wasn't only military people who were in receipt of this largesse, but agents, middlemen, and some journalists as well.

He sat back. Working with the military could be at times a dirty business. It went with the territory, since it was used by society to prosecute its own dirty business. If this information got out, the company would be pilloried in the press, and the size of the protests outside the building would mushroom. While he didn't condone such practices, he knew it to be a necessary evil. Once the company had recruited the super-salesman, the files would be passed over to them.

He opened the next folder, wondering if another hand grenade would fall out. He groaned when he saw the name Jerome Potter. Chapman recalled watching the man walk out to his car on the day he received his marching orders. The financial press labelled it an injustice, but only for a few days before the subject disappeared and life carried on as before: the king is dead, long live the king.

He didn't have an interest in finding out if Jerome's sacking had been underhand or unfair, it was water under the bridge in his book, but a series of emails from Jerome's son, Lucas, caught his eye. Reading through them, the son claimed Jerome's ousting had been fraudulent, and that Roger stole his shares in a company he helped to build. He demanded restitution: for Roger to hand back his father's original shareholding.

Roger had sent a terse reply, but Chapman's blood ran cold when he read Lucas' response. The final paragraph stated:

> *Maitland you are nothing but a liar and a thief. You have sullied my dead father's name and reputation. I'll give you one last chance to make this right, or I will do everything in my power to bring down you and the company.*

TWENTY

Henderson turned off the A31 and headed towards Farnham in Surrey. The journey had taken almost two hours, a bit of driving and a lot of roadworks and slow-moving traffic.

'I wonder why he stays out here,' Walters said, 'and hasn't gone back to Nottingham, the place of his birth and where I imagine the rest of his family lives.'

'Maybe it's got something to do with all the military vehicles we passed on the road.'

'The low-loader with the Challenger Tank on its back has got to be one of the strangest.'

'Between here and Wiltshire there must be dozens of military installations: training camps, depots, barracks. Quite a few are based around Aldershot, which is only up the road.'

'Which means visits from old comrades who are still serving will be easier.'

'Plus, he's closer to army hospitals and post-operative care. You would think they'll be more competent at dealing with gunshot wounds and other physical and mental issues caused by combat than any civilian hospital.'

They were visiting Jay Warren, one of the soldiers injured when their platoon came under attack from one of Vixen's drones. The detectives believed someone injured by the drone, in Warren's case putting him in a wheelchair, would be more embittered about the incident than someone who wasn't. Such an incapacity would for the most part absolve him from any direct involvement in Roger Maitland's murder, but meeting him could give them an insight into the depth of feeling prevalent among his former comrades.

Warren lived in a semi-detached house in Adams Park Road. A large piece of land with trees and a pond opposite the house gave the road its name. He didn't know how mobile Warren would be, but if he had chosen the house for this reason, it looked a fine spot to spend a warm afternoon.

They approached the door of his house and pressed the doorbell. It was a Ring video device and he imagined it would be a godsend to any disabled person. With it, they could first check the identity of the visitor on their phone, and not stumble about reaching for crutches or struggling into a wheelchair only to find the caller had come to the wrong house, or it's a local politician handing out election leaflets.

'Yeah?'

'We're detectives from Sussex Police, Mr Warren,' Walters said into the video screen. 'We spoke on the phone.'

'Oh yeah, I remember. Come on in.'

With a click, an electronic lock disengaged and Henderson pushed the door open.

'Make sure the door snaps shut,' Warren shouted.

They walked into the room where the voice had come from and found Jay Warren sitting in an armchair, a folded wheelchair at his side.

He had a muscular build with the beginnings of a tubby stomach, and sported a beard. Not a bushy one, liable to collect the remnants of the previous days' meals, but a close-clipped version matching his short, black hair.

After introductions, the detectives took a seat on the settee.

'That's a clever door you have,' Henderson said.

'Yeah, it is. Getting in and out of the chair is no problem, but it all takes time, you know?'

Henderson nodded. 'I guess you must get fed up sitting in the same chair for too long. I know I do.'

'Too true, mate. You guys want a drink or something? You've been driving for a couple of hours, I imagine.'

'I'll do it,' Walters said, standing. 'What would you like?'

'A cup of coffee would be good,' Warren replied. 'White, no sugar, thanks.'

'Coming up.'

'See, when I was serving, me and my mates were swallowing five, six thousand calories a day. Patrolling in the fucking heat of Afghanistan saps your energy like nothing I've ever experienced before. That's why, and because of the poverty too, the locals are so bloody thin. Now, with me doing fuck-all but sitting on my arse, if I ate even half as much as we were consuming at the time, I would never be able to lever myself out of this chair.'

'I'll bet. Do you manage to get out a lot?'

'Did you notice the blue Mini outside?'

He nodded. 'The one with the hand controls?'

Warren smiled, revealing a fine set of white, even teeth. 'You're a detective, right enough. I take the chair down the ramp and into the road. The tough bit is getting into the car then folding up the chair.'

'So, I take it you only go out if you've got a good reason?'

'Got it in one. Thank God for internet shopping,' he said, nodding at the closed laptop on the occasional table beside him.

Walters came into the room bearing three mugs. She handed one to Warren. 'Thanks mate, you're a star.'

'Jay, as we said on the phone,' Henderson said, 'we're investigating the murder of Roger Maitland, Chief Executive of Vixen Aviation. We'd like to talk to you about the attack on your platoon by one of their drones.'

'I don't mind talking about it, as it happened years ago and I've accepted my fate. For the first two years, I felt angry, so bloody angry, I blamed everybody: Vixen for making the fucking drone in the first place, the prick of a squaddie who didn't know how to program it, the army, Deke our corporal, for not getting me airlifted in time.'

'It must have been hard for you,' Walters said.

'Too true, at least until I met Doctor Phillipa Wenstrom, a clinical psychologist based in Aldershot. She turned me around. She got into my head like a worm and pulled all the anger out. A year of counselling with her and I came out a new man. I mean, I still boil up now and again about my wife divorcing me, my family not coming to visit, and the only people who come calling being my old platoon buddies.'

'Do you recall much about the incident?'

'I remember it all, clear as day. A couple of us were wearing helmet-cams and I look at the footage from time to time.' He reached for his phone, and with surprising dexterity, found what he wanted in a few seconds and tossed the device over to Henderson.

'Have a look yourself.'

The video lasted about five minutes, as the boring patrolling part leading up to the incident had been cut. It started with a lot of confusion, and shouts of: 'Drone incoming!' The drone began firing, the sounds of many people running, then a voice said, 'When did the fucking Taliban get hold one of those badass motherfuckers?'

The soldiers retreated behind a rock and the detectives saw bullets zipping off the stone; ruthless and relentless. The soldiers fired back, but no sooner had one of them pointed their rifle at their adversary, than the drone swung round to target them.

The noise and chaos went on for several minutes, before someone shouted, 'Got the bastard, it's stopped firing!' The video ended thirty seconds later.

'That's quite a video. You can sense the panic and the fear,' Henderson said.

'I look at it now and again to cheer me up. Remind me of the fine soldier I used to be.'

'Do you mind if I make a copy?'

'No problem, mate, fill your boots.'

Using Airdrop, Henderson copied the video to his own phone, rose from his seat and handed the device back to Warren.

'You said during your angry phase, Jay,' Henderson continued, when he'd returned to his place on the settee, 'you had a list of all the people you blamed for the incident. In the cold light of day and twelve years on, who do you blame now?'

'The army,' he said, without hesitation. 'They put an inexperienced lieutenant with only bum-fluff on his chin, and a private with less brains in his head than I have in my arse, in charge of a dangerous battlefield weapon. They fucked up big time. They denied responsibility, of course, but they, and Vixen,' he moved his arm in a sweeping motion, 'coughed up for most of this.'

'Would your comrades in the platoon agree with your analysis?'

'The guys in the video are me and my mates from Squad B. We were part of a bigger platoon of about thirty-five, but the seven of us were in the vanguard, okay?'

Henderson nodded.

'If you hear anything from anyone outside Squad B, it's bullshit; they weren't there. Only our squad was attacked by the drone, and thanks to us, we managed to down it.'

'Understood. So, would your comrades in Squad B agree with your conclusion about the army being responsible?'

'Deke Allen's still serving, so I guess he's neutral. Fellini George is the same as me, stuck in a wheelchair, but he's turned into a miserable old fuck. I wouldn't bother talking to him. Kieran Stock and Brad Luther have always blamed Vixen. They said the drone malfunctioned and the army were engaged in a cover-up. I don't buy conspiracy theories. If I did, I'd have a fucked-up brain to match my fucked-up legs.'

TWENTY-ONE

At the end of the morning update, Henderson stayed behind to examine the information on the whiteboards. The majority of the team were of the opinion the interview with Jay Warren had been beneficial, as they firmly believed one of the beleaguered army squad had to be responsible for Maitland's murder.

Henderson wouldn't be jumping to any early conclusions. Nevertheless, he wanted to meet Brad Luther and Kieran Stock. The two men were the only members of the squad who came away uninjured, and also reportedly believed Vixen were at fault. They were proving difficult to track down.

This didn't come as a surprise to him. Former infantry soldiers, including his brother Archie, had often experienced situations and events that would seem alien to ordinary people. This included being involved in combat and seeing comrades injured or killed, having to use obsolete equipment, and being commanded by officers who knew a lot less about a given situation than you did yourself.

In addition, there were the more mundane but nevertheless unusual settings not common in civilian life: eating in a mess hall with dozens of others, attending briefings by native-looking intelligence officers, and the testosterone-filled experience of being with fighting men all day. No wonder former soldiers often found it hard to settle back into civvy street. If suffering from PTSD, they might find themselves homeless and living on the streets. If they missed the buzz of doing something dangerous, they could now be involved in security or some form of criminal activity.

'Gov?'

He turned to see Phil Bentley walking towards him.

'Hi Phil, what's up?'

'I've been accepted into the *Soldiers of Peace* inner circle.'

'Well done, mate.'

'I think the demo at the oil terminal in Shoreham sealed the deal. I got a bit carried away and went toe-to-toe with this huge oil worker who shrugged his shoulders at my nerve.'

Henderson laughed. 'You need to be vigilant at those protests. They sometimes turn nasty.'

'Don't I know it? The way the SOP guys bait the workers, it's a wonder they don't have a big ruckus every time they demonstrate.'

'When's the next meeting?'

'Friday.'

'Be careful. If they're as bad as we think they are, they'll be on the lookout for undercover journalists and cops.'

'I hear you. See you later, gov.'

The DI decided he'd seen enough and turned to walk back to his office. Looking over the sea of desks, he spotted Harry Wallop waving, a phone stuck to his ear. As Henderson approached, the handset was returned to its cradle with a thump

'We're on. She's over in the Interview Suite.'

Claudette, an escort from *Brighton Tide*, didn't look to be in the same drop-dead category as Amber, the woman Harry Wallop had met. Aged about mid-thirties, the lines of a perhaps difficult life etched on her face, she had jet-black hair, the same colour as her clothes. It didn't mean she wasn't attractive; she was good-looking with a voluptuous figure, making it obvious why some clients would prefer her company, but he imagined she would appeal to an older group than those interested in Amber.

It wasn't a formal interview as Maggie Webster, Claudette's real name, hadn't been arrested and so the recording devices weren't activated.

'Thank you for coming in,' Henderson said after introductions.

'Didn't have much bloody choice, did I? He made me,' she said, nodding at Harry Wallop, sitting beside the DI.

The accent sounded northern, Lancashire, if forced to guess.

'We're part of the team investigating the murder of Roger Maitland.'

'So I gather.'

'You knew Roger rather well, I understand.'

She sighed. 'I've done nothing to be ashamed of. I know what I am, what I do. I'm comfortable with it.'

'I'm not here to judge. Tell me about Roger.'

'Like what?'

'You know, the sort of relationship you had.'

'We didn't any sort of relationship. It was purely business.'

'Okay. Tell me about your business relationship. Describe it for me.'

'He liked a few of the girls at the agency: me, Gabrielle and Marcella, and for a bit of light relief now and again, Cindy.'

'How often did you get together?'

'Three or four times a month.'

'Always at his house in North Chailey?'

'No, sometimes he would be hosting a meeting at the Old Ship or the Grand and he'd ask me to be in his hotel room when it finished. Other times, I'd come to the dinner after the meeting.'

'Are you aware of the kind of work he did?'

She gave him a look that said, *do you think I'm a total idiot*? 'Of course I did.'

'Tell me.'

'He's head of Vixen Aviation and they make military drones, but that's it. He didn't tell me any military secrets or anything. I mean, I would hear bits and bobs about military stuff over dinner, but nothing worth selling to the Russians or Chinese, so don't you go accusing me of doing anything treacherous.'

If he was being honest, Henderson hadn't thought of this as a line of enquiry. Clearly Maggie had, as she had become quite animated.

'You were with him on the Saturday night of his murder.'

'How do you know? I hope you're not accusing me of killing him.' She stood, the chair falling back on the floor. 'I know my rights. I can walk out of here anytime I choose.'

'Yes, you can leave whenever you want, but I need some questions answered and if it not now, it'll be sometime in the coming days. Don't push me or I'll have you arrested.'

She righted the seat but didn't sit. 'It's not illegal to be an escort.'

'I know it's not, but if you're unwilling to answer questions about the death of Roger Maitland, it makes me think you've got something to hide. Do you?'

'No, I bloody don't.'

'Well then, sit down and let's discuss this thing like adults.'

With a grumpy face that spoke volumes, she retook her seat and faced him, scowling.

'May as well do it today. It's a bugger travelling out here to Lewes.'

'I'll ask again, were you with Roger the night he died?'

'Who told you I was?'

'No one told us. We discovered several black hairs in Roger's bed. If you won't tell me, I'm sure a comparison of DNA samples will.'

Henderson knew an easier way. Maggie's hair was an unusual shade of black and regimentally consistent with no grey bits, suggesting it had come out of a bottle. Traces of dye were found on the hairs found in Roger Maitland's bed. All the DI needed to do was ask Maggie which brand she used.

'Okay, yeah, you got me. It was me in his house.'

'How did the two of you hook up?'

'He called me about half ten Saturday night, saying he was in Brighton. I live and work around the city so he drove over and picked me up.'

'What happened when you arrived at his place?'

'You want a blow-by-blow account?'

'No, I don't think we need the fine detail, the basics should be enough.'

'When we got there, the lights were on and the house felt warm. He said he did it with an app on his phone as he left Brighton, if you can believe it. We had a drink then we went upstairs and did what he paid me for. When it came time to go, I took my money, went out to my Uber and he drove me home. How does that sound?'

'What time did you leave?'

'About half one, quarter to two.'

'When you left Roger's house, did you lock the front door?'

Henderson knew the answer to this as the big door to Oakwood House had two deadlocks. Pulling the door closed without being in possession of the key meant it would be shut with regard to wind and rain, but not to someone who wanted to come in and murder Roger.

'Of course I bloody didn't. It needs a couple of keys.'

'Maggie, you're the last person to see Roger alive. You also knew when you walked away from the house, the door would be left unlocked.'

'What are you trying to say? I killed him, or got a mate to do it? That's ridiculous. Roger could be a bit of a strange bugger, right enough, but in a funny way I quite liked him. He paid me five hundred notes a month for a couple of hours' work. Why on earth would I kill him?'

TWENTY-TWO

No sound broke the silence of the Chapman household. At a time in the not-so-distant past, it would resonate with a cacophony of disparate noises – big boots on the stairs and across the upper floor, music playing at high volume, and loud voices when their three boys, Denzil, Rob, and Stuart, were either arguing or trying to communicate through the walls of their bedrooms, too lazy to walk a few metres down the hall.

Several weeks back their youngest, Stuart, finished an economics degree at the London School of Economics, and decided to stay in the city until starting a new job at Deutsche Bank in June. It meant, for the first time in over twenty-seven years, he and his wife Keri were on their own.

It could be a dangerous time for many couples. Having spent years talking to, at, and through the children, couples of their age often had got out of the habit of communicating with one another. Despite working in a fascinating and important industry, involving him in many meetings, important decisions, and numerous late nights and weekends, he and his wife made time to chat. It meant he didn't feel guilty when he left the house after their evening meal and walked to his office in the garden.

For a man with a fine workplace on the top floor of Vixen House, and a superior one now he had moved into Roger's, his neighbours had questioned the necessity of a garden office. He couldn't see the need either, except for his secondary career as a writer. He'd had three business books published. They were all aimed at managers with five to ten years' experience, keen to learn a number of new techniques which would allow them to manage better, keep them abreast of the latest thinking, and ultimately help them move up the organisation.

The books had been written, in the main, from his own experience. In his time at Vixen, he had nurtured twelve Vixen drones to market, from first seeing them as a drawing on the back of an envelope, to a finished product that had buyers from Germany, France, Italy and the UK eagerly lining up to buy them. He also read a number of new management books every month, looking for any novel approach which he would extract and interpret for his own audience. To avoid any accusations of plagiarism, he credited the ideas to their developers, and rather than use them wholesale, he instead created examples to explain their rationale.

He opened the door to his office and walked in. Judging from the warmth of the air, the heating timer had been doing its job. He placed the laptop he carried on the desk, plugged it into the power source and lifted the lid.

He had never suffered from writer's block or a lack of motivation, as he had a lot to say, and only having a short window in which to write he wanted to make the most of it. In addition, being a natural planner, any time he felt stuck all he needed to do was to consult his planning sheets and the way ahead would be clear.

He wrote for a half hour solid, the only interruption being Keri when she brought him a decaffeinated coffee in his favourite Yeti insulated cup.

His phone rang.

'Dan,' he said, when Daniel Hill's name popped up on the screen. 'How are you?'

'I'm fine, mate. Where are you?'

'Garden office.'

'Writing another of your weighty management tomes? What's it about this time?'

'It's called *Managing Up*. It sets out a number of strategies to inform your boss you are a committed and competent individual, ready to take their job when he or she decides to move on.'

'Christ, don't give a copy to any of my guys, whatever you do. Steve and Will are desperate to step into my shoes.'

Chapman didn't broadcast his second career to all and sundry at Vixen. Roger could be a harsh judge of anything he believed took an employee's eye off the ball. He had told Dan and no one else, and the manufacturing director had always been a keen reader of his first drafts.

'Is Keri around?'

'No, she's in the house watching a series about the Nazis.'

'Your wife certainly loves her history programmes, but I'm glad she's not around to hear this. Am I right in thinking the police have spoken to you about Roger?'

'And to Lester.'

'They didn't speak to me, so I phoned them.'

'You did?'

'Yeah. I wanted to find out more about what's going on. You and me have been saying all along we suspected one of those protestors of killing him. If so, my money's on that *Soldiers of Peace* character with all the tats on both arms. He gave Roger verbals whenever he walked out to his car; more than anyone else in the building.'

'You're right, he's a mean son of a bitch. What are the police doing about them?'

'They wouldn't say, but they're on their radar, whatever that means.'

'I suppose they'll get around to it at some point.'

'I said to this cop, the papers are saying someone stabbed him, but they didn't say with what kind of knife. She said, "I can't tell you anything about it." She softened a bit when I told her I knew Roger well and I wanted his killer caught. So when I asked her, do you mean thin, like a stiletto? She said, "No, wider." Do you see what I'm driving at?'

'No.'

'A thin blade indicates a street punk, some geezer in a tight suit who doesn't want the blade showing in the line of his smart jacket. Maybe a pimp or someone from the escort service Roger is said to use.'

It wasn't like Dan to pull his punches. He knew full well how the former head of Vixen behaved. About ten years back, he and Roger had enjoyed a close relationship, much in the way Lester had more recently. After a good day at the MOD, Roger and Dan would go on a bender before picking up some booze and a couple of prostitutes and taking them back to Roger's place.

'A thicker blade indicates a hunting knife,' Dan continued, 'but it's also the kind of knife used by soldiers.'

'I don't think you've got enough evidence to make these assumptions, Dan.'

'Maybe not, but I think it sort of points away from the *Soldiers of Peace* mob.'

'Why, and to what, or to whom?'

'The friendly fire incident of 2011.'

It had happened before Chapman joined Vixen, but he'd heard about it. Not only did he conduct his own due diligence prior to joining, he also talked to the coding team, as they always made a point of adding a small approval box to the control software of all the drones. He thought they were being ultra-careful, but they said it would prevent *another* friendly fire incident, a term which would alert anyone still in the dark.

'You think one of the soldiers did it?'

'One of our drones killed two and seriously injured another two. What more motivation do they need? I think one of the guys who survived is out for revenge.'

'I–'

'Don't you see, Adrian?'

'What?'

'One of those guys killed Roger. Mark my words, he'll be coming for us next.'

TWENTY-THREE

Henderson and Walters were in Crawley about to meet another former soldier. Lucas Potter wasn't a member of the army unit attacked by the drone as Jay Warren was, but instead, the son of Jerome Potter.

'I suppose it's inevitable this guy joined the army,' Walters said. 'He must have grown up in a house full of army talk; there'd be brochures for military kit lying around, and his weekends would be spent at air shows or army gun demonstrations.'

'For sure, and stuff like that rubs off, even when you don't realise it.'

They parked in Crawley Leisure Park and walked along London Road towards the offices of Potter Security.

'I never come to Crawley to shop or go to the cinema,' Walters said.

'Why would you, when you live in Brighton and it's got all you need?'

'I dunno, maybe for a change?'

'This is impressive,' Henderson said as they approached Lomond House, a building of six floors, constructed of red brick with smoked glass windows. 'I always think of security firms as being housed in grubby offices above a dry cleaner's or under a railway arch.'

'This lot must be doing something right.'

They climbed the stairs and buzzed the Potter Security intercom. Being kept waiting outside a secure door guarded by a sophisticated entry system, somehow felt fitting for an appointment at a security company.

A few minutes later a tall bloke called Al led the Sussex detectives into Lucas Potter's office. Lucas was smaller in stature than Henderson expected, with untidy sandy-coloured hair, clean shaven, but well-built and muscled. He also had an impressive military record, as research had told them Potter had been awarded medals for bravery in Afghanistan during the three tours he spent there.

The view from his office in a corner of the room wasn't bad. From one window, it looked over the office block across the street. The other window looked over Crawley Leisure Park with a cinema, restaurants, and bowling alley. Potter had his back to it, just as well as the constant movement of people and traffic might have been a serious distraction. On a credenza close by were a series of framed photographs: Potter in uniform with his army buddies, his colleagues from Potter Security, his partner, Henderson assumed, in a British Airways uniform.

'What do you do here, Mr Potter?'

'Our main work is providing airport security. This can vary from patrolling the perimeter, working airside to check the warehouses and around planes, to being in the airport itself, checking passengers. Whatever they need. We also provide guards for office blocks, sporting venues, entertainment arenas; you name it.'

'How did you get started?'

'You've heard about my dad and what happened at Vixen?'

'Yes.'

'He received a big payoff when he left the company. He gave me a hundred grand to set this place up. If he was still alive today, it would have been my pleasure to pay him back.'

'Business is good?'

'Never better.'

'I'm leading the team investigating the murder of Roger Maitland in North Chailey, a week last Sunday.'

'Okay.'

His face hadn't changed in all the time they had been talking, and registered no emotion when the DI mentioned Maitland's name.

'We are speaking to everyone who knew him, trying to build a picture of the dead man.'

'I'll give you a picture: a greedy, grasping, narcissistic shell of a man. He lacked empathy and common decency, and I'll never understand how my father and him were ever friends.'

'Do you think your father was treated badly by Roger?'

'Of course I bloody do. Dad had the idea of setting up Vixen in the first place, he even thought up the company name. He'd written most of the AI software and needed to find someone like a designer or an engineer who could put his ideas into practice. He wanted to design intelligent robots for industry. Not the dumb, repetitive ones, like those you see in car assembly and paint shops, but robots able to take decisions autonomously.'

'I didn't know.'

'It was Roger who came up with the idea of making military drones after talking to one of his former lecturers at Imperial. I have to admit, and with the benefit of hindsight, it was an inspired decision as they've built a large and successful business on the back of it. You see, Dad at heart had always been a pacifist. Making military drones butted up against all the principles he believed in.'

'How did they fall out?'

'A couple of years before the drone shooting incident... Have you heard about it?'

Henderson nodded.

'A few years before the drone incident, Dad complained about how Roger ignored him in meetings and demeaned him over any mistakes he made. I only found out bits of it when I came home on leave as I was serving in Afghanistan at the time.'

'I understand.'

'When the drone attacked the patrol, it all went haywire.'

'Were you anywhere near the drone incident?'

'No, the attacked patrol was what we called grunts, foot soldiers. We in the Royal Artillery were in a different sector hundreds of miles away, but we heard about it. Without knowing the circumstances, all my guys suspected operator error. Any time we came across Vixen drones, they were as good as gold.'

'When you say everything went haywire, do you mean at Vixen?'

'Yeah. Roger blamed faulty AI for the shooting. He went to town on Dad, not inviting him to important meetings, bad mouthing him in front of people, and to cap it all he reduced Dad's departmental budget.'

'This is before the army's board of enquiry exonerated the company?'

'When their judgement was announced, Dad felt exonerated and confident Roger would lay off, but he didn't. He accused Dad of trying to sabotage the company, which is beyond ludicrous. Dad regarded it as his baby. To cut a long story short, Maitland invoked a clause in Dad's contract allowing him to dismiss him, forfeiting his Vixen shares in the process. Vixen, in case you're not aware, is worth about eight hundred million today. Maybe during Dad's time, about two or three hundred million, but big bucks however you look at it.'

'It's a lot of money.'

'You're telling me. I mean, Dad received a big payoff. It meant him and mum didn't go hungry, but can you understand why I think Maitland is nothing but a robber and a thief?'

'Did your father never think of taking him to court?'

'He was angry when it happened, livid I would say. We all were. He'd had testicular cancer in his late forties and, following a course of treatment he got the all-clear. In his fifties, at one of his regular checks, they found it had returned and had spread to other parts of his body. He was undergoing chemo for the second time and in no mood to spend what he regarded as the final days of his existence sitting in a stuffy court room facing Maitland.'

'Where were you a week last Saturday night, Sunday morning?'

'You think I did it?'

'We are asking the same question of everyone we meet.'

'I suppose you think I've got four hundred million reasons to murder him?'

'No, as I don't imagine killing him, although you may know better, would return your father's share of the company to you or your mother.'

'I'm sure it wouldn't. Give me a second.' He tapped the mouse on his desk computer and looked at something; his diary, the DI assumed.

'We had no emergencies over the weekend, only on Saturday morning after a postman spotted a suspicious package outside the headquarters of a Saudi bank in Docklands. With it being quiet, and my partner, who's cabin crew with British Airways, not working, she cooked her special curry. Afterwards, we put on a movie, and about midnight went to bed.'

TWENTY-FOUR

Thursday night at a hall in Brighton's North Laines, Phil Bentley attended a meeting of the *Soldiers of Peace*. The hall looked busy when he walked in, but rather than receiving non-committal looks and guarded stares as he expected, he received a wave from some and smiles from others. What a difference being in the 'inner sanctum' of the *SOP* group had made.

He took a seat on one of the benches and waited. The evening was a chance to hear Brian Connolly, a leading light in Greenpeace, and a few years back in CND, give a speech entitled: *Protesting Effectively*.

Bentley was having his doubts SOP were the violent group the murder team thought they were. Yes, they were more vocal and 'in your face' than other protest groups, but while some aggressive shouting and intimidation came to the fore in the two protests he had attended, he hadn't seen any violence.

The leader of SOP, Simon Deacon, stood on the little stage.

'Good evening fellow Soldiers of Peace.'

This elicited a muted response from the thirty-plus people gathered.

'I'm glad so many of you made it here on what is proving to be an extremely wet one in Brighton this evening to hear one of the icons of the UK protest movement. He has led sit-ins, marches to Parliament, manned barricades at road blocks, and boarded ships on the high seas. This man has done the lot. He's here to talk to us about *Protesting Effectively*, so please give a warm welcome to: Mr Brian Connelly.'

This time, the crowd really responded, a mixture of clapping, yelling and banging on tables. Connolly had silver hair, worn a bit too long for a mid-sixties man, with a jowly face and a bit of a paunch. Bentley expected as much, as he had looked him up on the web. However, when he opened his mouth to speak, the voice sounded strong and authoritative, his message delivered with the verve and energy of a thirty-year-old.

Despite Connolly's talk being about a subject Bentley only pretended to like, he felt captivated. If he was one of the university students here, or with the guys in good jobs who cared about the environment, poverty, and social issues with a passion, his smile and cheering would be as broad and loud as theirs.

Connolly spoke for forty minutes and ended with a heart-felt exhortation to get out there and make a difference. The hall erupted in a cacophony of sound lasting a couple of minutes. It reminded him of some videos he'd seen of the adoration shown by followers of evangelist preachers in the US.

'What an amazing talk!' the guy next to Bentley said. 'To still have all that enthusiasm for the issues after so many years is beyond astonishing.'

'I loved it,' Bentley said, 'so inspiring.'

The accolades and the retelling of examples made by the speaker carried on as Phil approached the table containing the tea urn and a couple of coffee pots. He had to wait in a queue, which included tonight's speaker in the company of Simon Deacon. Phil didn't have to fake his responses too much as he'd enjoyed the speech too. He didn't agree with the overall message, but the pictures Connolly painted of doing good and making changes sounded sincere and punchy, without being patronising or preachy.

Phil returned to his seat. He would chat and drink his coffee for the next ten minutes, before heading home. He imagined everyone else would be planning to do the same.

'Hi Luke.' It was one of a few guys he knew were in decent jobs and didn't quite fit the profile of a typical protest group member – rebellious student or the angry unemployed. His name was Ben, while Phil had adopted a pseudonym he had used in the past: Luke Grayson. He kept Luke's social media profile up to date with a post about every couple of weeks; not sufficient to suggest an active user, but enough to inform the mildly curious he still existed.

'Hi Ben, how are you?'

'Inundated at work. I barely managed to get away tonight. I'm so glad I did. Brian Connolly did a better speech than the majority of guys I see fronting management and motivational training courses.'

'I'll bet. If he wasn't talking about such contentious subjects and giving most captains of industry palpitations, he could carve a successful career as an entertaining after-dinner speaker.'

He laughed. 'I've been to a couple of those. The best I've seen is Alex Ferguson being interviewed by a comedian, whose name escapes me. They had the audience roaring and laughing for most of their forty-minute chat.'

They talked for a few more minutes as Phil finished his coffee. He considered making a move home when Dave King approached.

He was a big guy with broad arms full of tats, and always wore an army-style jacket with lots of badges. He would stand at the front of any protest, so the people being targeted noticed him first, and he was the person local photographers wanted to snap. If truth be told, the SOP leader liked his prominent position too as it gave the group a threatening edge.

'Luke,' Dave said, 'can I talk to you a minute?'

'Sure.'

'You're down for the meet at the oil delivery depot in Lewes next Tuesday. You still up for it?'

'No problem.'

'Right mate, come this way, and grab your jacket. We're going outside.'

They trudged through rain-sodden streets before stopping in front of three garage lock-ups. Dave pulled out a key, opened the middle one and pushed the up-and-over door.

'C'mon,' he said to Phil, ushering him inside. He switched on the light and hauled the door closed.

Phil tensed, believing he had walked into a trap, fooled by Dave's false bonhomie. He imagined being beaten up and exposed as an undercover cop. To be fair to Dave, it didn't look like the best place to attack anyone, as the centre of the space was dominated by something large, hidden under a black sheet.

'Give us a hand, mate.'

Phil helped him remove the cover. It revealed an aggressive-looking Jeep Wrangler with an array of high-set front lights, larger than average tyres, and steel bars reinforcing the inside of the passenger cabin.

'Quite a machine.'

'She is. Her name is Ruby and she only comes out on special occasions; the oil depot in Lewes fits the bill. We'll get there nice and early and use her to block the gates. Then, after we cut through the fence,' he said, opening the rear door of the car, 'we'll slash the tyres of their trucks with these little babies.'

Phil looked inside. The box contained six or seven lethal-looking machetes, and beside them, several hunting knives. Any thoughts about the SOP being an ineffective talking shop disappeared like smoke under the gap at the bottom of the up-and-over door.

TWENTY-FIVE

Sussex had been battered by heavy downpours for the best part of the previous night and early this morning. In Hazelmere in Buckinghamshire, the streets were equally sodden, and any parks and waste ground Henderson and Walters passed had a smattering of large puddles.

'This looks like a lot of British towns,' Walters said as they travelled through the south-western stretches, 'an old village with lovely stone houses, surrounded by a host of new housing developments. New houses are so standard looking, we could be in Norfolk or Devon or anywhere else for that matter.'

'You're starting to sound like me.'

'Am I? Is that a good or bad thing?'

'As a detective trying to climb the greasy pole, I suppose it's not too bad. As a woman in the market for a new boyfriend, I'd say it's a definite no-no.'

'Maybe that's my problem. I thought it was the high standards I set.'

They turned into Ashley Drive.

'I think these houses are a bit older than the ones we saw earlier,' the DI said, looking at two rows of red brick houses with tiled roofs. 'Maybe built in the 1950s.'

'They're semis right enough, but look on the large side.'

They parked outside the home of Brad Luther, one of the surviving soldiers from the drone attack on the army platoon. He had escaped uninjured, but his comrade Jay Warren had said Luther believed Vixen were responsible.

'Do you think money from the army and Vixen bought this one as well?'

'I read an article on the web that said the whole platoon got money from Vixen and the MOD, but those not disabled got less.'

Makes sense.'

'Therefore, I don't imagine it was enough to buy a house like this.'

Luther's wife answered their knock on the door. After a brief introduction she hurried out, saying she was late for a dentist appointment. Brad stepped into the frame and, after shaking hands, led the two detectives to a seat on the rear deck, overlooking the garden.

The weather was cool, the temperature too low for sitting outside, but the patio had a roof and heaters at each end, both of which were lit. A few minutes later, they also had a mug of hot coffee in front of them. Their reason for being outdoors soon became apparent when Brad dumped his cigarette packet and lighter on the table.

Henderson opened the discussion. 'I'm leading the team investigating the murder of Roger Maitland, Chief Executive of Vixen Aviation, about two weeks ago.'

Luther looked clean-shaven with a mop of untidy brown hair. He wasn't a bad-looking bloke with blue eyes and an open, honest face, but the large scar on his cheek did nothing to enhance it.

'I can't say any tears were shed in this house when we heard the news,' Luther said, reaching for a cigarette and lighting up.

'You blame Vixen for the drone attack?'

'You bet I do; one hundred percent. Vixen must have known at some point in time, the army being the army, they would order an inexperienced soldier to take the reins of that drone. It doesn't take a detective like you two to deduce that.'

'Didn't the findings of the army's Board of Enquiry, absolving Vixen of any negligence, maybe not change your mind, but temper your opposition somewhat?'

'No chance. You think the army played a straight bat? No fucking way. They looked at Vixen, what they'd done so far, and what they were planning, and decided they wanted more of their technology going forward. No way would they want to jeopardise such a good relationship.'

'Not even for two dead and two seriously injured soldiers?'

'Not even for ten dead soldiers.'

'Do you think there's a strong case for incorporating drones into the military arsenal?'

'Yeah I do. The great thing about the army is the comradeship of being with mates. Every day you're filled with this fear of not knowing where you're going or what's around the next bend, and the absolute joy of surviving a firefight or returning from a dangerous patrol.'

He lit another cigarette and took a deep drag.

'On the other hand, I do recognise drones can be put into areas where we wouldn't want to go, and with their aerial view of things, they get a better picture of what's going on. I'm no Luddite, I'm not frightened of change, and I appreciate what they're good at, but they won't replace boots on the ground. To my mind, their role is to make us more effective.'

'Do you still keep in touch with other members of the unit?'

'Charlie Park and me were best buddies. I kept my eye on him when we were taking shelter from the drone. He popped up from behind a rock to let off a shot when a bullet from the drone went straight through his helmet, killing him stone dead.'

'Through his helmet? I thought those things were designed to protect you.'

'Oh yeah, they'll save you from the rocks thrown by the boys in the village, or a bit of flying shrapnel from an IED, but no bloody use at all with a direct hit from an armour-piercing bullet.'

'Is there anyone else you talk to?'

'Yeah, I call Jay Warren every couple of weeks. He doesn't know it, but I do it when I'm feeling crap. I call him Mr Cheery, and this from a bloke who pisses in a bag and rolls around in a fucking wheelchair. It's nothing short of remarkable. The boy deserves a medal just for that.'

'Did you take your concerns to Vixen?'

'I spoke at the Board of Enquiry, and sent a couple of letters to Roger Maitland, then emails when I'd got the hang of them, but he gave me the corporate bullshit: *There's been a BOI and Vixen weren't to blame. I'm sorry for what happened to you and your mates*, yada, yada yada.'

'How did it make you feel?'

'Angry, but Sandra, who you met earlier, pulled me out of it. She says the past is gone; we can do nothing about it. If you dwell on it, it will eat you alive, and she's right. I've got her and two lovely kids. I don't need anything else.'

'I understand. Brad, we're trying to track down another member of your unit, Kieran Stock. Do you still keep in contact with him?'

'Kieran Stock? There's a name I haven't heard in a long time. After the incident, me, Fellini, and Jay got out of the army. Two choices: be pensioned off, or stay. We all left but Deke and Kieran stayed. Kieran only lasted another couple of years before being invalided out. He'd been serving with undiagnosed PTSD. I think he spent something like nine months in rehab.'

'Not good. Have you any idea where we can find him?'

'Haven't a clue. To be honest, I didn't like him much. When soldiering, what you need beside you is men you can rely on. You're looking for qualities like dependability and conscientiousness. Kieran had neither of those qualities; he was either an awkward bastard or a maverick, take your pick. He had his own way of doing things and he gave Deke, our corporal, a bloody hard time, questioning him about where we were going, or debating the point of the operation. In the mess, we voted him the man most likely to step on an IED. He liked that, can you believe it?'

TWENTY-SIX

Friday night, Phil Bentley walked away from *The Cricketers* pub in Southwick. Inside, members of *Soldiers of Peace* were still celebrating their early morning visit to the Lewes Depot of Burnston Oil. They had cut through the fence and damaged the tyres of many of the tankers parked inside. The group had been so successful damaging the tankers, Dave decided there wasn't any point in blocking the entrance with Ruby as the vehicles weren't going anywhere.

The only thing left to do was to take lots of pictures. They were sent to a news agency for all interested newspapers and websites to publish, and to post on social media showing the world what a great protest group they were.

The twelve or so SOP members in attendance went back to their day jobs, those who had one, others to their university lectures, and for the rest, back home or to a pub. They had arranged to meet up at *The Cricketers* in the evening, a pub close to where SOP leader Simon Deacon lived, to crow over the media coverage and celebrate.

The mood in the pub was, without doubt, and who could blame them, self-congratulatory. The main newspaper in the Brighton area, *The Argus,* had a front-page story condemning the senseless act. A piece also went out on the BBC regional news programme, *South Today*, with film of the damaged tankers and an interview with the pissed-off depot manager.

Phil had participated in the raid and didn't hold back. He used the bolt cutters to cut the wire fence, and grabbed one of the machetes to slash the tyres of one tanker. In addition, he ran behind a post holding an aggressive Alsatian which had its teeth into the leg of an SOP guy. Bentley hauled the dog off the guy and wrapped its long chain around several objects to shorten its reach. Phil was lucky it didn't turn on him, but the dog was so focussed on mauling the SOP guy.

Many of those who turned up to the pub this evening lived within walking distance, others had booked an Uber or arranged a lift. For his own reasons, he did none of those things and drove. As a result, most of them were as pissed as rats by nine; he on the other hand felt stone-cold sober.

It was a hard act to perform: look part of the group while they were getting legless and you weren't. By the time a couple of members had left to stagger home, around ten fifteen, he decided to make a move. He received friendly hugs and handshakes for his participation in the Burnston Depot Attack, as the papers were calling it, and so he walked out feeling assured his undercover role was safe for another couple of weeks.

Despite his active role in the raid, he had a problem reconciling in his own mind protesting about something he didn't like, with committing criminal damage. Of course, protesting was a slow process and produced few short-term results, but in the long-term it changed some people's minds. Attacking an oil depot put the tankers out of action for no more than a day or so, but would have caused resentment in many quarters.

He had parked his car several streets away in the car park of the local library. He didn't want anyone knowing the car he drove, despite it being a nondescript Vauxhall Astra. He used it for work and someone might see him in the company of a uniformed cop or driving into a police station. His reasons for not parking the car outside a pub could be sidestepped: he needed a walk to clear his head, he preferred to put the car in a better-lit place, but being seen associating with a fellow cop could not.

Away from the pub, he walked along Southwick Square; not so much a square, rather a road lined with closed shops: post office, barber, newsagent, sweet shop.

He passed the car park behind the shops and, on the point of walking past a public toilet block, something struck him on the shoulder. It didn't feel a heavy blow, as it didn't knock him down, but it hurt like hell. He turned to face the phone snatcher, mugger of drunks, or whoever it might be, when a big fist came barrelling towards him, smacking him in the face and bursting his nose. He fell this time.

He tried to stand, but his knees had turned to rubber. *Wham!* A kick in the stomach caused him to double-up. *Wham!* Another kick, this time on the hands trying to protect his body.

Big hands grabbed the front of his jacket and pulled. His bloody nose caused his vision to wobble, but the face and beery breath of Dave King was unmistakable.

'You fucker, I knew you was dirty the moment I clapped eyes on you. If I ever see your ugly mug again, or you write about us in your fucking rag of a newspaper, you'll get this.' He reached into his jacket and whipped out a vicious-looking hunting knife. The knife disappeared back into his jacket and he let go of Phil's and stood.

About to walk away, he turned and came back. He drew his leg back and aimed his boot at the inert man's balls.

TWENTY-SEVEN

Saturday morning, DI Henderson drove to Mile Oak. A big murder case normally threw up a number of leads, and if they were lucky, a few suspects. In the Maitland case, the opposite was true. The victim could have been killed by any number of people: a Vixen protestor, a soldier from the drone shooting, a pimp connected to the prostitutes he often used, or the latest one, the son of Vixen's co-founder.

He couldn't put his finger on why, but Lucas Potter's excuses weren't convincing. He talked in warm terms about his father, but when it came to the subject of his dismissal from the company, he appeared to be holding back a lot of pent-up emotion. In the case of his alibi, he'd trotted it out like an actor, as if the lines had been rehearsed numerous times.

Potter didn't lack motivation. In addition to feeling outraged at the way his father had been treated by Maitland, the issue of the forfeited shares weighed heavily. If the company had been unsuccessful, teetering on the brink of bankruptcy, the shares wouldn't be worth the paper they were printed on.

At the time of Jerome's dismissal, the company was worth around two-to-three hundred million pounds. Latest estimates valued the company at eight hundred million, so the Potters' share would be worth four hundred million now. This wouldn't leave Lucas and his mother 'comfortable'; it would rocket the pair into the multi-millionaire class. Stephanie could afford an elegant Georgian mansion apartment in Sussex Square, while Lucas could give up working and run a charity for ex-veterans, or do nothing but drink mojitos in the pool of a smart villa in Barbados.

The ex-vets charity idea wasn't the result of Henderson's fanciful meandering. The three directors of Potter Security were Lucas, Al Cowan, and Tony Sherman, all former soldiers, and on their website, they made a virtue of employing former service personnel as security guards. In terms of suspects, Henderson put him near the top of the pile.

Phil Bentley lived in Truleigh Drive, Mile Oak. Its neighbour, Portslade, could be a bit of a rabbit warren of similar-looking houses, and he knew from experience, an easy place to get lost. Despite his extensive knowledge of local streets, he used the sat-nav.

Phil's house, like those on either side and across the road, was chalet-style: a semidetached bungalow with rooms built into the roof. They were close to Mile Oak Recreation Ground and the sports centre, a building the DI knew Phil visited a couple of times a week to supplement his rugby training. He wasn't sure Phil would be going back there any time soon.

The door opened and Helen, Phil's wife, stood there with two-and-a-half-year-old Katie hanging around her legs. He had met them both a few times before, but not enough to expect a gleeful smile from the child or a hug from her mother. However, the look he received from Helen when she said, 'You'd better come in. He's in the lounge,' was frostier than he'd expected.

'Hello, Phil. How are you?'

'Oh, hi gov, good to see you. I'm bruised all over and my face is a bloody mess.' His voice sounded like he had a bad cold, not helped by the strapping across his nose.

'You're not kidding. Did you get seen in A&E quickly?'

'You wouldn't believe the dirty looks I got from the nurses, thinking I'd been involved in a drunken pub brawl. I saw a doctor about half an hour after I arrived, and I told him about being a cop. Only then did their attitude mellow.'

'I suppose they see so much of it, and in most cases it's self-inflicted, so a cynical approach is more or less guaranteed.'

'Yeah, I guess you're right.'

'What's the diagnosis?'

'Broken nose which they reset, and severe bruising to my ribs and back.'

'Nothing else damaged?'

'No, I got lucky in a way. Hang on a sec, gov. Helen, love,' Phil called, 'can you make me and the boss a cup of coffee?'

The DI couldn't quite make out Helen's reply as she mouthed something to Phil, but he understood enough to realise she was agitated.

Henderson turned. 'Helen, if you have something on your mind, just say it.'

'He could have been killed!' she hollered, her face red with anger as she stomped into the lounge. 'I might have lost my husband and Katie her father. I blame you for sending him into a place where he could come to harm!'

'I told you before, Helen,' Phil said, 'I agreed to do it. I could have said no.'

'Yeah, but if you did, how would it look in front of your colleagues?'

'When we decided to investigate this group, we had the option of using surveillance and research,' Henderson said, 'but I felt the quickest way to find out more was to put somebody in there. I take full responsibility, but if I'd thought there was any chance of Phil being beaten up, I wouldn't have done it.'

'If he'd squared up to me,' Phil said, 'I don't think I'd have come off second best, but he jumped me and caught me by surprise. He's a big guy, but he drinks too much and he has a soft underbelly.'

Henderson turned back to Phil, accompanied by a clattering background noise as Helen went back into the kitchen, banging a variety of utensils in the process. 'You know the person who attacked you?'

'His name is Dave King. He's the big guy who wears fatigues and stands at the front of all the *Soldiers of Peace* protests.'

'The bloke with all the tats who looks like a former soldier?'

'Yeah him, but he's been nowhere near the services, the discipline would kill him. He's a builder's labourer, works for the most part on new housing developments.'

'If you know where we can find him, we'll bring him in and press charges.'

'Good to know, but I need to tell you something else. When he finished breaking my nose and bruising my ribs, he threatened me with a knife.'

'Oh?'

'Yeah, not with any old knife, this looked to be a serious hunting knife with a broad blade.'

'Interesting. Is this his role in the group, beating up undercover cops?'

'I don't think he knew I was a cop, he thought I was a journalist.'

'What made him think that?'

'Maybe in the pub with me reading *The Argus* too much and commenting on how they'd done such a good job reporting the depot attack. In fact, I was only looking at it as a result of being fed up talking to a bunch of piss artists. With hindsight, I should have got drunk, same as the rest of them.'

Helen walked into the room and placed a mug of coffee in front of Phil, and another beside the DI. A better outcome than he expected, as he'd imagined she would slam it down on the coaster. Perhaps a sign she had calmed down somewhat, or didn't want coffee stains on her nice wooden floor.

'It goes without saying,' Henderson said, 'I'll terminate the *Soldiers of Peace* undercover inquiry, but at least we've got something useful out of it. We'll pull in Dave King and take a closer look at his knife.'

'There's a couple of guys I'm friendly with in the group who weren't at the pub and won't be aware I've been kicked out. I'll contact them and find out where King is working at the moment.'

'Good man. Give Carol a call when you do,' Henderson said, standing. 'I'd better get back to work. How long have you got off?'

'The doc said I should take next week off, but I'll be back in the office on Tuesday.'

'No, Thursday.'

'Wednesday.'

'Okay, Wednesday it is. See you then.'

TWENTY-EIGHT

Henderson drove in the direction of Lewes. Phil Bentley's undercover operation would be viewed as a partial success with the identification of Dave King as a suspect, but at the cost of having one of his officers laid up for several days with painful injuries. However, it would be hailed an unmitigated triumph if Dave King proved to be Maitland's killer.

Although Phil had done undercover training and had infiltrated a couple of similar groups before, he wasn't what the DI, and most police forces, would regard as a proper undercover officer. These guys had Henderson's full admiration, as to infiltrate organised criminal gangs they would dress like their targets, change their hair and beard to look like them, and try to talk like them. In some cases, they were in situ for several years, building strong relationships with their targets, and in a few of the cases that had made the national press, marrying one of their members.

He called Carol Walters.

'Hi Carol, I'm on my way back to the office.'

'Good, everyone's in.'

'I dropped by to get an update on Phil's injuries.'

'How is he?'

'Nothing too serious. He's been beaten, got a broken nose and some nasty bruising on his ribs, but otherwise okay. Should be back at work on

Wednesday, although I imagine he'll be a bit stiff in his movements.'

'It's good to know he's okay and not badly injured. His cheery demeanour will be missed around the office.'

'It's not all bad news. The guy who jumped Phil is a bloke called Dave King, the guy with the tats who fronts the *Soldiers of Peace* demos.'

'I remember him.'

'He threatened Phil with a knife similar to the one we think was used on Roger Maitland.'

'Did he now?'

'We've got enough to arrest him for the assault, and with the suspicion that he might have murdered Roger Maitland we should be able to obtain a search warrant and give his house a good going-over. I want that knife found and sent to the lab for immediate testing.'

'Got it. Where do I find him?'

'Phil says he's a labourer on new housing developments. He knows some guys in the SOP group who might not have heard about his altercation with King, and may know where he's working. If they do, he'll call us with the details.'

'If they don't?'

'I guess it's down to calling the site managers at all the sites in the area and asking if a man fitting his description works there.'

'Do you know how many new housing developments there are in Sussex? Dozens, I would say. Every time I travel through a town or village, there's always a new development sprouting up on the outskirts.'

'If King tends to work for one builder, as some of those guys do, it should make the search a whole lot easier.'

'I'll await the call.'

'Okay, I'll catch you later.'

Henderson spent the rest of the journey with the radio turned low. He needed time to think. He had pencilled-in Lucas Potter as a good fit for Maitland's killer, but now Dave King shifted into the frame. His membership of SOP, a group whose stated aim was to stop Vixen producing military drones, added weight to his motives. If he had indeed killed Maitland, in terms of the stated aims of the SOP, he had done a better job than he realised.

The death not only robbed Vixen of its chief executive, it also eliminated the company's main point of contact with the MOD and military. Henderson didn't know much about military contracts, but reading between the lines during his discussions with Adrian Chapman, Maitland's vast selling experience would without doubt be missed, making him a difficult man to replace.

It was a more tenuous link than Lucas Potter, but he knew how members of protest groups were often motivated by more than could be explained by common logic.

He walked into his office, took off his jacket, and was about to sit down behind his desk when Walters appeared.

'You didn't take long.'

'Phil's house in Mile Oak is close to the A27.'

'That's up Portslade way?'

'Yes, at the far end.'

'Get lost in that warren and you'll grow a beard by the time you find your way back. While you were out, Phil phoned.'

'Did he?'

'Yeah, he sounds better than his injuries first suggested.'

'It's all the rugby training he does, he's tougher than he looks. Did he manage to tell you Dave King's whereabouts?'

'He did. He said he's working on a Calman site near Billingshurst.'

'They work Saturday mornings?'

'They do indeed. A patrol car is heading to that very place as we speak.'

'Well done, Carol. Let me know if and when they find him.'

'Will do.'

'Before you go, what's the story on our missing soldier, Kieran Stock?'

'He's off the radar. Didn't Brad say he had PTSD?'

'He spent nine months in rehab. I assume he's now...I guess cured isn't the right word, but you know what I mean.'

'Even with rehab, he might still be suffering. If he's living on the streets, changed his name, or maybe moved abroad, it could prove difficult finding him.'

'Understood, but keep looking. We need to find him, even if only for elimination purposes.'

TWENTY-NINE

Not the best start to a Monday morning for Henderson to be sitting in his boss' office waiting for him to finish talking to his secretary. During any major investigation, he kept Sean Houghton updated at regular intervals. This one felt different; Houghton had asked for the meeting.

'Ah, Angus, how are you?' the CI asked, as he breezed into his office, pushing the door closed behind him. 'All set for another busy week?'

'Yes indeed.'

He took a seat in his large leather chair, another benefit of being the next rung up, as well as a bigger office and desk. However, in Henderson's mind it made the office environment too comfortable, making it hard to step outside into the cold to chase down villains.

'There are two things I want to talk to you about. The first is Phil Bentley.'

'I saw Phil on Saturday. He's had his nose broken and his ribs are bruised, but otherwise he's okay. He should be back at work Wednesday this week.'

'I'm pleased to hear it, although it could have been much worse.'

'Maybe, but maybe not. Phil said he thought it was a warning shot to a suspected journalist to say he'd been rumbled. This is a protest group who are trying to protect their own, not some serious organised crime group who would think nothing of murdering an undercover cop.'

'Nevertheless, it was a risk you were not required to take.'

'What makes you say that? We knew nothing about *Soldiers of Peace* before this, now we know plenty.'

'I'm sure there must be other ways.'

'There's a load of information on the web, but a lot of disinformation as well. Yes, they are a protest group who resort to property damage on occasion, but some of the things ascribed to them aren't true. For example, we were told they had broken into Vixen's offices and damaged some computers. When Phil asked someone about it, they said it wasn't them, but they were happy taking the credit for it.'

'Even still. One of our officers ended up in hospital.'

The DI didn't risk eliciting Houghton's ire by pointing out Bentley had been an out-patient in A&E and hadn't spent a night in hospital. Henderson felt sure Phil's wife would never have allowed him anywhere near their house if that were the case.

'Not only did Phil's undercover operation provide us with more information about *Soldiers of Peace*, he also found us a suspect for Roger Maitland's murder.'

'Oh?'

'The guy who attacked him is a bloke called Dave King. Phil saw him with a knife similar to the one used to kill Roger Maitland. Plus, being a member of SOP, he has, by definition, a grudge against Vixen.'

'Interesting. Give me a summary of where we are.'

'We are currently concentrating on three main fronts, one less than we were before as we don't believe the killer came from within his family group. They are: the soldiers attacked by a rogue Vixen drone; Lucas Potter, son of Jerome Potter, one of the co-founders of Vixen Aviation; and now Dave King from *Soldiers of Peace*.'

'I understand the motives of the first and last on your list, but what would Jerome Potter's son gain from Maitland's death?'

'Nothing more complex than pure revenge for the way his father had been treated.'

'Remind me.'

'Jerome and Roger Maitland set up Vixen, dividing their shares in the company fifty/fifty.'

'Okay.'

'When Maitland sacked Jerome, blaming him for the rogue drone strike on the army patrol, he forfeited all his shares. The shareholdings were reduced when the company was floated not long after Jerome Potter was sacked, but however you look at it, Jerome missed out on a bumper payday.'

'He had the power to do that?'

'He invoked a clause written into both of their contracts. Don't forget, when they were first drawn up all those years ago, Vixen was a small company with a similarly tiny order book. I don't imagine either Potter or Maitland in their wildest dreams believed it would grow into what it is today: an eight hundred-million-pound company with sales in over twenty countries.'

'I suppose not, but missing out on a four-hundred-million-pound payday is enough to send anyone off the rails. Although I don't imagine killing Maitland would in itself encourage Vixen to hand the Potter shares back to the family.'

'Hence I believe the motive is not financial, it has to be revenge. However, now with a new man at the helm—'

'Adrian Chapman, isn't it?'

'Yes. He's temporarily in the top chair and might take a different view of the situation from Roger. I don't see him offering Jerome's widow the lost shares, but perhaps more compensation than they received last time.'

'It's a curious case this one,' Houghton said, rising from his seat and pacing the office floor. 'Here's Roger Maitland, a prominent businessman, and working for a company with a name, in some people's eyes at least, that needed a bit of polishing. To improve its image, he did the rounds of society and charity dinners and hobnobbed with plenty of local politicians.'

'I've seen loads of pictures on the web of him doing just that.'

'The thing those pictures don't show, and I'm speaking from personal experience, is that there always seemed to be a distance between him and the people he knew. He received little praise for the number of charities supported by Vixen, and the good causes they funded. I used to think it was because he worked for a military supplier, but asking around since his death, I now believe it was something else.'

'Oh?'

'Women said they found him "creepy", not because he went over the top and put his hands where he shouldn't, but just a vibe. I remember one told me at a charity dinner, he would be making small talk with her, and a minute or so later, would be guffawing like a docker with men over a dirty joke or a story like they were in a pub after a rugby match.'

'Perhaps he was a man's man. You know, more relaxed in the company of men.'

'Certainly it accounts for some of his behaviour, and hanging out with military types didn't help, as they can often give an air of aloofness, but there was something else. He was a well-known womaniser, and I've seen it happen at first hand when he left many a social gathering with a new woman on his arm.'

'We've looked into this. A prostitute was at his home the night of his murder, and it seems he used them on a regular basis. We also found, when we analysed his phone, he went out with a succession of women he met on internet dating sites. We've tracked down the taxi that came to his house the night of the murder to pick up his escort. The time of her departure checks out. In addition, she didn't appear to be covered in blood or displaying a nervous or anxious disposition, so she's been ruled out.'

'That's a shame, but doesn't he sound like a bull in a field full of cattle?'

'The problem is, no one has come to the fore complaining of any wrongdoing, except for his penchant for rough sex. We thought maybe an angry pimp or irate husband would appear, as I'm sure married women weren't immune to his charms, but they haven't.'

'Keep it on the back burner. Here was a guy sailing too close to the wind, or should I say, flying too high towards the sun. He must have upset someone.'

THIRTY

Adrian Chapman was gazing out of the window in his home office at the bottom of the garden. The new management book he was supposed to be writing stared back at him from the screen of his laptop. Since Roger's death two weeks ago, progress had been snail-like.

Passages he'd assumed would be easy to write when he first outlined them, appeared on the page of his Word document as if his six-month old MacBook had been fitted with an 8086 processor. Concepts and theories he knew so well he could recite them in his sleep were wrung from his memory like trying to entice a dog from under a table during an electrical storm.

It wasn't the loss of the big man that was worrying him, or his attendance at Roger's funeral earlier in the day, although from a business perspective, it did leave a huge hole. In fact, it had inspired him in other ways. The sudden departure of a key executive and how to manage the organisation without them would be the main topic of his next book.

He hoped the hole could be filled by the recruitment of a super military salesperson, a subject he would raise for approval at the forthcoming board meeting. In the meantime, he had to prove to them he had the abilities and skill to fulfil all the other roles of the chief executive, and so far, he believed he had achieved this.

From a personal standpoint, he would not miss Roger one bit. Chapman had been recruited by Jerome Potter and, from the outset, Roger had been hostile. Chapman couldn't believe it, as any racists he had come across until then wore football shirts or NF t-shirts and gripped plastic glasses of cheap lager in their tattooed hands. They did not walk around in two-thousand-pound Pierre Cardin suits and buy their shirts in batches of five from a bespoke tailor on Jermyn Street.

Chapman also did not like the way he spoke about female members of staff behind their backs. He never used out-and-out sexist or misogynistic terms, forcing the other attendees at the meeting to report him to the Ethics Committee, but sly digs: 'she thinks that way because she's a woman', 'her mind's not on the job, but on her bloody kids' exams'.

As a manager, Roger led by example. When he came back to the office with a new contract under his arm, he rallied the troops and encouraged everyone to get behind him to meet its demands. Yes, Chapman would miss Roger as a brilliant and hard-to-replace military liaison, but he would not regret his passing as a person.

The reason he couldn't write and why the death of Roger played so much on his mind, was because he believed he would be next. It wasn't only the call he'd received from Dan Hill the previous week when he'd raised the same concerns, but on finding a file concerning the sacking of Jerome Potter, including a batch of emails from his son.

He had to admit, now being aware of most of the facts, Jerome's dismissal from the company had not been handled well, and he would have objected to it if it had happened today. Roger did it, he realised now, because of greed – he wanted control of the company, to have it all to himself. In subsequent marketing publications whenever the origins of the company were mentioned, Jerome's role was downplayed and Roger's elevated. Now, he understood Lucas Potter's frustration after Roger sent him a 'piss off and don't bother me again' style of email, and refused to answer any further communications.

The tone of Potter's emails didn't sound as money-grabbing as might be expected from a man deprived of millions of pounds, but more focussed on looking for redress to a wrong done to his father. Lucas didn't stipulate what form this reparation would take, but Chapman imagined several: a written apology by the company, a sum of money, a wall plaque on the way to the staff canteen, a puff piece in a military or aviation magazine praising the dead man, or maybe a job at Vixen for the Potter widow.

If only Roger had been more conciliatory and selected and implemented one of those, Potter's vendetta against Vixen might have been stopped in its tracks. Instead, Lucas Potter's emails became more threatening with each new missive received.

He'd clearly run out of patience with Roger, now it was Chapman's turn to pick up the poisoned chalice. It was only a matter of time before Lucas contacted him, but what would he say? Could he reach out to Potter and stop him before the hand of fate touched Chapman's shoulder as well? Could he find an olive branch and use it to prevent another needless death?

He glanced at the clock above his head: 23:10. Where had the evening gone? He saved the document without looking at it, and closed the cover of his laptop. If he looked over what he had written it would only make him depressed. He sat for a couple of minutes trying to drive the negative thoughts from his mind. When the feeling passed, he switched off the desk lamp, plunging the garden office into darkness. He opened the blinds and looked out of the window to see if light illuminated their bedroom. The house looked to be in complete darkness, suggesting Keri had gone to bed and was now asleep.

Before heading out, he liked to spend a little time in the dark looking to see if any nocturnal animals had wandered into the garden. It was a large space, so often a fox or badger would walk in, although for the last few nights he'd spotted nothing more exotic than next door's moggy.

He waited about ten minutes, but nothing appeared. About to give up and head out, he spotted movement at the back of the house. He couldn't be sure at this distance, but he could make out something black climbing on the bins close to the kitchen. At first, he thought it resembled a large cat, but he knew nothing puma-sized lived wild in Hove, or for that matter in the UK. When he spotted what looked like a hand reaching for the top window in the kitchen, he realised it was a person.

He curbed his first reaction, to call the police or run out shouting, as it would wake the neighbourhood and for all he knew, it could be something harmless. Perhaps it was the boy from a few doors down who was known to smoke too much weed, trying to sneak into the wrong house as he had forgotten his key once again.

He reached for the office door and opened it with as little noise as possible before stepping out. He pulled the door closed in a slow, deliberate movement, making the least noise possible. In his heightened state and moving into the cool night air after the warmth of the office he experienced a slight shock to the system, but he soon regrouped.

He headed to the side of the garden and up the gentle slope towards the house. His movements were quiet, not difficult with a plane flying overhead, the sound of a couple of cars on the road outside, and the hooting of owls in trees nearby.

He edged closer and realised his first instincts were correct, he could see a person in the shape of a burglar. He had levered open the top window in the kitchen with a metal bar, still in his hand. In his other he held a long thin wire, or possibly another metal bar. 'Hey you!' Chapman hollered. 'What the hell are you doing?'

The burglar looked round, but Chapman couldn't see his features for the balaclava covering his head and most of his face. The guy jumped down from his perch on the bin and came towards Chapman. Before he could put up hands to defend himself, the guy whacked him on the side of the face with something hard and punched him in the gut. He fell to his knees, not only from the blows, but from the shock of being hit.

He tried getting up, but the guy kicked him in the chest, causing him to fall backwards. From his prone position, he heard the sound of feet running across the patio and out to the front of the house. Moments later, a car started up and drove away.

THIRTY-ONE

Henderson drove away from Kelly's house in East Hoathly. The journey to Hove would take about twice as long as his drive from there to his office in Lewes. In fact, his route this morning would take him around Lewes.

The previous evening had been quiet, a few drinks and a meal at a local pub. In a major investigation, like the murder of Roger Maitland, the temptation could be to devote every waking hour until a satisfactory resolution could be reached. At times, it was a good idea to take a step back and clear the head for a couple of hours, and often the facts of the case would appear in a new light.

No startling revelations had made their appearance as yet, but a call from a sergeant in the uniform division, who knew about the case he and the team were investigating, alerted him to the break-in at Adrian Chapman's place. He headed to the house now as he wanted to view the crime scene for himself, and later he hoped to talk to the man himself if he felt able. Walters would take the morning update meeting.

It had been a windy night but it had blown itself out by morning. It left the rural roads around Kelly's village strewn with small sticks, the occasional branch, and covered the edges of the road with mud which had slid down from the banks at the side.

Fortunately, no such impediments appeared on the A27 as he headed west.

Adrian Chapman lived in a big house in Mallory Road in Hove, befitting a senior executive in a successful company. Local police were treating the incident as a burglary, so no crime tape or police cars in evidence. With the murder of Vixen's former chief executive still fresh in his mind, Henderson would decide for himself.

A woman answered his knock on the door, dressed in what Henderson imagined to be work clothes; white blouse, tight black skirt and matching black shoes. Her hair was light brown and short. If similar in age to her husband, fifty-four, she was doing something right, as her unblemished face and slim figure gave the impression of someone younger, perhaps mid-forties.

'I'm Detective Inspector Henderson from Sussex Police,' he said, holding out his ID. 'I called earlier.'

'Hi, I'm Keri Chapman.'

They shook hands.

'Do come in.'

She led him into the lounge and invited him to sit down. She sat in a chair opposite.

'I don't imagine everyone receives this sort of service from the police after an attempted break-in,' she said, sweeping a hand in his general direction. 'I suppose it's connected with Roger's murder.'

'You're quite right. Anything untoward happening to one of the senior directors of Vixen would be flagged to my team. Talking of Roger, did you know him well?'

'I didn't come across him as often as other directors' wives. Adrian thought him a racist, although it didn't bother me too much. I'm HR director for a chemical company and I've met many strong characters at the plants we own, and Roger was a lot like them; confident to the point of arrogance; boorish, even.'

'Interesting.'

'He was a man's man. Happiest when talking to other blokes about football, drones, women, and cars, but bored stiff when speaking to a woman about children or domestic issues, or someone like me about business matters. I wouldn't want to be left alone with him, and I know quite a few of the other wives felt the same.'

'What can you tell me about the attempted break-in?'

'Come and I'll show you.'

They stepped outside. The garden looked large, unusual for a house in the middle of Hove.

'Who uses the home office?' he asked, indicating the wooden and glass construction at the far end of the garden.

'It's Adrian's man cave, as I call it. It was when he was working out there that he caught sight of the burglar.'

'What does he do there?'

'If you can believe it, Inspector, the place is kitted out with all manner of goodies: Sky television, Wi-Fi, water for the coffee machine, and a toilet. He's supposed to be writing a management book, but for all I know he spends his time watching cricket.'

'I see. Tell me about the attempted break-in.'

'We'd returned home from Roger's funeral around eight.'

'Broadstairs in Kent, I believe?'

'Yes, it's where Roger had been brought up and where his father and mother are buried. It took ages to get there as it's on the far side of the county, so when the others said they were retiring to a pub that Roger loved in his youth, we had to decline. It would have meant not getting home until after midnight and I had an important meeting to attend this morning.'

'Which I imagine you've cancelled.'

'You're right. When we arrived back at the house, neither of us felt hungry, but I made Adrian a sandwich and he took it with him when he went over to his cave. He said he finished up his writing about eleven fifteen, by which time I had gone to bed, switched off the light and sat for a few minutes waiting for a fox, a frequent visitor to our garden. It was then he noticed a strange movement. He didn't call you guys as he thought it might be Rob from a few doors down trying to get into the wrong house, but instead, decided to investigate himself.'

'Not always the most sensible course of action.'

'As hindsight has proved. When he confronted this person, rather than run off in fear as Adrian expected, he smacked him in the face with the metal bar he had been holding and punched him in the stomach. I found him lying here on the patio,' she said, pointing, 'when the noise woke me.'

'How is he?'

'At first, we both thought his jaw had been broken, as he couldn't speak without slurring, but the doctor at Brighton A&E put it down to the swelling in his jaw and throat. They gave him an injection to reduce the swelling, so he was able to tell me what happened. They kept him in overnight as he could be suffering from concussion, and to allow the inflammation to subside. I'm heading into work for a few hours after we're finished here, and I'll pick him up at four. He won't be at Vixen for a couple of days, but knowing him he'll be working on his laptop as soon as his head clears.'

'Where did the intruder try to break in?'

She pointed at the main window in the kitchen. 'The area around the top of the window is damaged where he tried to lever it open with the bar that he hit Adrian with. According to Adrian, the guy was about to insert a long stick or wire inside so he could pull up the handle of the main window. Easy when you know how.'

Henderson tried to visualise it. A couple of tall bins were nearby. Push one under the window and do what Keri had just described, and soon the main kitchen window would be open, leaving a space big enough to allow an average-sized person to enter.

'You'll need to have the window fixed.'

'That's what the guys in the patrol car said. I think as I've waited in for them, and for you, it's Adrian's turn to wait in for a handyman to come and fix it.'

'I think he might be glad of the distraction. Recuperating from such an injury can be quite boring.'

'You don't know Adrian as well as I do, Inspector. If you did, you would realise nothing will keep him from work, especially with the chief executive's job dangling in front of him.'

THIRTY-TWO

Henderson went off in search of Walters. He found her standing in the coffee area, staring into space while the coffee machine dribbled hot liquid into her cup.

'Morning Carol.'

'Morning gov. I swear this coffee machine gets slower and slower each day.'

'I imagine it needs to be cleaned now and again.'

'It gets wiped down and the drip tray emptied every night.'

'I mean, inside the machine. What do they call it... descaling?'

'How do you do that?'

'You put a sachet of descaling chemicals through it, assuming this one works the same as the one I have at home.'

'I'll ask Sally to take a look at it. She's good with technical stuff. How's Adrian Chapman?'

'Kept overnight in hospital with suspected concussion'

'That bad?'

Henderson went on to explain about his meeting with Keri that morning, the burglary, Adrian challenging the intruder and how he received his injuries.

'He's got a swollen jaw where the burglar hit him with his jemmy, and suspected concussion, but his wife said he'll be let out later today.'

'And they say burglary is a low-level crime.'

'Some forces are getting serious about it,' he said. 'The logic being, if we catch burglars and graffiti artists, who are often teenagers, the shock of a court appearance or some time in detention will deter them from a life of crime.'

'Does Adrian Chapman's intruder fall into this category?'

'It's difficult to say. If the burglar had gone there with the express intention of killing him, which would link it inextricably to the Maitland case, he had the perfect opportunity to do so when Chapman confronted him.'

'True, but maybe the intruder panicked when this strange guy came up behind him, or he didn't recognise Chapman in the dark.'

'It's possible, but I'm loath to ignore coincidence.'

'I agree.'

'For this reason, I'd like you to organise surveillance at his house. I'm not thinking here about a round-the-clock operation, but from about seven, when I imagine he comes home from the office, to about midnight.'

'No problem. Now you've got yourself a coffee, shall we go down and talk to Dave King?'

He looked at her, a startled expression on his face. 'He's in custody? Last update I received, he legged it from the building site where he'd been working.'

'We picked him up this morning from his house. They were early and caught him in bed. While one of the cops stood guard as he put his clothes on, the other took a snoop around. Under the stairs he found a rag with a couple of knives and a machete inside.'

'Even if traces of Maitland's blood are found on one of the blades, a decent defence lawyer will have it thrown out for being discovered during an unauthorised search.'

'I know, but after being turned down for a search warrant, what choice did we have? If it's the murder weapon, it gives us a green light to turn over his place and try to uncover something else. If not, he's in the clear.'

'When will forensics be able to look at it?'

'It's fast-tracked, so the day after tomorrow.'

'Bang goes my departmental budget. The timing shouldn't present a problem, though, as I intend keeping him in custody for the attack on Phil.'

'Shall we go and find out what he's got to say for himself?'

'How did the update meeting go?' Henderson asked, as they walked to the custody suite.

'The meeting itself, or how I handled it?'

'Both.'

'I think I did a good job, but you need to ask someone in attendance if it's an objective opinion you're after. The headlines are, we are still trying to trace Kieran Stock, our last remaining soldier, and we're still waiting for BA to send us their flight rosters.'

'The last to verify Lucas Potter's alibi, which if I remember rightly, is he spent the evening in the company of his partner.'

'It's about all we can do, short of canvassing their neighbours. His partner is long-haul cabin crew, so if she was in the UK at the time of the murder, his alibi has a good chance of sticking.'

'But if she had gone overseas before...'

'We can call him a liar.'

Dave King appeared to be as large as Phil suggested, six-two or three, and muscled, evident with his sleeves rolled up and his tattooed arms crossed. It looked intimidating at first sight, but on closer inspection, the DI noted the flabby jaw and the start of a decent beer gut. He didn't expect a man of limited means such as King to have a top-notch solicitor by his side, and he'd been right, but Kay Todd would do a decent job.

Walters started the recording equipment before they made their introductions.

'Mr King,' Henderson said, 'do you know why you're here?'

'Somethin' about beating up a bloke I've never heard of. Have you guys run out of suspects, so now you've come around to me?'

'No, we haven't. You are accused of assaulting Phil Bentley in the car park of Southwick Library last Friday.'

He shook his head. 'Never heard of him.'

'You might know him as Luke Grayson.'

He shrugged his shoulders theatrically. 'Don't know that bloke either.' His body language suggested otherwise.

Walters opened the file she had brought with her. 'I am showing Mr King a photograph taken by a CCTV camera at Burnston Oil depot in Lewes, where a group of *Soldiers of Peace* protestors had assembled close to the main entrance. Isn't this you, Mr King?' she said, pointing at the photograph of the SOP group, blown up to show King and Bentley in conversation.

'Yeah, that's me. Not very inconspicuous, am I?' he said, a self-satisfied smirk on his face.

'Who is that you're talking to?'

'Ah, yeah, right, that's Luke. I don't think anyone ever told me his last name.'

'So, you admit you do know him?'

'Yeah, he's a member, or should I say, used to be.'

Walters produced another photograph. 'The CCTV camera outside Southwick Library took this one. It features you as well, Mr King, does it not?'

The picture showed King taking a kick at a prostrate Phil Bentley curled up on the ground.

'Oh, I dunno. Might be someone else.'

'If you don't like this picture, Mr King, we have plenty more. The whole attack captured on video.'

'Fuck it, it's me, aw' right? He's a fucking undercover reporter trying to do a number on us. Couldn't let it happen, could I?'

'Why, what were you planning?' Henderson asked.

'It's confidential, like. I'm not saying.'

'He's not an undercover reporter. He's a serving police officer.'

'C'mon, pal, you can't pin that on me. Can he?' he said to his brief. 'I didn't know.'

'My client is quite correct, Inspector,' Todd said. 'He believed Mr Grayson to be a reporter. He wasn't aware he was a police officer.'

Henderson considered this for a beat. 'Okay, I accept your explanation. Where were you, 6th May, two weeks last Saturday night?'

'I object to this hostile line of questioning.'

'It's no problem, mate, I can handle it. I went to The Cricketers pub in Southwick. I go there just about every Saturday night. After, we head back to Simon Deacon's place where we play music until we're knackered and go to bed, or if we're really pissed we pass out where we're sitting.'

'Your alibi will be checked,' Henderson said, gathering his papers together. 'In the meantime, you will be held in custody while we gather more evidence on the assault charge. We'll leave you now to consult with your solicitor.'

THIRTY-THREE

'Hi babe, how are you? We've just landed.'

'Great to hear you're back.'

'I've just had the crappiest flight imaginable.' Rosie's voice dropped a couple of octaves. 'An American, a bit worse for wear, tried hitting on me every time I walked past.'

Lucas Potter laughed. 'What are you saying, Rosie, a man has to be drunk to fancy you?'

'What? No. What can I say, I'm jetlagged.'

'Did you enjoy LA?'

'Brilliant. I told you about the tickets Ros had for the Metallica concert?'

'Yeah, you did.'

'Me, Jess and Ros went. They played all the old favourites: *Sandman, Unforgiven, Nothing Else Matters*, as well as some of their new stuff. We were so close to the stage we could see all their faces, but for the next two days I couldn't hear a thing.'

'I wish I'd been there,' he said in a low voice.

'What did you say?'

'I think you're still deaf.'

She laughed. 'Stop messing about you idiot.'

'I said, I wish I'd been there.'

'You could have been, if you worked less hours and were more willing to spend some of your hard-earned loot.'

'I have to work to keep you in the style that you seem to have become accustomed to.'

'Yeah, yeah. Hey, I'd better go, Zara is calling. What time will you be home?'

'Late. Me and Al have a problem to fix.'

'Oh, one of those. I will refrain from enquiring further.'

'Ask no questions and you'll be told no lies.'

'I know, I know. See you later, babe. Love you.'

'Look forward to it. Love you too.'

He was still cradling the mobile when Al Cowan breezed in.

'Difficult call?' he asked.

'No, quite the opposite.'

'Rosie's back in town?'

'You got it.'

'Grab a jacket, mate, I'm starving.'

He got up from his desk, reached for the coatstand and picked up the jacket he had worn that morning.

'You'll need something heavier. I checked the forecast; it's gonna be a cold one tonight.'

He put the lighter garment back on the peg and selected the quilted anorak he used whenever out on a job. They headed out of the office, the last to leave, and walked to a pub nearby. Potter Security was situated near the centre of Crawley with plenty of shops and pubs within walking distance.

The two men ordered soft drinks while perusing the menu.

'I think I'll go for the rib-eye,' Cowan said.

'Like you did the last time, and the time before. There's no need for you to look at the menu, I could order your food for you and save you the bother.'

'I blame the army: repetition, repetition, repetition.'

'Too true. It's a hard lesson to break. Rosie does it for me. If she sees me doing something time and again, she'll pull me up about it.'

Potter and Cowan left the pub an hour and a half later. Outside, daylight was fading fast. The drive to the Heathrow area would take at least another hour, so by the time they arrived, it would be dark. Potter had been checking sunset times and knew when the shipment was due to go out. What he didn't feel confident about was cloud cover. A day of sunshine would leave the sky clear at night, while heavy rain clouds would blot out the stars and moon. The forecast looked to be in their favour with much of the latter. He hoped it would be accurate

The drive north didn't attract the attention of the forces of law and order, as Potter took it easy. Not a simple thing to do in the Jag, as it behaved like an overactive dog straining on its leash, encouraging him to put his foot down. He and Al were like an old married couple. They'd known one another as long as many couples were together, so they slipped with ease in and out of conversation topics, and silences weren't pregnant with tension.

In the army, sitting in the back of a Warrior armoured vehicle, silence ruled. Not in case they gave their position away, but it allowed each man to deal with their own fear and anxiety about what could be coming up next. It didn't pay to dwell on the negative, so he used to think about good things from home. He hadn't met Rosie by that point, so more often than not, he imagined taking revenge on Roger Maitland.

The warehouse they were heading towards wasn't in Heathrow itself, but in one of the numerous industrial estates that had sprouted up all around the vast airport site. Twenty minutes later, he parked the car with a view of the front of the unmarked warehouse and killed the engine. Despite driving a decent car, it wouldn't stand out. They were in a line of other cars, some more expensive than his, no doubt left by travelling businessmen who baulked at paying high airport parking charges.

They didn't have long to wait. Once a week, GH Transport delivered a load of electronic goods from a huge warehouse in Holland to this place at Heathrow. The company renting the warehouse would then distribute the goods to independent retailers around the country. Trouble was, some of the goods often went missing. Lucas had suspicions about Karim Gunda and Trent Bonham, the Potter Security guards on the site.

Potter and Cowan made a move with the arrival of the GH Transport truck. The workers at the warehouse and the security guards only had eyes for the truck and didn't notice them making their way into the shadow of the nearest building.

They watched for about half an hour as the lorry reversed inside, the goods were unloaded unseen and, now empty, the truck departed. A few minutes later, the workers shut the doors to the warehouse and locked them, before heading to the car park and their lift home.

None were carrying suspicious packages, as Potter and Cowan had confirmed on previous visits, hence the suspicion now fell on the security guards. Having supervised the unloading and that nothing had been stolen by the workers, the security guards would now check that the warehouse had been securely locked. They would do this, and a number of others in the nearby area, periodically during the night.

What happened next stunned Potter so much he wouldn't have been able to speak, even if he and Cowan hadn't decided to maintain silence. Bonham walked over to the warehouse door while Gunda dashed off, as if to retrieve something. Rather than shake the door to ensure its secure status, Bonham opened it with a key. He threw the door open, and seconds later, Gunda appeared driving his old Nissan Sunny, and reversed inside.

'The thieving bastards,' Cowan growled under his breath. 'This could cost us the contract.'

'Yeah, too true. Let's go and put a stop to it.'

Potter and Cowan approached the part-open and unlocked warehouse door. A glance under told them the lights were on and the middle part of the loading bay was occupied by the faded red Nissan.

'You head to the right of the car, I'll go left.'

Cowan nodded.

'Walk, don't run.'

He nodded again.

Potter opened the door and the two men walked inside the well-lit warehouse. At the rear, rows and rows of shelving were heaving with boxed electronic products: cameras, DVD players, mobile phones, laptops, and much more besides.

In the seconds it took Potter to stride the length of the car, he understood what they were doing. Bonham held in his hand a shopping list, and when he found what he wanted, he extracted it and passed it to Gunda, who loaded the items into the open boot of the Nissan.

When almost level with the rear of the Nissan, Potter hollered, 'Stop what you're doing!'

Gunda, closest to them, took one look at Potter and ran the other way. He didn't get far when a punch in the face from Cowan stunned him, before another on the side of the head landed him on his back.

Bonham walked towards them after putting down a DVD player. 'C'mon guys, it's not what you think.'

'Enlighten me.'

'It's excess stock, destined for landfill.'

Bonham moved closer and stopped. Potter made up the distance between them in a flash. 'You're a lying bastard and I don't want anyone like you working in my organisation.'

Potter punched him in the gut, causing him to double over, before kneeing him hard in the face. He fell to the ground groaning, blood streaming from a damaged nose.

'The famous Potter double-tap,' Cowan said, smiling. 'Haven't seen it for a while.'

'You might be seeing it a few more times before this night is through. Let's grab these two scumbags and take them into the back. I want to find out who their customers are, and if anyone else in the organisation is involved.'

'With pleasure, mate; it'll be just like old times.'

THIRTY-FOUR

Henderson and Walters were back at Vixen Aviation. This time, no protestors were outside the factory building, or at the offices. Perhaps the arrest of Dave King had spooked the various protest groups and they were away licking their wounds.

'It's strange not having them here,' Walters said, as she got out of the car. 'Not a single piece of litter or a torn placard to remind us of their presence, which is kind of sad.'

'It's what these big companies are like. No sooner have builders, graffiti artists, or protestors disappeared, a clean-up team rushes out and removes all vestiges of their presence.'

'Can't have their beautiful, manicured lawn sullied by bits of rubbish, can they?'

A few minutes later, they were shown into Adrian Chapman's new office. Its occupant wasn't there, but they were assured he would be along in a few minutes. They sat in the visitors' chairs.

'It looks like Mr Chapman has stamped his identity on this place,' Walters said.

Perhaps the photographs of Chapman's wife and kids on the desk, arty street scenes on the walls, and the absence of clutter on any of the flat surfaces made the difference. When the DI had previously walked past the office on his first visit to Vixen, military paraphernalia had dominated: helicopter and plane pictures on the wall, model planes on cupboard tops, and on others, drones.

'Good morning detectives,' Chapman said as he entered. 'Any news on finding Roger's killer?'

'Nothing new to report, I'm afraid. But how are you? That bruise on your face looks really nasty.'

He touched it. 'It still aches and I'm still on these,' he said, holding up and rattling a small bottle of pills.

'Should you be at work?' Walters asked. 'After all, the attack happened only two days ago?'

'I would like to say I'm fine, but I don't think I am. I still have double-vision on occasion and my mind goes blank without warning. However, an important meeting is scheduled for this afternoon which I can't afford to miss. I'll be heading home when it finishes.'

'We have news of your burglary.'

'Good. I'd like to hear it.'

'We've arrested and charged the culprit. It's slightly connected to Roger's murder in the sense that the burglar had read about it and figured your house would be empty on the day of his funeral, and you would probably come home late after staying behind afterwards for a few drinks.'

'Not an unreasonable assumption.'

'When he came along at the time he did and saw the house in darkness, he must have felt vindicated and took his chance.'

'No other connection to Roger?'

'None.'

'That's a relief.'

'Mr Chapman, what I wanted to talk to you about this morning, now you've had an opportunity to look through Roger's things, have you found anything which might lead you to suggest a theory as to who murdered him or the reason behind why he was killed?'

He steepled his fingers and looked pensive for a few moments. 'I haven't looked through it all, but from what I've seen, I can't say there is.'

'You don't sound so sure. If you like, I could bring in a forensics team to do it for you.'

Henderson had considered doing this with a warrant, but for the moment, they had enough leads to follow.

'No, no, that won't be necessary. I suppose I should show you this.'

He reached into the drawer at the side of his desk and extracted a file.

'You've heard what happened to Jerome Potter?'

Henderson nodded.

'His dismissal was unfair, in my opinion. Reading between the lines, Roger wanted the company all to himself. Money wasn't the sole driver; he had plenty and didn't feel motivated by adding more. I think he sought kudos, the adulation of military men and fellow chief execs in the defence industry.'

'I see.'

'What you have to understand is working with the military is a very macho experience. Roger had no problem standing toe-to-toe with colonels and generals, but in the latter years that Jerome worked for the company, he believed him to be a liberal intellectual who had no place at his side. Nowadays, he couldn't be more wrong. The military of every nation are desperate for AI engineers to program smart munitions, IT geeks to hack into enemy computers, and computer nerds to safeguard their own systems. In many respects, Roger was the dinosaur and Jerome the visionary, but he couldn't see it.'

'And what about Jerome's departure?'

'He left with a two million pay-off, and while it's a lot of money to most people, it's peanuts when you consider if he had stayed, his shares would have then been worth somewhere north of four hundred million.'

'What do you intend to do about it?'

'I'm in two minds. If Jerome was still around, the decision would be easy. I'd invite him to return to the company and offer his shares back. Now, with a widow and son, the options are less clear, in particular when Lucas Potter sends emails like these.' He handed Henderson a file that had been lying on his desk.

'This is a file Roger kept on Lucas Potter. The emails started off in a conciliatory tone, but in a matter of months, they became more and more threatening.'

Henderson speed-read the contents, not too difficult as the emails were short. The early ones inviting Roger to explore various avenues, the latter demanding action or suffer the consequences.

'I understand what you mean,' Henderson said.

'Of course, Roger's robust replies only succeeded in fanning the flames. Roger thrived on confrontation, and I'm afraid the Potter boy had met his match.'

'I'd like copies of these.'

'No problem.' He stood and took the file back from Henderson. 'Give me a minute.' Chapman left the room.

'Has BA come back to us?' Henderson asked Walters when they were alone.

She shook her head. 'Still waiting.'

'Chase them up when we get back. We need to find out if Potter's alibi stands up to scrutiny.'

'Will do. The content of the emails sent to Roger Maitland sound like a clear motive.'

'They do, for sure, but it begs the question: why kill Maitland now? It's not as if Potter was still in the army and heading off for months on tours of duty.'

'He isn't part of the Army Reserve, is he?'

'It's a good point, as some former soldiers are.' Henderson said. 'We'll ask the next time we talk to him, which I think will be sooner rather than later, because even if his partner verifies his alibi, we still need to talk to him about those emails.'

'It's possible Potter made the threats and one of his buddies killed him. He must know loads of former colleagues who have the requisite skillset.'

'I'm pleased to say this morning isn't looking like the write-off we thought it might be.'

THIRTY-FIVE

Following the meeting with Adrian Chapman, Henderson returned to his office. He sat at his desk with the Roger Maitland forensic report open in front of him. He'd read it several times, but didn't uncover anything else, other than it had been a vicious attack, multiple stab wounds, and done with a large knife. No hair follicles, fingerprints, or items capable of yielding DNA were found, the only exception being the hairs belonging to Claudette.

An assumption he'd made at an early stage in this investigation was the killer understood Maitland's movements. This, he believed, from many nights watching his house; but was this right?

On the Saturday night of Maitland's death, the killer must have seen the car arrive and two people enter the house. He would have had no idea if the woman was staying over or would leave when she and Maitland had done their thing. This was where luck played a part.

He must have been patient, waiting until the couple were sound asleep, or for the woman to make her way home. If she didn't leave, he would have taken the decision either to come back another time, or enter the house and kill them both.

This suggested the killer didn't need to keep Maitland's house under surveillance for any length of time. It was possible, providing he knew something about Maitland's fondness for using escorts, he might have gone to Oakwood House for the second or third time on that fatal Saturday night. This altered the DI's thinking somewhat. At first, he suspected many days and hours of hiding out in the woods surrounding Maitland's house, and enduring much of the bad weather they had experienced of late.

This implied the skills and experience of a soldier, but as he now believed the surveillance part to be optional, the killer might well be a civilian. This would point to the person with the most to gain from Roger Maitland's death: Adrian Chapman.

A fly lay in that particular ointment; Chapman's reward didn't look so grand: a larger office, a bigger salary, and possibly control of the company if the CEO job became permanent, but still a salaried man. Roger's shares in Vixen would go to his wife Sonia, and the rest of his assets to his daughters, Laura and Katy. None of those women were on their list of suspects.

Henderson picked up some papers, about to walk into the Detectives' Room to find Walters, when she appeared at the door.

'I've been having a rethink about our murderer,' he said.

'Oh yeah?'

Henderson explained his theory.

When finished, Walters said: 'Does this take Lucas Potter out of the frame?'

'Far from it, he's still there. However, if he produces a watertight alibi and we cross him off our list, we needn't limit our search to another ex or current soldier. This person might well be a civilian.'

'I see your logic, but take your pick from a long line of suspects.'

'How do you mean?'

'The more I learn about Roger Maitland, the more I think he sounds like an odious individual, capable of upsetting a great number of people.'

'I agree, but don't you think there's a big difference between him being rude or offensive to someone, and riling them so much they decide to stab him to death?'

'I suppose you're right.'

'Why did you come to see me?'

'Dave King's knife has been tested and no trace of Roger Maitland's blood has been found.'

'Oh.'

'Also, his alibi checks out.'

'What is it,' he said with a sigh, 'the word of *Soldiers of Peace* leader Simon Deacon, or a fellow boozer at the pub he drinks in?'

'Yeah, Simon Deacon, but also the barman at his local, the Cricketers Pub in Southwick.'

'Two points I'd make. He's a regular at the pub and so he's likely to be friendly with the bar staff. Also, if he goes out drinking as often as he says he does, one Saturday night will merge with another.'

'The barman Sally spoke to didn't like King one bit and would have been happy to drop him in the shit. He remembers the Saturday night in question, as King had an argument with the fruit machine. He kicked and thumped it so much, the barman had to go over and stop him. He got a black eye for his trouble.'

'Good enough for me, but I still want him for the attack on Phil.'

'Of course.'

'When's his court appearance? Tomorrow, isn't it?'

'Yeah.'

'Contact the CPS. Tell them what we've discussed; he's only up for the assault on Phil. We'll drop the suspected murder charge.'

'In which case, it's likely he'll get bail.'

'It all hangs on whether he knew about Phil being a cop or not. If he did, I'm certain he would be remanded, but since he denies it and we've no proof either way, I think you're right, he'll walk.'

THIRTY-SIX

Adrian Chapman left the office and walked to his car. If he was confirmed as the company's chief executive at the next board meeting, he probably should treat himself to a better one. He liked his BMW 5 Series, but Roger drove a large Mercedes and it cost a whole lot more than his. Perhaps he was a bit young for a luxury sedan, so instead he could opt for something a bit sporty: a Porsche or maybe an Aston Martin.

That afternoon's meeting went well. The delegation from Interpol were keen to explore the possibility of using armed drones in their fight against organised crime gangs. In particular, they wanted a drone to go into a building or warehouse before any of their officers, and clear the way. At this early stage of their deliberations, they focused a lot on control and security.

Control, in their minds, meant having complete power over a drone's actions. In their world, no uniforms were worn by the combatants to delineate them, so they didn't want to give the drone authority over life-or-death decisions. Brett McQueen, Vixen's AI Manager, assured them the targeting part of the AI program could be turned on or off, and this had been demonstrated to their satisfaction in dramatic fashion.

Brett trained one of the Interpol guys to use a drone before sending it into the conference room. It hovered above the meeting attendees with its weapon pointing at Chapman. With the central control AI switched off, the drone was instructed to select all targets in the room. The gun pointed at Chapman, but didn't fire.

Security to Interpol meant if the control unit and drone fell into enemy hands, it couldn't be used against them, or indeed, to terrorise the general public. The latest version of the Vixen control unit was equipped with fingerprint recognition, with facial recognition as an option, and despite repeated attempts by the Interpol team to activate the system, they couldn't.

When the detectives had come to see him that morning, Chapman was still suffering from the effects of his confrontation with the burglar. At the meeting and afterwards, he felt well enough to continue working, much to the annoyance of his secretary, who told him several times to go home. In fact, tonight she had left the office before him.

He had been reluctant to show DI Henderson the Lucas Potter file, as it could be construed as washing the company's dirty linen in public, something Roger vehemently warned the management team never to do. In another sense, laying it open as he did, gave it credence; making it real. All the while it had been in Roger's possession, Chapman had not been appraised of its contents and so it failed to bother him. Now, with its vicious claims and counterclaims exposed and the police having their own copy, it worried him.

Yes, the threats were aimed at Roger, but Lucas returned with a more venomous and barbed attack after receiving Roger's belligerent responses. He took one key question from the whole sorry mess: did Lucas Potter only have a beef with Roger, or did it include other members of the Vixen management team? If the latter, he and the other directors would now be in the firing line.

He pulled into the driveway at the front of his house. Switching off the engine, his mind went over the events of the last couple of days as the components and bodywork cooled. If Keri had been home she would have been puzzled by his strange behaviour. She knew the sound of the car and would have been drawn to the window. Instead, she was out as her choir was performing Handel's *Messiah* in the chapel at Brighton College in a few weeks' time, and tonight was an important rehearsal.

He stepped out of the car a couple of minutes later. It wasn't yet dark, so not difficult to look around for a strange car or loitering strangers. They lived in an area with many large houses and ample space between them, so someone who shouldn't be there would be obvious. It saddened him to move from house to car without seeing or talking to a neighbour, but it was the life they had chosen for themselves.

The next hour or two he spent relaxing with a drink, before turning on the oven and sitting down to enjoy the spicy cottage pie Keri had left for him. After eating, he put his plates and cutlery in the dishwasher, tidied up the kitchen, then headed into the lounge.

Darkness had descended and, without switching on a light, he moved to the window to close the curtains.

He glanced at the garden, neighbouring gardens, the area around his car. The attempted burglary had made him nervous of the person coming back; unfinished business or revenge for being arrested. The rational side of his brain told him this was unlikely, a street kid like him knew harassing a victim would give him a longer sentence, but it didn't stop Chapman fretting. He hoped the feeling would pass as his injuries healed.

He looked along the road and spotted a new arrival: a dirty grey Vauxhall that hadn't been there when he'd come home. The red glow of a cigarette an indication of someone sitting inside. He realised the light from the kitchen, not shining directly behind him, but out of the lounge door and down the hall, might be framing him, so he moved and hid behind the curtain.

What was this person doing? Watching him? He had a good view of the house, but for what purpose? Waiting for the best time to strike?

He risked a glance. The cigarette no longer in evidence, but the glow of a street light told Chapman the car was still occupied. He ducked down, his hands trembling, body shivering, his mind a jumble of frightened thoughts.

Pull yourself together, Adrian, the authoritative voice of the management writer said in his head. *You work for an aggressive armaments manufacturer, so why are you scared of a guy sitting in his car?*

How he wished he had brought one of their drones home. They were near-silent in operation and capable of sending back pictures to his phone of the person sitting in the car. It would tell him if the driver had a silenced pistol cradled in his lap, or a bottle of chloroform and a gag on the seat beside him. Would he allow the drone to shoot him if he had? It posed a difficult ethical question, and one he hoped he would never face. Perhaps he would deal with the subject in one of his future books. The title of it could be: *When You Want to Kill a Rival.*

He decided he no longer wanted to be a victim, cowering in a corner like a beaten dog, waiting for his fate to befall him. No, he would take the fight to his aggressor.

Crouching low, he headed upstairs. Using only the light from his phone, he dressed in a black jumper and dark trousers, and fastened up black trainers to match. He sneaked out the back door and closed it with minimal noise. He wanted to move behind the target, no way would he approach it from the front.

The windows in the house next door were in darkness. Brad was an aeronautical engineer who travelled the world, while his partner Sam, often worked late. He climbed the fence separating the two properties and a minute or so later, walked down their driveway to the road.

He pretended to walk away, but when he had put a good distance between him and his watcher, about thirty yards, he crossed the road and, keeping low, speed-walked towards the watcher's vehicle.

When a couple of car lengths away, he ducked behind a parked car and moved into the road. Keeping low, he sped towards his watcher. When he reached the target car, he hauled the driver's door open, wrapped his arm around the guy's throat and pulled hard.

'What the fuck are you doing here watching me? Are you here to kill me?'

'No! I'm...agh!'

'What are you saying, you bastard? Who do you work for?'

The driver's hand was snaking into his jacket pocket. Fearing a gun, Chapman released his hold and jumped back in alarm.

He whipped out not a Smith and Wesson or a Glock, but an ID card. This did not compute.

'I'm a cop, you fucking idiot,' the man said. 'Did nobody tell you, I'm here to make you feel safe. I didn't realise I'd be the one put in danger.'

THIRTY-SEVEN

Lester Grange stood beside his car watching Adrian Chapman drive off. Both men had attended the Interpol meeting earlier in the day. While he went for it with a boyish enthusiasm most often reserved for football, women, and alcohol, he thought Adrian seemed a bit off the pace.

It couldn't be the death of Roger bothering him, or was this him being disingenuous? It wasn't as if Adrian and Roger couldn't work together, they did at a business level, but Roger always held him at a distance. At heart, the reason for it was plain to him: his former boss's racism. He had seen enough of it in the army to recognise it without too much trouble. Grange hadn't objected to it at the time as he believed it served a purpose – stopping Adrian from getting too big for his boots.

He was an ambitious guy, Adrian; nothing wrong with that in his book, but as Roger would often say, he hadn't yet earned his spurs. You didn't just waltz into the MOD and demand a contract. It had to be earned and deserved. The product demonstrations needed to go well, the prices had to be competitive, and the promised delivery dates realistic. In addition, he had to spend time building relationships with all the key players. This didn't happen overnight, as Grange found out when he first joined Vixen. It took years.

Plus, Adrian would find it harder than say, himself, as they were also guilty of harbouring racial grudges.

He opened the car door and climbed inside. The smell of leather a constant reminder of how fortunate he'd been. When he left the army, he didn't have a job or a clue about what he would spend the rest of his life doing. The vision of him being homeless, unable to rejoin civilised society, had haunted him, but it had succeeded at spurring him on. A chance meeting with Roger at a regimental dinner changed his life. He didn't want to go, despite still having his dress uniform, as he couldn't afford to pay for any drinks. His wife borrowed the money from her sister and from then on, he never looked back.

He owed Karen big-time, but in the end she couldn't adjust from the needy ex-squaddie requiring a leg-up to move into Civvy Street, to the confident businessman he had become. Perhaps her empathetic and giving nature meant she needed to help a victim to make her feel whole. The guy she'd left him for definitely fell into that category. A rock guitarist, he made a meagre living as a solo performer, this without a repertoire of decent songs, and a singing voice any hyena would be proud of.

Grange took time adjusting to living alone. In the army, his clothes were washed, his food cooked, and he was told when to sleep and when to wake up. Karen had assumed this role, and perhaps this had been a contributing factor to her leaving. When she did, it forced him to learn a whole plethora of new skills.

Whilst learning, and sometimes to escape the travails of domestic drudgery, he often made use of a laundry and ironing service. A few weeks ago, he added the services of a cleaner and a gardener who both came to the house once a week, and many of his evening meals were delivered by Just Eat or Deliveroo.

When relaying this to women he met on dating sites, some wouldn't come right out and call him pathetic, but it often led to the date coming to a premature halt. He'd learned the lesson and nowadays he portrayed himself as a domestic god. His dates now lasted longer and a fair number came back to the house and slept with him, but he knew it would present a stumbling block to any long-term relationship. It was fortunate none as yet had come up to the mark.

While driving, he often listened to Radio 5 Live. They were previewing a Premier League match: his team, Manchester United, were soon to kick-off against Chelsea. As soon as he arrived home, he threw off his jacket and switched on the television. He hadn't missed much, as the players were on the point of lining up for photos. No way would he cook tonight. He pulled out his phone and tapped the Deliveroo app. He fancied Indian: Chicken Tikka, Pilau Rice, naan bread. He made his selections in a matter of moments, before dashing through to the fridge in the kitchen and grabbing a couple of beers.

Eight minutes in, United scored and he almost knocked over his beer in celebration. He had grown up in Oldham and even with a dozen senior football teams within a short travelling distance from his home: Bolton, Bury, Oldham, Rochdale, to name a few, he felt no contest when his father took him to the Theatre of Dreams and he saw United for the first time.

He grabbed his phone again, this time intending to place a bet on Paddy Power, convinced this would be a three- or four-nil demolition job, when the doorbell sounded. He looked at his watch, although he didn't need to as a few minutes before he'd looked at the clock on the television to see the amount of game time played: twenty minutes. Deliveroo were often quick, as he lived in Lindfield, close to Haywards Heath and its many restaurants, but this had to be a record.

He left his phone on the settee and walked to the door. Being in such a rush, he didn't switch on the hall light, believing the light in the porch outside would be enough. He opened the door. A guy stood there but he didn't look like a delivery rider. He wasn't carrying a large insulated bag or searching through it for his meal selection. In fact, he couldn't see him well at all, as he was dressed in black, wearing gloves, and with a black hat pulled low over his eyes.

Grange opened his mouth to say something when the guy's hand shot out. He didn't comprehend the action until he felt a sharp pain in his gut. He hadn't been punched as expected, but the warm flow of blood told him he'd been stabbed.

'Why the fuck did—'

The arm shot out again and stabbed him once more, then again, then...

He staggered backwards into the hallway but he couldn't escape the knife. He dropped to his knees, fell to the side and slumped against the wall. His body felt cold, but something warmed him. He realised, before he shut his eyes for the final time, it was his own blood.

THIRTY-EIGHT

DI Henderson climbed out of his car, stood for a moment and looked around. The call had come at the civilised time of eleven in the morning. A woman from Lester Grange's department at Vixen had driven to his house in Lindfield to find out why he'd failed to turn up for an important meeting that morning and wasn't answering his phone.

They discovered the reason soon enough when Sarah Johnson, a distribution assistant in Lester's department, pulled into the driveway. The door was locked, but when she peered through the frosted glass at the side of the door, she spotted a bloody corpse lying in the hall. If someone had been walking past the house at the time of the murder, he doubted they would have seen anything, as the garden was surrounded by a high and thick hedge.

Lindfield, Henderson imagined, had been a separate village at one time, as they had driven past a well-tended open area with a large pond and several shops, pubs, and houses around it. Over the years, its larger neighbour, Haywards Heath, had grown as a consequence of being located on the main train line from Brighton to London, so it became hard to tell where the boundary between the two had been.

Henderson and Walters made their way towards the house where a small collection of police officers, a pathologist, and SOCOs had gathered near the door, forming an untidy semi-circle close to the body. Something else caught the DI's eye.

'What the hell is that?' he said to Walters, pointing.

At the side of the house sat a white plastic bag. They headed towards it.

'I dunno. It wouldn't do any harm to peek inside.'

'You think?'

'If there's an explosive device inside, I don't think it'll be wired to the bag itself otherwise it would go off when the bombers picked it up.'

'I'm not usually this cautious by nature, but because we're dealing with a defence contractor with aggressive demonstrators outside their building, it has moved the goalposts somewhat.'

Henderson leaned over. It didn't look like gardening waste, the bag too flimsy and pristine to have been left out for weeks in variable weather. Perhaps it was a delivery. He spotted a piece of paper inside the bag. With care, he reached over and removed it using his fingertips.

'For lunch,' he said to Walters, 'how would you fancy a nice bit of Chicken Tikka, Pilau Rice, with a piece of naan bread on the side?'

'What?' she said, laughing, the tension leaching from her body like sweat from a marathon runner.

'It's from the Oriental Palace in Haywards Heath. What's it doing here at the side of the house?'

'It must be a delivery from the likes of Deliveroo or Uber Eats. If they can't contact you, they leave it in a safe place.'

'Makes sense, but what does it suggest?'

'He died before taking delivery.'

'Going by the timestamp on this,' he said, waving the receipt in the air, '20:42. I think it gives us, with a fair degree of accuracy, the time of death.'

Henderson walked to the front door, stepped into the hall and took a look at the body. Like Roger Maitland, Lester Grange had been stabbed by a vicious killer, four wounds in all, done with a broad bladed knife, but he wouldn't be jumping to any conclusions just yet. He left pathologist Grafton Rawlings to complete his examination and headed into the house.

While Walters chatted to one of the SOCO team, Henderson wandered through the house. It didn't take long to realise Lester Grange lived alone. It wasn't because the place looked untidy, as it didn't, it lacked a feminine touch and none of the rooms on the ground floor at least contained anything to suggest more than one person stayed there.

Walters walked towards him as he stared out of the back door at the garden.

'I'm told Sky Sports was playing on the TV when the SOCOs turned up,' she said. 'Also, they found his phone lying on the settee.'

'So, he's watching the Man United-Chelsea match last night on TV, as I was, and decided rather than start cooking and risk missing the match, he'd order something from the Oriental Palace?'

'We'll be able to confirm once we've analysed his phone and talked to the Oriental Palace, but it looks that way. He then hears a noise–'

'Maybe the ringing of the doorbell.'

'Could be. He hears a noise or gets up to answer the door. When he opens it, the killer is standing there.'

'He stabs him. Lester Grange falls back into the hall. The killer pulls the door closed and walks away.'

'Sounds about right.'

'I think the killer walked back into the road rather than make their escape through the back garden.'

'What makes you say that?'

'Look out there,' he said, nodding at the rear garden. 'A tall fence encircles the property. No doubt a good screen and burglar deterrent when first erected, but the panels are sagging and showing signs of rot. Any attempt to climb and it would give way under the strain.'

'I see what you mean.'

'Which makes me think our killer left by the front driveway, so get a team down here doing door-to-door enquiries right along this road. See if you can find anyone who saw or heard anything around the time of the murder, and with luck, they might have a bell or security video system. I'd like to see any footage you find.'

'Will do. Are we saying Grange's murder is related to Roger Maitland's?'

'It's hard to think otherwise, wouldn't you say? They're both directors of the same company, they were good friends, they were both stabbed multiple times with a broad knife.'

'In which case, it should narrow down the range of suspects.'

'Maybe yes, maybe no. Roger may have wronged someone close to him, and Lester supported him or stood by while he did it. I don't think we can dismiss it out of hand, but I agree, it's more likely to be someone or something where the paths of the two men cross.'

'If it's so obvious the two deaths are related, our friends in the press will spot the connections too.'

'I'm thinking the same thing. Let the games begin.'

THIRTY- NINE

'This is Lester Grange,' Henderson said, tapping the picture on the whiteboard behind him. A handsome face looked back, with strong bone features and unmarked skin, surprising for a man who had endured the rigours of combat. 'Aged forty-six, he lived alone following a separation from his wife, Karen. He's an ex-soldier, and of late, Distribution Director at Vixen Aviation.'

Henderson took a sip from his coffee cup. The team were quiet, absorbing the news and about to make the obvious connection.

'He's been stabbed four times with a broad knife at his home at West Common in Lindfield, around 20:40 last night. A colleague from Vixen discovered his body this morning, when she came to the house to find out why he hadn't attended an important meeting. He's also a close friend of Roger Maitland.'

'It's the same MO as Maitland,' Vicky Neal said. 'It has to be connected.'

'It's got to be Roger Maitland's killer,' Sally Graham said, 'same vicious stab wounds and the use of a similar knife.'

'Both men working for Vixen does it for me,' Harry Wallop said.

It went on like this for about thirty seconds before Henderson called a halt.

'I agree, there are too many similarities for us to ignore. It means we need to analyse where the lives of the two men crossed, which will be a great deal, in my opinion.'

'There's no way his murder isn't connected with the company,' Wallop said.

'You would think so, Harry, but I'm not limiting the search. Lester and Roger were big drinking buddies, and Lester told us discussions about business were often far from their minds. I think there's a good chance the killer could come from that side of his life.'

'Maybe.'

'Vicky, I want you to shake down Lester Grange's private life. His ex-wife is called Karen, and if my memory serves me well, they had three kids.' When Walters and Henderson met Lester Grange at Vixen, a posed family portrait had been on display in his office. His wife, a good-looking blonde, looked a few years younger than Lester. With having such attractive parents, the kids seemed to follow the family line.

'Call the Human Resources Department at Vixen. They'll have the contact details.'

'Will do.'

'Harry, I want you to coordinate the information we collect from the door-to-door team. If anyone has a door camera or personal security system, see if it gives us an image of the killer, or perhaps their car.'

'No problem.'

'Carol and I will go back to Vixen, although I hate to think what the atmosphere will be like after losing two of their senior people.'

'They will all be thinking,' Phil Bentley said, 'they're next.'

'It would be good to reassure them,' Walters said, 'but as we're not sure yet what motivates the killer we can't.'

'No, we can't, and soon I expect to receive flak from the likes of Adrian Chapman for not doing enough to make them feel safe.'

'And this from a manufacturer of killer drones?' Sally Graham said.

Henderson returned to his office. He sat for a few minutes going over the interview he'd conducted with Lester Grange two weeks before. In fact, it wasn't the words he'd said that interested him, but the impression they'd left.

It was of a rumbustious, former platoon commander and the loud and boisterous Roger Maitland getting together over copious amounts of alcohol. Henderson knew companies like Vixen wouldn't hold back on providing entertainment for their customers, so they would be participating in many evenings of heavy drinking with people from the army and MOD. In the more serious sessions, a bit of drug-taking could be introduced, and from what he had learned about Roger, the appearance of attractive women, perhaps in the form of prostitutes.

This would be the sort of scenario where things could go disastrously wrong. Here, the DI let his imagination run riot. One of Maitland's party could have fallen into a river and drowned, a drunken officer might have discharged a weapon, or one of the women present could have complained of rape.

Looking at the issue from the other side, someone so appalled at their behaviour could have threatened to report their activities to the authorities, and the men could have agreed to silence them.

He now believed the answer lay somewhere in such a scenario. It felt a more convincing motive than any provided by the Maitland family members, the *Soldiers of Peace* protestors, or the soldiers from the rogue drone attack. However, he couldn't ignore the summary dismissal of Jerome Potter. It came a close second.

FORTY

Henderson took a sip from his pint of Harvey's Best Bitter. He savoured it, but he wouldn't have any more. Even though Kelly offered to drive this evening to allow him to relax more than he had been doing these last few weeks, he decided against it. In the middle of a murder investigation, a call could come through at any moment demanding his immediate attendance somewhere else.

They were at The Cock Inn, in a place called Ringmer, close to where he worked in Lewes. Neither he nor Kelly had been to the pub before, but based on what he had seen so far, it impressed. The food was homemade, although he hadn't tasted anything yet, and the beer was one he liked.

To stop their relationship becoming stale by only going to the same restaurants or pubs whenever they went out for a meal or a drink, they made a point of visiting a different pub each time. This one on the advice of Carol Walters, having been taken there on a date.

It turned out her companion for the evening was a real-ale fiend, and with this pub being on the CAMRA Ale Trail, one of his favourites. He'd proceeded to regale the DS for several minutes about the ins and outs of brewing a real ale and the benefits of using various types of malts and yeasts. Needless to say, he didn't make it to a second date.

The pub was far enough away from the Falmer campus at the University of Sussex for Kelly not to bump into some of her students or colleagues. Kelly had taken a look around just to make sure. The issue Kelly wanted to talk about could have been discussed in the car, but for most of the journey Henderson had been talking on the phone to Sean Houghton about Lester Grange, bringing him up to date

'So, this is about a student of yours?'

'One I taught last year.'

'What happened?'

'Her friends were getting no answer from knocking on her room door or from her phone, so they called Security, assuming they had a spare key. They didn't and dithered about breaking down the door, quoting Health and Safety regulations and issues of student privacy. When at last they managed to persuade them to enter the room, they found her lying on the bed, dead, a drug overdose.'

'Deliberate or accidental?'

'They're certain she did it on purpose.'

'Did the delay outside the door contribute to her death?'

'The pathologist didn't think so. She believed the poor girl had been dead for several hours.'

'It's such a waste. Why do you think she did it? Did she struggle with the course or hadn't she settled into university life?'

'No, she was popular and bright, one of my best students, in fact. That's how I first noticed her. The essays she produced were clear and the key points well argued.'

'What do you think lay behind it?'

'Her parents split up part-way through her first year.'

'A tough situation for anyone to cope with.'

'Indeed, and even though we think it affects small children more, it can devastate this age group. The whole foundation upon which they've built their studies crumbles in a moment: financial support for fees and accommodation, a place to return to at the end of term, somewhere to go when the course finishes to allow them to look for a job. When this safety net is suddenly pulled away, it's no wonder many feel lost and abandoned.'

'Nevertheless...'

'I know what you're going to say, it affects different people in different ways.'

'It does. Faced with the same situation, some will start a weekend job and try to fill the financial void created by the divorce, while others, unable to concentrate on their studies, will leave university altogether and start working. For them, suicide isn't an option.'

'You're right. No doubt she exhibited some signs only her parents or siblings would have been aware of, perhaps they should have prepared their daughter better to receive such bad news.'

'Hello folks, I have your meals,' a smiling young woman said. 'So, who's having the Sussex smokie?'

'That's me,' Kelly said.

'And I take it the chicken and leek pie is for you, sir?'

'Indeed it is.'

'Would you like any accompaniments?'

'Not for me,' Kelly said.

'Same.'

'How about drinks?'

'A small glass of Sauvignon Blanc for me, please,' Kelly said.

'Nothing for me, thanks.'

The waitress departed.

'It's you who needs the succour of an alcohol dose tonight, Kelly. On hearing such news, I'm not sure why you volunteered to drive.'

'I think your need is greater than mine. The last few weeks have been so stressful.'

'It's been difficult, I can't deny, but nothing tops the death of a student.'

She shrugged. 'Yeah maybe, but despite knowing her quite well, a lot could have happened in the six or seven months when I haven't been teaching her.'

'I guess.'

Henderson dug into the pie. It tasted excellent and it looked as though the trek out to this pub had been well worth it.

'How's the investigation going?'

He paused for a moment, chewing his food. 'I'm asked this question half a dozen times a week by senior officers, journalists, members of the public, and I always find it hard to respond without using platitudes. You know the kind of thing: enquiries are continuing, we're pursuing a fresh lead, when something happens you'll be the first to be informed, or something else equally bland and noncommittal.'

'I suppose it's all background noise and speculation until you arrest the person responsible.'

'If we had a definite lead or someone had given us the name of the perpetrator, we wouldn't be talking about it, we would be out arresting them.'

'It's the same —'

Henderson's phone rang. He looked at the display. 'I'd better answer this.'

'You carry on, I've got a meal to eat and fish goes cold so fast.'

'Hello Carol,' he said. 'Don't you realise this is Friday night? What are you doing in the office?'

'I hadn't planned to go out anywhere tonight and there's work to be done, although I'm not in the office, I'm at home working on my laptop.'

'Where's Nick?'

'Gone.'

'What, away on a work assignment?'

'No, I mean gone-gone.'

'Ah, I see.'

'British Airways got back to us.'

'Ah yes. Potter claimed he spent the night in question at home with his partner.'

If Henderson sounded a tad circumspect, it was because he was in a public place and didn't know who would be in earshot.

'Well-remembered, gov, but listen to this. The Saturday night in question, his globe-trotting stewardess partner... Are we still calling them stewardesses, or are they now stewards?'

'Actresses are now actors, so you could be right. Let's settle for female flight attendants.'

'Whatever she's called, the Saturday night of Maitland's murder, she was in Las Vegas from the Friday night before the murder, until Wednesday of the following week.'

'So, the slippery Mr Potter lied.'

'He certainly did.'

FORTY-ONE

Once again, Henderson and Walters were seated in Adrian Chapman's office. Since their last visit, he had made further strides at putting his own stamp on what had once been Roger Maitland's with a new desk and some other furniture.

'It looks like he believes he's a shoo-in for the top job.'

'You would hope so as it would be a waste of money buying all this stuff if the new man decides to junk it.'

'It's fortunate the protestors stayed away,' the DI said. 'I think tensions are running so high, someone might be tempted to come out to them with a baseball bat.'

'Or, if they're really angry, they might be tempted to send out one of their killer drones.'

He laughed. 'For sure, that would get rid of them, maybe forever. It's not good news about Potter not being available, is it? Do you think he's trying to avoid us?'

'His flight is due back Monday. If he only went for a short break to be with his missus, then he'll be on it. If on the other hand he's made a break for it...'

'We'll issue an international arrest warrant.'

'I don't think there's enough evidence.'

'No, but you have to agree, he's a bloody good fit. He made threats, and did so in writing, there's big money involved, and he hated Roger Maitland. I think we've got plenty.'

'All true but circumstantial.'

'We'll cross that bridge when we come to it. On Monday, as I said in the car, position a couple of officers at Gatwick to meet Potter's flight when it arrives. We'll arrest him before he reaches the terminal building.'

'On what charge?'

'Did you wake up in an arsey mood this morning, or have I said something to offend you?'

'Just playing devil's advocate.'

'In which case, take your pick: suspicion of murder; conspiracy to murder, or as an accessory. I think we have enough to convince any magistrate.'

'Okay. I admit he's a good fit for Roger Maitland, but what about Lester Grange?'

'One thing at a time. Don't forget, Potter runs a company with dozens of guys like himself; ex-squaddies trying to make a career in civvy street. One of them might well be willing to do something for Potter in return for money or keeping their job. I'm not suggesting they would commit murder for him, but they could be helping him in other ways.'

'Hello detectives. I can't say I'm pleased to see you again,' Adrian Chapman said as he walked into his office. They stood and shook hands.

'We're sorry to be back here as well, Mr Chapman,' Henderson said, retaking his seat. 'As you might expect, we're here to talk about Lester Grange.'

'Do you know if he's been killed by the same person who murdered Roger? I bought loads of newspapers and I thought they would tell me, but they don't.'

'It's not for general dissemination, but we are treating the two deaths as related. This doesn't mean we're assuming they were killed by the same person, as I believe it's too early to make those sorts of assumptions.'

Chapman looked puzzled for a moment. 'They're related but not necessarily killed by the same person? I don't understand.'

'Think of it this way, the two men may have been killed for the same reason, but one or multiple people might be involved.'

'Surely the same person killed them; Lucas Potter in my book?'

'Not necessarily. Unlike a bullet wound where we can accurately determine if two bullets came from the same gun, we cannot ascertain this from a knife. We can say a wound is wide or narrow, the blade used serrated or smooth, but it could have been made by any number of blades.'

'I think I can appreciate where you're coming from.'

'Tell us about Lester.'

'He joined Vixen six years ago from BAE Systems at Wharton where he did a similar distribution job. When he started, he and Karen were still together. They have three children.'

He stopped and took a drink from the cup beside him.

'He was an ebullient, glass half-full sort of guy with bags of energy. This enthusiasm transferred to the staff in his distribution team, who at the time were a bunch of lazy sods. With Lester in charge, it became the best-run division in the company.'

'Impressive. What about his relationship with Roger?'

'They didn't hit it off straight away. Roger had always been slow at allowing friends into his life, and he left Lester to find his feet in the organisation for a while. When he realised how well he'd got the distribution area running, he embraced him with enthusiasm, praising him in meetings and approving whatever expansion plans he decided to put into his budget.'

'Did he take him to customer meetings?'

'That was part of Roger's plan. We have a number of former servicemen working in the company, as I'm sure you're aware. We are keen to employ them as they recognise and understand the demands of a military organisation, and they speak their language. Roger wanted someone with all that experience by his side at customer meetings. He'd tried various individuals, and for several years it was Daniel Hill, our manufacturing director.'

'Oh.'

'Daniel and Roger were very close, going to meetings, demonstrations and even socialising together, but even then he felt Dan never possessed the requisite knowledge and gravitas.'

'Until Lester came along?'

'Lester had seen service in Afghanistan, been in firefights, had comrades blown up by IEDs and others shot, so it gave him a high level of kudos with the brass hats.'

'I can imagine.'

'Putting on my commercial hat for a moment, it's safe to say this business grew with Lester around. It became easier to gain access to the key decision makers, and often purchasing decisions were made faster. I'm not talking here only about UK military, but the Roger and Lester show got us into markets we had never been in before, such as Scandinavia and the Far East.'

'Did they socialise together away from work?'

'Yes, they both liked to gamble and frequently went horse racing or to a casino, and they were both members of the same gun club.'

'What about customer entertaining?'

'It isn't what it used to be, what with the stricter tax rules and corporate governance directives.'

'Mr Chapman, that's the answer I would expect you to give a journalist, not two detectives investigating the deaths of two of your senior colleagues.'

'I suppose it made me sound a bit like Roger. We'd have management meetings after Roger and Lester returned from days of drunken debauchery with an order under their arm. Roger would regale us with some of the goings-on, but with the warning that whatever we heard in the meeting, it would go no further.'

'I can imagine. Like most societies, we have an uneasy alliance with the military. If too much is revealed about their methods, or how big contracts are awarded, the trust could be broken.'

'It's something we are acutely aware of, but I think we've discussed Lester enough. I want to know how this killer is picking his targets and who will be next. Not only that, what are you doing to protect us?'

FORTY-TWO

The group made their way outside. The slow pace reminded Phil Bentley of the crowd leaving the Amex Stadium after a big match. They were in Ship Street, in the middle of Brighton, the third pub they'd visited since seven thirty that evening. Most of them were heading home, not because they were old and tired, especially with an average age of only twenty-eight, but because many had young children, or they had work in the morning.

Phil Bentley knew the age of the group because he went to school with every single one of them. Three years ago, one of his former classmates put a post on social media about having a class reunion, and despite thinking only ten or twelve would show, thirty-odd turned up. This had been their third annual get-together, and they still had a respectable attendance of twenty-six.

'What a night,' Ben Wright, standing beside him said. 'I was jammed in between Jessie Buckman and Alice Goodyear. I wouldn't risk it for Alice as she talks too much, but I'd take a chance on Jessie. She's a right belter, and what a sense of humour. I always remember her as the studious type who said nothing in class, but oh how's she's changed.'

'A lot of us have.'

'And a lot haven't, like you mate,' he said punching Bentley playfully on the arm. 'You still play rugby, you're still with Helen, and now you're a grown-up version of the prefect you used to be.'

Bentley laughed. 'I've been called many things, never that.'

'I wanted to ask you–'

'Boys!' Daisy Padolski shrieked. 'Come to *Escape* with us. It's gonna be brilliant!'

'I can't,' Ben said. 'I need to be in Southampton tomorrow by ten.'

'That's a shame. What about you, Phil? Although I seem to remember the last time we danced, I advised you to take some lessons.'

'Cheeky mare. If my memory serves me well, it was *you* who trampled on *my* foot, but I'm sorry I can't come either. I'm on an early shift tomorrow.'

'Couldn't Helen make it tonight?'

'No, we'd arranged for her mother to come and babysit, but she came down with some mysterious virus and called off at the last minute.'

'What a bummer, she would have enjoyed it. Well,' Daisy said in a pseudo-TV voice, 'it's a straight no from Ben, and another no from Phil. Okay, saddos, I'll just have to go and find somebody else who likes to dance. Enjoy a good life!'

They loitered outside the pub for a few more minutes before Phil said goodbye to everyone and walked with a few others to a bus stop in North Street. He timed it well as he didn't have long to wait for his bus. Living where he did at the extreme end of Mile Oak, with views over the South Downs, only one bus went all the way, unless he fancied a twenty-minute walk.

He had the companionship of two others as the bus crossed the Old Shoreham Road, but after a succession of stops, he was the last of the class of 2013. He dozed as the bus wound its way through Portslade, but was sufficiently awake to realise who it was that stepped aboard at the previous stop: Dave King, the guy from *Soldiers of Peace* who had beaten him up.

When King rose from his seat as the bus approached St Helen's Park, Bentley followed. King headed into the park and moments later, Bentley found out why he had decided to traipse across damp grass rather than walk around the road, when the guy lit up a spliff. This would be enough to arrest him on suspicion of possessing, or perhaps selling drugs, but he didn't need an excuse tonight. What he planned was simple: cold, vindictive revenge.

He ran up behind him, and even though he didn't think he was making much noise, King turned to see what the sound might be. Bentley punched him on the side of the head. He fell, not so much from the weight of the punch, but due to him being unbalanced.

'You fucker!' he screeched as he lay on the deck, trying to shift his brain into gear.

King peered at his attacker and despite the dim light, recognised him. 'You bastard! You think being a copper can save you now?' He reached into his jacket and pulled out a knife. 'Maybe you fancy a bit of this!' Before he tried to lash out or scramble to his feet, Bentley kicked his hand and the blade spun away.

He leaned over and punched King in the face; on the nose, the same as he'd done to him. He felt the tissue and bone shift inwards and soon it gushed with blood. King uttered something unintelligible. To shut him up, Bentley swung a leg and kicked him in the balls. Payback.

Bentley walked out of St Helen's Park, satisfied no one had seen this little incident. Houses surrounded the park, but those closest had their line of sight obscured by some trees, and the others were too far off to determine anything in detail.

The case against King would be prejudiced if it could be proved the copper he was accused of attacking had in fact beaten him up. With no witnesses, it would be King's word against his. Added to this, King had been drinking and smoking cannabis. Any decent lawyer would put the suggestion to the court that in his addled state, a picture of his accuser must have popped into his head like a ghostly apparition. With a smile on his face, Bentley set off for home.

FORTY-THREE

Henderson walked out of Sean Houghton's office. The number of suspects was narrowing, pleasing the CI, but he was concerned that no one was a definite fit. If pushed, Houghton would finger Lucas Potter.

Two officers were at Gatwick waiting for the arrival of the 09:10 British Airways flight from Orlando. Potter had joined his partner's trip on Thursday to enjoy a long weekend, taking in some of Florida's delights, including some welcome sunshine with not much of it around in Sussex.

He looked at his watch: 08:40.

The team at the airport were under instruction only to arrest Potter as a last resort. He would be asked to come down to the station to answer some questions, but if he refused, he would be arrested.

For both a suspect and the police, answering a few questions came with little baggage. A suspect wouldn't feel compelled to engage a lawyer as it gave them an opportunity to clear up any misunderstandings. If arrested, a lawyer would be present and the interview would be required to follow procedures laid down by the Police and Criminal Evidence Act.

He returned to his office and looked through his email inbox for the main documents relating to the murder of Lester Grange: the pathology and SOCO reports. He read them in detail, but to his disappointment, uncovered nothing new. The way the murder took place probably accounted for this. The killer didn't enter the house, so no forensic data would be found on furniture or the carpets. From Henderson and Walters' visit to the crime scene, they reasoned the killer made his exit via the front path, so no fibres or hairs would be trapped on the garden fence.

From a door video camera a couple of doors down from Lester Grange's house, they caught a fleeting glimpse of a black-clad figure of average height and build walking past. They deduced little else, other than his brisk but not overly hurried pace. With being in possession of an accurate time of death, the DI's first inclination was to pull CCTV footage from town cameras and identify his car.

In this respect, Lindfield behaved like the village it once had been: it had no such cameras; the nearest were in Haywards Heath. The advantage they had in knowing the time of the killer's escape made no difference as they didn't have any idea about which direction he took. Looking further afield where there would be cameras didn't help, as it became muddled by the inclusion of dozens of roads and cars.

There were no shortcuts. The team he had going door-to-door around Lindfield would continue their endeavours and with luck, they might throw up something the murder team could use.

'Deep in thought, gov?'

He looked up to see DS Walters standing at the door.

'Been looking at Lester Grange's forensic report.'
'Anything new?'

He shook his head.

'Such a shame. On a more positive note, Lucas Potter is now sitting in the Interview Suite.'

'Is he?' He looked at the clock on the wall: 10:55. 'Is that the time already?' he said almost to himself. 'Did he come without a fuss?'

'He did indeed.'

Henderson picked up his folder and stood. 'Let's go and watch him squirm.'

For a man who had been in Florida only a couple of days, Lucas Potter appeared tanned and relaxed. He supposed the nature of his work meant he wasn't an office-bound desk jockey, but out visiting warehouses, Gatwick Airport, and all the rest, at all times and in all weathers.

'Good morning, Mr Potter. Thanks for coming in.'

'I don't think I had much bloody choice. It's a fine way to spoil the effect left by a damn good holiday.'

'How was Florida?'

For a moment he seemed taken aback by Henderson's convivial tone.

'Eh, yeah, yeah, great.'

'What did you do?'

'We visited a couple of parks, not the ones for the kids like Disney and Sea World, but the movie parks, you know; Warner Brothers and Universal.'

'I imagine you also did a bit of sunbathing.'

'We had a car so we went over to St Pete's for the afternoon and did nothing but lie in the sun and drink Bud.'

'Mr Potter, the reason we wanted to talk to you is that on the night of Roger Maitland's murder, you told us you were at home with your partner, Rosie Carruthers.'

'That's right. I said we had a meal and watched a movie. Why, do you have a problem with it? Do you need me to a sign an affidavit or something?'

'According to Rosie's employer, British Airways, she couldn't have been with you that night. She departed for Las Vegas earlier in the week.'

Walters passed over a copy of the flight roster supplied by BA.

Potter picked it up, glanced at it for a couple of seconds, before reaching into his pocket and pulling out his phone. 'This isn't right,' he muttered as he scrolled though his apps, looking for the calendar or an email, Henderson assumed.

They left him for a few moments.

'Ah, I see what's happened. Rosie was due to be off that weekend, but she sent me a copy of an email she received telling her to report for the Las Vegas flight as someone had called in sick. I didn't read it at the time, and forgot later, so I hadn't updated my calendar.'

'When we spoke to you a week last Thursday, the murder of Roger Maitland had occurred only ten days before. I'm surprised you couldn't remember such an important detail and tell us then.'

'Well, I didn't. What does that prove? I've got a bad memory?'

'Where were you?'

'Nowhere. Stayed home. I made a meal and watched a movie. Instead of Rosie being with me, I did it on my own.'

'Can anyone verify it?'

He gave Henderson an exaggerated, exasperated look. 'Of course no one can bloody verify it. There was only me.'

'Let me try you with another date. Wednesday night, the day before you flew to Florida.'

'That's an easier one. I went on a stake-out the day before, Tuesday. Some of our guys had been stealing from a warehouse at Heathrow. It turned into a late one as I ended up at A&E.'

'Anything serious?'

'One of the guys we nabbed pulled out a knife. I got a slash across the stomach. Nothing too deep.'

'Not enough to stop you flying to the US?'

'No, and Rosie will confirm I stayed home the next night. I'm not a good patient, I'm afraid. I had a hot bath and an early night.'

FORTY-FOUR

'Didn't Lester Grange do well for himself when he left the army?' Sally Graham said.

'What makes you say that?' Vicky Neal asked.

'Well for one, he was in the army for about twelve years, so he wasn't always a big earner. We've seen where he lived, a decent-sized house in Lindfield, and now I see where his missus, or ex-missus lives, I have to say I'm impressed.'

They were in Courtmead Road in Cuckfield, a private road with no through traffic. Moving only a row of houses away from a busy road with buses, cars, and boisterous schoolchildren, it turned into a tranquil oasis, chockful of large, detached houses.

'I suppose so. I thought of him as nothing more than an overpaid company director. Even though Grange had been a platoon sergeant, I think you're right, no one joins the army for the money.'

'All the same, divorce is an expensive business, don't you think? Buying two houses and having to pay twice for electricity, council tax, and all the rest.'

'I wouldn't want to do it.'

Neal guided the car into the driveway and parked beside a Range Rover. Judging by the gleaming exterior, either an old car well maintained, or one purchased recently. Her money would be on the latter, but hard to tell with the private registration.

An attractive woman in her early forties opened the door. She had shoulder-length, thick brown hair and wore a body-clinging dress showing off to good effect a slim, but curvaceous figure.

'Karen Grange?'

'Yes.'

'Hello, we're detectives from Surrey and Sussex Major Crime Team investigating the death of your husband. Can we come in?'

'Yes, please do.'

She pointed them into the lounge while she went into the kitchen to make coffee. If she had been distraught, Neal would have made it for her, but she appeared to be fine.

The house looked old on the outside, but modern and airy on the inside. A family picture on a bookcase showed Karen with three children, the youngest around seven or eight, and the oldest, sixteen or seventeen.

'Have you always lived here?' Neal asked, when Karen came back into the room.

'Six years, ever since we moved down from Lancashire.'

'Where are you from?' Neal asked.

'The same neck of the woods as you by the sound of it.'

'I'm from Wythenshawe.'

'We were almost neighbours. Timperley.'

'Do you think you'll move back up, now, with Lester...?'

'That's what all my friends are asking, but I tell them, why would I? Tom turned one a few weeks after moving here, so he's more or less a Sussex boy, while my other two, Kayleigh and Gemma, have lost their accents and would hate to move back. So no, I have no plans until at least the kids are off my hands. Although if your kids are customers of the bank of Mum and Dad, like mine are, that time may never come.'

'As I said earlier, we're part of the team investigating Lester's death. Are you aware of anyone who might have had a grudge against your husband?'

'He's my ex in all but name. The divorce papers are lying over there,' she said nodding over to the table beside the window, 'waiting for my signature. Anyone with a grudge?' She paused a moment pondering. 'I don't think so. Lester lived life to the full. If he couldn't bring his energy and enthusiasm to something, he would try something else.'

She took a sip of tea.

'That applied to work, DIY projects around the house, even the kids. A day at the park with him and they'd either come back completely worn out or scared out of their wits. He didn't do anything in between.'

'Why did the two of you split?'

'Well, the thing that first attracted me to him, this loud, bursting with energy bloke who could be a one-man party if he put his mind to it, became the thing that eventually wore me out. A constant need to be on top of my game every minute of the day or he would sulk. A man never content to read a book, or sit with me in a pub and talk. He would rather scan the faces all around or look at his phone.'

'Did he have any enemies?'

'Not in his home life, mainly among fellow parents from the school our kids attend. As for the work he did at Vixen, he didn't say much about it to me.'

'No?'

'He was full of it when he first started working there, talking about the new people he met, the things he got involved in. Six months or so later, when Roger began including him in customer visits, it became all, *'I can't tell you as it's covered by the Official Secrets Act,'* or *'It's top-secret, if I tell you, I'd have to kill you.'* Some of it rang true, as they were dealing with stuff only a few people knew about, and some cutting-edge technology, but on the other hand, it was his way of not letting me have a peek into his dirty world.'

'What's dirty about it?'

'Some of the contracts Vixen are involved in are worth tens of millions of pounds, which will keep the folks at the factory in paid employment for the next three, maybe four years, so they're a big deal. To be awarded them, Lester and Roger had to throw everything at it. I mean, despite having a close working relationship with their MOD and army contacts, they still wanted to be wined and dined.'

'Like lots of other businesses, I suppose,' Graham suggested.

'You're right, except for the sums involved. Don't forget, many of the folk they were dealing with were hard, former military men who took no prisoners, and it would be game over if they spotted any weakness.'

'Are you aware if they got up to anything illegal?'

'I don't think so, but I can't say for sure as Lester would only tell me so much before he would clam up. He told me a little about the heavy drinking, the people taking cocaine, although Lester never did drugs, and the women.'

'The women?'

'They would be drinking in some private club and at some point in the evening, a group of women would appear. They had been arranged by Roger, of course, but Lester swore the pleasure was all for the customer, not for him and his boss. As you can imagine, I found this hard to believe. It was this, and the secrecy surrounding the work he did, that in the end finally broke our marriage.'

FORTY-FIVE

Lucas Potter lived in a small cul-de-sac in Horley, set out in a horseshoe shape. At this moment, Carol Walters had a team of officers walking around each of the houses knocking on doors. They were asking if anyone had noticed whether the lights were on in the Potter household on Saturday night, three weeks before. It was a tough question for some, in particular the retired, unemployed, or those caring for small children or an ailing relative, when one weekend often merged with another.

The houses were of that ubiquitous new house design, but of the larger, detached 'executive' variety and perhaps no more than about five years old. It looked ideal for a busy couple like Lucas Potter and Rosie Carruthers, with him working long hours and her being away for days at a time in the Americas or the Far East.

With only a tiny garden at the front, few onerous tasks were required to be undertaken, and all the things that demanded attention in an older house: boiler, roof, electrics, pipes in the loft, were fairly new, keeping routine maintenance to a minimum. That said, despite having not much to work with, some of their neighbours had gone to town with numerous planters, climbing plants, and a variety of ornamental sculptures.

Of course, Walters and her team of uniformed officers were looking for something more concrete than half-remembered lights. They wanted someone who had spoken to Lucas as he arrived home, someone walking their dog late at night and remembering seeing him at the window, or perhaps a neighbour admiring his new car and remarking to him about it.

To assuage suspicions and not blacken the Potter name with their neighbours, she had concocted a story about a burglary in the area and reports of lights in the Potter household when she knew the couple were out. It covered the bases, although there would always be one who would have heart palpitations whenever the word 'burglary' came up in conversation.

DI Henderson wasn't as convinced about Potter's guilt, believing the killer emanated from the boisterous social life led by Lester Grange and Roger Maitland. The problem here was finding the evidence. Roger didn't reveal everything of the activities in which they were involved to the rest of the Vixen management group, and instead fed them a few tame titbits, while Lester said little to his wife.

To complicate matters, the two men had probably attended a large number of such meetings. The DI had no way of telling which one had descended into such a level of debauchery, something bad or illegal might have happened. Even if they tracked down the attendees of such meetings, what were the chances they would be willing to admit their involvement in anything nefarious?

Her phone rang.

'Morning gov.'

'Morning Carol,' Henderson said. 'How goes the door-to-door?'

She looked at her clipboard. 'Two no-shows and one who was sure he couldn't recall seeing his car.'

'It's not much.'

'No, it isn't, although I'm more hopeful at the house one of the guys is about to go into a few minutes from now. It's the tackiest garden in the close, more pots and gnomes than you can shake a wand at.'

'It sounds like someone with a lot of time on their hands.'

'Yep, and money to burn.'

'You've got the team pulling his phone records and bank statements?'

'Yep, if today throws up nothing, he might have made a call or bought something with his credit card, proving he didn't stay at home.'

'Keep plugging.'

'You sure?'

'What makes you say that? Do you think you're wasting your time?'

'I thought you weren't convinced Potter made a good fit for our killer?'

'I'm not one hundred percent, but his motive for killing Roger Maitland is as good as any we've come across.'

'But not for Lester Grange.'

'One thing at a time. Let's shake down his alibi as much as we can; see where it leaves us.'

'No problem.'

'Catch you later.'

'Cheers gov.'

The copper knocking on the door of the tacky house received no reply. He then did the right thing and walked around to the back of the house to find out if the owners were in the garden or conservatory. It was a bright and sunny day, but with a cool breeze, one of the few decent days they'd experienced this spring. When driving to Horley she couldn't help but notice the amount of people outside washing their windows and cars, and weeding their gardens.

Walters heard what sounded like a loud conversation taking place. She was thankful it didn't sound like the shocked shrieks of a woman sunbathing topless, only to spot a young, open-mouthed PC gawping at her. It didn't feel warm enough for those sorts of activities; instead, the good-natured sounds of someone raising their voice as they were at the far end of the garden.

A copper walked towards her.

'Hi Sarge. Number five is a gobby middle-aged bloke who didn't sound best pleased at being disturbed from viewing daytime television. He said he couldn't remember what he was doing the previous week, never mind three Saturdays ago, and took no interest in what his neighbours were doing as he believes they are all a bunch of self-obsessed tossers.'

'Somebody got out of the wrong side of bed this morning,' she said as she noted the comments down on her clipboard.

'I'll go over and do number seven now.'

'Thanks.'

'Sarge!'

She looked up after she finished writing the word 'tossers' on her response form.

The copper who had gone into the tacky garden house now stood beside the householder at the front door. He waved her over. She threaded her pen into the clipboard holder and walked towards them.

'This lady has a door video system,' the PC said when she approached.

'Good morning, madam, I'm Detective Sergeant Walters, Sussex Police.'

'Cindy Davidson. My husband installed the doorbell thingy system. I don't think he set it up right as it shows practically the whole street, not just our doorway.'

Walters glanced at the PC who gave her a faint, knowing smile. *Here lives a nosey bugger*, they both thought, keen to find out what his neighbours were up to, particularly the pretty girl across the way: Rosie Carruthers.

'Your officer said you were interested from about seven thirty on Saturday night, three weeks back?'

'That's correct.'

She fiddled with her phone for a minute or two before handing it to the DS. 'At least he's got it set up so the video only activates when detecting movement, otherwise we could be here for hours.'

It took Walters a few seconds to orient herself. The picture looked outward from the front door of the house with a good view of the garden area and all the pots and statues in the garden. Across the road and a little bit to the left, the herringboned driveway of the Potter house and all its windows.

'The picture quality is all right,' Walters said, 'it's better than many town centre CCTV cameras.'

'Yeah, it's not bad, but in my experience, you get what you pay for.'

Walters watched a fox come ambling past at eight ten. At eight forty, a car entered the close and parked at another house. At ten thirty, a man walked his dog. At eleven twenty, the appearance of another fox. All the time the video played, the driveway of the Potter house could clearly be seen. No car appeared on the driveway and no lights or movement were visible inside the house.

FORTY-SIX

Sergeants Walters, Neal, and Wallop walked into Henderson's office. He picked up the file from the desk and joined them at the small meeting table.

'To make sure we're all on the same page,' Henderson said, once everyone was settled, 'let me recap. This morning, Carol conducted a door-to-door operation at the cul-de-sac where Lucas Potter and Rosie Carruthers live in Horley. On the Saturday night of Roger Maitland's murder, he said he and Rosie were at home all night. Her flight roster at BA proved this to be false as she had flown to Las Vegas a few days before. He then told us he had been home alone, but what Carol found suggests otherwise.'

'The woman in the house opposite,' Walters said, 'has a door camera. It only activates when it detects movement, and on the four occasions it did so on that Saturday night, no car could be seen outside the Potter house and no lights were visible in any of the windows.'

'Well done finding this out, Carol,' Neal said. 'What a liar Potter has turned out to be.'

'If he's innocent,' Wallop said, 'what the hell is so important or secret he doesn't want to say where he was? It has to be something illegal.'

'It's a good point Harry.'

'He's got motive enough,' Neal said. 'Maitland point-blank refused to offer him and his mother further compensation for his father's sacking. With him out of the way, Adrian Chapman sounds like a more amenable individual.'

'I agree with you, Vicky,' Henderson said. 'With Roger out of the way, you would think he would start a dialogue with Adrian, but as far as we know, he hasn't.'

'If this had been his intention,' Walters said, 'why would he kill Lester Grange?'

'This is why I'm not one hundred percent sold on Potter,' Henderson retorted, 'but I can't let him get away with providing another dodgy alibi

'Not to mention,' Neal said, 'if it is Potter, and he's got an agenda we know nothing about, the other directors at Vixen could be in danger.'

'If that's the case,' Wallop said, 'I would bet next on the list would be Daniel Hill, the guy in charge of manufacturing. Roger and him were big buddies in the past, but they sort of drifted apart when Lester came along.'

'This is what worries me, Harry,' Henderson said. 'If it's not Potter, and we waste time and resources on him, we might miss something else and put Hill, or one of the other directors, in the firing line.'

'We can't protect them all,' Walters said. 'We don't have the manpower.'

'Which is why we need to arrest Potter, pull his alibi to pieces and find out once and for all if he's our killer. First of all, we need to put him under surveillance.'

'Why?' Wallop asked, looking a tad perplexed. 'Couldn't we just pick him up at his house or place of work?'

'No, Harry. He's a hands-on sort of business owner, so he's out checking the warehouses his staff are supposed to be guarding, and with the security people at the airport. I don't want to send a team to arrest him at his house or his offices in Crawley only to find he isn't there.'

'Point taken.'

'I'll set it up,' the DI said. 'Where are we on the other loose ends?'

'We're still looking for Kieran Stock,' Neal said, 'one of the soldiers from the patrol attacked by the drone.'

'Keep on it.'

'Even though we're now going after Lucas Potter?'

'He's the last active member of the army unit and if he checks out, we can close that as a suspect group. So yes, keep trying to locate him. Okay?'

'Yes.'

'What about door-to-door enquiries in Lindfield, Harry?'

'Nothing else has surfaced other than the fleeting glimpse of him on a neighbour's door camera. I think the killer got quite clever about where he parked his car. He didn't park outside the victim's house as it might have alerted a neighbour, but in a nearby street. His only risk was being seen walking, and who remembers a single Joe out for an early evening walk?'

'Good point, but it doesn't help us one bit. We're working on the assumption their deaths are linked and the connection must be where the two men dovetailed. Carol and I believe we've found one: the socialising the two men did when trying to secure military contracts. Vicky, have you come across anything in the personal lives of the two men to suggest the motive might be there? I'm thinking here about their love of sport; they're both members of a gun club, and they sometimes went to a casino.'

'It's been in my mind all the time I've been interviewing the various family members, but nothing they've said hits the mark. A few, like his soon-to-be ex-wife, Karen, talked about the socialising they did for work and understood, at times, it verged on debauchery, but Lester didn't elaborate on any of the details.'

'It's a such frustrating aspect of this case. I feel for sure something might have happened during those boozing and womanising sessions, but no one seems to know a thing about it.'

'Or they're not saying.'

'Adrian Chapman changed the subject when we spoke to him about it, not because of good acting skills, more a recognition he didn't know much.'

'I agree,' Walters said.

'Well, if no one's got anything else, I'll await news of Lucas Potter's arrest.'

FORTY-SEVEN

An unmarked Sussex Police pool car slotted into a parking space in the large car park, close to Nuffield Health in West Green, Crawley. Parking where they shouldn't on double yellow lines, sat a police patrol car from the local nick. The surveillance team put in place by DI Henderson had spotted Lucas Potter enter the gym at 10:05am and this little posse had been assembled to arrest him.

'It's a handy gym for him,' DC Seb Young said. 'His office is no more than five minutes away.'

'I'm wondering why he uses it at all,' DC Sally Graham said. 'According to DS Walters, they have a gym in the office.'

'I heard that too, but I took it to mean a couple of cardio machines and maybe some weights, to help overweight security guards to lose a few pounds. It doesn't sound like it'll stretch to a full cardio workout like you can do in a place like this.'

'Do you go to a gym?'

'Yeah, but not a fancy one like this. It's in the local leisure centre.'

'I've never been into gyms. I'm not built for lifting weights and too much cardio makes my head spin.'

'If you went a couple of times a week and started lifting weights, you would soon get into the swing of it.'

'And what would I do with a set of overdeveloped arm or leg muscles? If a large perp comes running at me, I'm not going to try and wrestle him to the ground, am I? I'll use guile and intuition, and if that doesn't work, it's a blast of pepper spray in the face and a whack on the knee with an expandable baton.'

'Ha, I wouldn't like to upset you.'

'No, you wouldn't.'

'He should be out by now, our Mr Potter. He's been over an hour. I can do my routine in about forty minutes, providing I don't become distracted by something on my phone or a pretty girl in tight Lycra.'

'We haven't missed him, have we?'

'I don't think so. The patrol car arrived no more than five minutes after the spotters reported him walking in. The fact it took us forty minutes to drive here is neither here nor there. We'll give him another ten. I know some people who do a forty- or fifty-minute workout then another twenty- or twenty-five-minutes showering, doing their hair, and making themselves presentable to the outside world. Maybe he's one of those.'

'And I thought girls were bad.'

'I don't mean all guys do it, only some. Me, I'm in and out of the changing room in ten minutes.'

She gave him a look as if to say, '*it figures*', but she stayed silent.

She looked out of the car window at the car park. Plenty of people were about for a Wednesday morning. She didn't have kids, but the absence of youngsters in the nearby town centre suggested schools hadn't broken up for half-term just yet. The car park had plenty of spaces, not only for Nuffield Health but also a ten-pin bowling alley, cinema, and a host of eateries. She couldn't see herself working out in a gym, and no way would she want to watch a film or go bowling this early in the morning as some people were doing. She looked at the car clock. 'Ten minutes are up. Let's make a move.'

'But–'

'No buts. I didn't want to arrest him in his underpants, but I'm getting impatient so we may have to. Radio the patrol car and tell them what we're up to.'

After instructing the Crawley officers to wait outside, the detectives walked inside the building. Graham showed her ID to the receptionist, Gemma, according to her name badge.

'We're detectives from Sussex Police. A man we would like to question entered this building over an hour ago. We'd like to locate him.'

'Would you like me to put out a call for him?' she asked, indicating the intercom system.

'No need. We'd like to take a look ourselves.'

'Oh, I'm not sure if I can allow it. You're not appropriately dressed and your presence might alarm some of our clients.'

'I wouldn't be asking if it wasn't important, but this is in connection with a murder inquiry.'

'Sorry, I didn't realise,' she said, her eyes opening wide in alarm. 'Go right ahead. The main gym is over there,' she said, pointing.

'Thank you.'

'I think you kinda freaked her out,' Young said as they headed towards the gym. 'Did you notice the tremble in her pointing hand?'

'No, I didn't. It wasn't my intention to scare her.'

'This place is bloody huge,' Young said as they walked into the gym. 'So much bigger than the gym I go to.'

It had about twenty of everything: treadmills, bikes, cross trainers and rowing machines, plus all the other accoutrements of such places: leg and chest strengthening machines, wall bars, ropes, loose weights, mats, and televisions high up on the wall.

She walked up one side and Young the other. When they met at the end, a shake of the head told her he hadn't spotted their target, and she hadn't either. Moving outside the gym, they came across a number of rooms and areas that also required checking: weights room, spin bikes, fitness classes, café, and the pool, but despite looking in every one, the missing man could not be found.

They discovered many potential hiding places: store rooms, staff rooms, offices, and if Potter was really trying to evade them, it would require more than two officers to find him. They returned to the entrance area and once again, Sally Graham stood at the reception desk. When Gemma became free, she came over.

'Did you find your missing man?'

'No, we didn't. Your system uses electronic cards. Can you look up a name for me and tell me when he came in and if he checked out?'

'Sure, no problem.'

Graham wrote down Potter's name on a piece of paper and handed it to her.

'Give me a second,' Gemma said, before turning to her computer and tapping her fingers with some dexterity on the keyboard. 'Ah, here we are. He checked in at 10:06 and hasn't checked out. Which is strange'. She looked up, smiling. 'That means he's still in the building.'

The detectives conducted another search, this time with one of the Crawley cops to help. Despite including ante rooms, staff rooms, and storage cupboards in their search, they returned with the same result.

Over two hours had elapsed since Potter entered the gym, and in Graham's opinion, he was deliberately trying to keep out of their way. No way would the businessman spend so much time away from his work. This was surely further proof of his guilt and DI Henderson would be glad to hear it, but not the news of him not being in custody.

FORTY-EIGHT

He knew they had come for him. Lucas Potter spotted the cop patrol car outside Nuffield Health fifteen minutes after he walked in. He also knew, with about the same degree of certainty, they wouldn't come straight in. They would hang about for the arrival of detectives from Henderson's crew, thirty-odd minutes distant in Lewes, and wait for him to come out – a cleaner arrest than doing it inside a busy gym.

He made his way to a fire door at the end of a row of fitness rooms, one he'd seen when he'd attended a Pilates class for the first and last time. It often lay open as some of the private trainers went out for some fresh air, although how clean the air would be in Crawley, being so close to Gatwick Airport and the M23 motorway, was anybody's guess. This suggested to him the door wasn't alarmed.

He shoved the bar up and stepped out. He was at the back of Nuffield Health, next to the place where deliveries came in, the opposite side of the building from where the cops were parked. He took a second or two to orient himself before heading in the direction of Ifield Avenue.

He made it without incident or having to climb any fences, as with so many businesses in the retail park, the original builders had to provide a number of entrances and exits. If a tall fence had barred his way, one he couldn't scale, he would have dumped his gym bag in one of the bins at the back of Nuffield Health, and walked through the main car park. With his baseball hat pulled down and his hands in his pockets, he would look more like a ten-pin bowler than a gym goer, and would be confident the waiting police wouldn't have given him a second glance.

Minutes later, Al Cowan pulled up in his BMW estate.

'Fuck me, mate,' Cowan said, as Potter climbed in. 'That's what I call cutting it close.'

'I can only agree, but I'm free as a bird now.'

'For the moment.'

'Aye,' he said, running a hand through thick sandy brown hair, 'they'll be back.'

'What are you gonna do?'

'As I said on the phone, I just need to buy some time. We have to finalise the deal with Jamil before they nab me. If we don't, we'll be stuck with a whole load of gear that would give me more jail time than anything these bloody Sussex detectives can throw at me now.'

'Yeah, but they're not going to lock you up, are they? They've got no evidence, you said.'

'When does something like that ever stop them? If they hold me even for a few days before realising they've got nothing, Jamil will fuck off back to where he came from, telling all his mates in the industry we're too unreliable to deal with.'

'It's the risk we run with this sort of enterprise.'

'You mean, the risk *I* run. This is my fault it's come to this, but if we can seal a deal tonight, then I can sort out my beef with the cops.'

They drove to a hotel nearby where Potter showered and changed into more suitable clothes, items Al had brought for him. With so many hotels and Airbnb's in the vicinity of Crawley and Gatwick Airport, no way could the cops watch them all. So they enjoyed a leisurely lunch, safe in the knowledge they weren't being watched. They left the hotel around four and drove to Ashford.

He didn't reveal to Al the reasons why he needed this deal; his friend would assume he still needed the adrenaline rush and was doing this for kicks. In reality, his business had been haemorrhaging cash. In a bid to make his dead father proud, he had expanded too rapidly. The money from tonight's deal would keep the business going for another six months, enough time to successfully complete a contract at Gatwick Airport, leading, he felt sure, to an even larger one being awarded.

When they arrived in Ashford, their plan was to kill the time until meeting Jamil by going for dinner, but neither of them felt hungry. Instead, they bought some sandwiches and headed over to the warehouse. To while away the hours, they checked the consignment and played cards.

Around nine, a knock on the warehouse door: one rap followed by two rapid hits; an agreed signal. Al pressed a button on the wall and the warehouse door rose with a slow rattle.

In drove a black Mercedes which no doubt contained Jamil, and directly behind it, the dark Range Rover of his bodyguards. Jamil Haddad, a Lebanese arms dealer, had offices in four major cities around the world. Most of the time his business dealt in legit goods, but on occasion, as if arms-dealing wasn't dangerous enough, he liked to take a few risks by dabbling in the black market.

The doors of the cars opened simultaneously as if controlled by an electronic switch, and out they stepped. Except none of them looked a bit like Jamil.

'What the...?' Potter gasped.

The men were dark-skinned and at first Potter thought they were Afghans, but when one of them spoke, it wasn't Dari or Pashto, languages he would recognise, it sounded more like Albanian.

'I see you have guns, lots of guns,' one of the men said walking towards him and Al. He spoke good English, but heavily accented.

'Where's Jamil? This stuff is for him.'

'Not any more. It's for us.'

Potter's mind raced; this did not compute. Jamil may have sold guns to this lot, but no way would he trust them to pick up his consignment.

The Albanian moved close to Potter's face, so close he could smell the thing he was chewing, a mix of aniseed and coriander.

'If you want the guns, do you have the money to pay for them?'

In response, the man turned to look at his team of seven, all armed with guns themselves. They had moved closer in, a respectful distance from the main man, but close enough to react if Potter or Cowan made a move.

'Hear that boys? They want us to pay for these guns.' He laughed, cackled more like, and his men did the same.

He turned to face Potter and, without warning punched him hard in the gut, then smacked him in the face with his fist.

'Aah!' he screeched, as he doubled over.

Out of the corner of his eye he saw Al react but before he could do anything, one of the Albanian crew whacked him over the head with the butt of his gun. Al dropped to the floor like a rag doll.

The guy who'd punched Potter, pulled him up by the hair. His eyesight was blurred and his jaw throbbed with the regularity of a strobe light. The hit felt harder than any fist he'd faced before. The bastard either had the muscles of Desperate Dan or was wearing a knuckleduster.

'What we gonna do is take these guns and the price we pay is not shoot you. Dead people not in the drug business are bad news. Makes cops look a bit closer; you understand?'

He would have nodded, but he didn't want his hair pulled any harder.

'You sit on your ass over there in the corner. If you move, one of my guys will shoot you. Maybe next time we bring some money, not today.'

FORTY-NINE

The door opened. Facing the small posse of police officers, a bleary-eyed figure wearing a lightweight dressing gown, now pulled tight in crossed arms; Rosie Carruthers, Lucas Potter's partner. Even without makeup, she looked attractive, but Henderson imagined the demands of long-haul travel: breathing the rarefied air inside a plane, the flitting back and forward between time-zones, partying the night away with the rest of the crew, and the snatched hours of sleep, would in time take their toll on her complexion.

'Yeah?'

'Morning, madam, sorry to wake you. Is Lucas at home?'

'No, he's away on business.'

'I thought he might be. We're detectives from Sussex Police and I have in my hand a warrant to search these premises.'

'What?' She removed the piece of paper in the DI's hand and looked at it. Her features contorted a little as she tried to concentrate, before handing it back a few seconds later. Either she was a fast reader or she gave up when the first section didn't appear to make much sense.

'I suppose you'd better come in.'

The team leader directed two of his searchers upstairs as the others examined downstairs. The house was detached, but with small rooms and straight walls, and no cubbyholes or cellars to concern themselves with, it would make the search, in Henderson's opinion, more or less straightforward.

'While we wait for Rosie to dress,' Henderson said to Walters, 'let's take a look outside.'

On a peg near the door, he spotted a key marked 'Shed'. He picked it up, unlocked the back door and stepped out on to the patio. It looked a fine spring morning, the sky replete with wispy clouds and bright sunshine.

When Sean Houghton discovered Lucas Potter still evaded them, despite conducting several searches of the Nuffield Health gym, he went ballistic. He accused Henderson of not believing in Potter's guilt and of somehow sabotaging the search. He believed Potter had slipped out before Graham and Young had arrived in Crawley, because the DI had not dispatched the two Sussex detectives fast enough.

Neither points were true. Graham and Young had been on stand-by ever since the spotter team were deployed to keep tabs on Potter. In addition, Potter couldn't exit the Nuffield Health building without using a keycard. Excluding a faulty card, unrecorded by the system, Potter had somehow got wind of the police presence outside and disappeared through a fire escape or the delivery entrance.

He would not win an argument with Houghton, so he soaked up the criticism and vowed to do better next time. In situations like this, the CI sitting in his office with only the bare bones of the case in front of him often saw a clearer picture of a case than those with their noses up against the glass. This time, with the evidence being more circumstantial, Henderson would wait for more of the race to be run, while Houghton, quite out of character, had already plumped for one of the leading runners.

The garden was small, befitting the 'executive' tag given to such houses, and as they didn't have children, it wasn't cluttered with a slide, swing, and paddling pool, only a rotary drier and shed. They walked over, unlocked the padlock and pulled the door open.

'God, this is the neatest shed I've ever seen,' he exclaimed, shocked at the absence of clutter. 'Are we certain this house isn't a rental?'

She laughed. 'No, they own it.'

'They've gone to town on the minimalist approach. All they have is a mower and a pair of shears.'

'Not forgetting the box of grass seed.'

He picked it up and gave it a shake, just to be sure.

'C'mon, Rosie should be able to speak to us now.'

He closed and locked the shed door and they walked back to the house. They found Rosie in the kitchen as the kettle came to the boil, with a selection of coffee mugs beside it waiting to be filled.

'Hello,' Henderson said, 'feeling more awake?'

'I am, thanks. I got home about nine last night after my flight got delayed. I slept for about eleven hours, but I still feel exhausted.'

'I'm sure the different time zones you're always flying between must play havoc with your sleep patterns.'

'You're right.'

'Where's Lucas today?'

'Why are you interested in him?'

'He's a suspect in our investigation into the murder of Roger Maitland.'

'You can't think he did it?'

'You know about his father?'

'I never met him, he died before we hooked up, but Lucas told me all about him.'

'You're aware he started Vixen Aviation with Roger Maitland?'

'Ah, I see now what you're getting at. You think because Jerome got booted out the company, his son went after Roger Maitland in revenge?'

'Doesn't that seem plausible to you?'

'No, it doesn't! If I lost my job, would I expect my dad or Lucas to kill the Managing Director of British Airways in response? No way. It's ridiculous.'

'Ms Carruthers–'

'Call me Rosie, you make me sound like my mother.'

'Rosie, Jerome wasn't just an employee of Vixen, he was one of its founding shareholders.'

'What does that mean? How does it change anything?'

'If Jerome hadn't been sacked, and instead held on to his shareholding in the company, the Potter family would now be worth around four hundred million pounds.'

She gripped the countertop to stop her falling. 'What? Four hundred million pounds! I had no idea.'

'Gov! Are you there?'

'Excuse me for a minute,' Henderson said to Rosie. He walked to the bottom of the stairs. 'Jeff, what is it?'

'You've got to come and take a look at this.'

He climbed the stairs.

Jeff met him at the top and led him into what looked like the master bedroom. 'We were looking in here when we found a box of army mementos under the bed.'

On the bed lay a plastic box with its sealable lid put to one side. It contained papers, a webbing belt and some medals.

Beside it, Jeff opened the folds of a piece of cloth to reveal a knife in a metal scabbard.

'It's a bayonet,' Jeff said, as his gloved hand withdrew it from its metal sheath. Henderson had come to the same conclusion from the unusual shape of the handle.

'If I'm not mistaken,' Jeff continued, 'it's one from the SA80 rifle and I think still in use by UK armed forces today.'

'Where did Potter get it; took it as a souvenir?'

'I would guess so.'

To most former soldiers, no more than a dusty prize of war, taken out once in a while to show the grandkids. However, it was a wide blade, similar in size to the wounds inflicted on both Roger Maitland and Lester Grange.

FIFTY

On Saturday morning Henderson drove into work. The search for Lucas Potter had intensified. Spotters were outside the house he shared with Rosie Carruthers, his office in Crawley, and the house of Al Cowan, Potter's best mate.

He had to be sleeping somewhere. The DI would need to be persuaded before having officers visit all the hotels, B&Bs, and Airbnbs around Crawley, a huge job with Gatwick Airport being so close by. Although his hand could be forced if Potter evaded them much longer.

The bayonet uncovered in his house had been fast-tracked through lab testing. If it contained the slightest trace of either Roger Maitland or Lester Grange's blood, it would be found, and they would have him. If so, the hunt for Roger and Lester's killer would come to an end.

The investigation had not captured the public imagination in the same way as some in the past, so he didn't need to check if any journalists were standing in the street before he drove out. Nevertheless, Roger had been a high-profile businessman, leaving Henderson confident if the knife proved Potter's guilt, or if the man in question was arrested, much ink and newsprint would be expended on informing the public of the news.

CI Houghton had taken a keen interest in the manhunt, although he would be missing today while attending a birthday party in Hampshire for one of his sons. His anger hadn't abated for Henderson 'letting him go' at Nuffield Health in Crawley. He still maintained the DI reacted too slowly when the spotters first tagged Potter. Despite the absence of any evidence of a card key exit, they did not believe he was still hiding out in the NH building, but had escaped through a back entrance. Potter's continued evasion of capture spoke volumes to the DI.

Henderson often enjoyed the drive from Brighton to Lewes. The journey was long enough to clear his mind of the trivia and travails of domesticity, allowing him to shift into work mode, but not so long it left him agitated to get started. He listened to the Today programme on Radio 4. The gravity of the stories sounded little different from the weekday broadcast, but the relaxed tone of the presenters suggested they had traded their smart suits and ties for jeans and jumpers.

When he arrived at Malling House, he dumped the things he had been carrying in his office and went straight into the Detectives' Room. He found detectives Walters, Bentley, and Graham sitting behind a triangle of desks, each with radio and laptop in front of them. Walters connected directly with the team at Potter's house, Bentley with those at Potter's office, and Graham with the team watching Al Cowan's house.

They were not only monitoring any activity at those locations, but also giving the spotter team guidance if any of the targets made an unexpected move.

'Morning all,' he said.

'Morning gov,' they said, almost in unison.

'What's the current situation?'

'There's no movement at his house,' Walters said. 'Judging by the lack of cars and with the curtains open, Rosie isn't at home either.'

'Do we know if she's on a flight? Perhaps she's with him?'

She shrugged. 'I've asked BA for the roster, but as they took so long to respond last time, I'm not holding my breath.'

'Sally?'

'We've seen a steady stream of workers walking into the building, which is to be expected as I don't imagine it's a regular nine-to-five business.'

'I think you're right. Nobody's turned up in heavy disguise, wrapped up in a hat and scarf when outside it's a fine and warm morning?'

She laughed. 'No such luck. The spotters have been told to look out for such a thing, but so far no one fits the bill.'

'Okay. Phil, how about Al Cowan?'

'Still asleep, all the curtains in the house drawn.'

'Not surprising, as it's early yet. The spotters have been in situ since what, yesterday evening?'

'Yep.'

'Potter couldn't have sneaked in through the back garden?'

'We don't have anyone watching the back of the house, so it's possible if he climbed over fences and the like. Couldn't we obtain a warrant?'

'Not without some proof: his face at the window or a neighbour complaining about someone sneaking through her garden.'

'I thought as much.'

The DI rose. 'I'll leave you to it. You all know what to do if he does show up?'

They nodded.

'Good. Catch you later.'

If Potter made an appearance, he wouldn't be sending any of his officers up to Crawley and risking Potter making an exit and the ire of his boss. Crawley Police had agreed they would send a couple of cars round at the first sight of their fugitive and make the arrest.

Instead of heading back to his office, he walked over to the corner of the room where the whiteboards containing pictures of their two victims and their connections to others were located. He often sat there during an investigation, the board in front of him, the facts pertinent to both victims clearly visible so he couldn't forget them.

He understood why Houghton, and many of his own officers, favoured Potter as the perpetrator. He had a clear motive and he behaved like a guilty person. With the alternative, someone from the business and social life of Maitland and Grange, they didn't have a motive and they were unable to name a specific person. Thinking about it now, he realised why he wasn't sold on Potter: the time gap between Jerome's sacking by Vixen and Roger's death.

It amounted to about eight years: he'd been dead for five, and he was dismissed three years before his suicide. Lucas was still in the army when the sacking took place, but he had been back in civvy street for at least the previous six years. Why not exact his revenge earlier?

So deep in thought, he didn't hear the shout. When Graham called again, he looked up. She waved him over. In the walk to the triangle of desks, he shifted his focus from Potter's strange behaviour to the manhunt for their target.

'What's happened? Has he been sighted?'

'He's just walked into the offices of Potter Security.'

FIFTY-ONE

Henderson couldn't wait to interview Lucas Potter. The man stewed in the Malling House Interview Suite, awaiting the arrival of his solicitor. The delay wouldn't be much if he had opted for a duty solicitor. After the Saturday morning hearings in the Magistrate Court, following the Friday night fights and punch-ups, by Saturday evening they were often left kicking their heels. Instead, Henderson was waiting for the Potter family solicitor, the firm used back in the day by Jerome when trying to negotiate his severance package.

Having completed a successful job, the search triumvirate of Walters, Bentley, and Graham had been disbanded and all except Walters allowed to go home and enjoy the remainder of Saturday. For them, at least, the weekend would not be a total write-off.

Such hold-ups were for the most part a waste of time, the nervous bit before the appearance of the big act. Instead, the delay gave him the opportunity to lay out his approach for the interview of Lucas Potter.

To be sure, his shaky alibis were more circumstantial information to add to the angry emails Potter sent to Roger Maitland. However, the knife found at his house, the first credible piece of solid evidence, could be the clincher they were looking for. As luck would have it, the results of the forensics tests would not be available for this interview, but promised the following day. Henderson had to ensure the prisoner would be held in custody at least for the next twenty-four hours.

His phone rang. He listened before replacing the receiver. He lifted the folder on his desk and went off in search of Walters.

'Hi gov,' she said, when he approached. 'Are we on?'

He nodded. 'His solicitor has turned up at last, and if you can believe it, he's dressed in a full DJ and dickey bow. The poor man would be attending a posh client dinner in Worthing if he hadn't received the call.'

She picked up her papers and together they walked towards the stairs.

'If he's been pulled away from something he was enjoying, I don't imagine he's best pleased to be here.'

'On the other hand, it might make him impatient for a quick result.'

'We shall see.'

They turned into the interview room. Lucas Potter's casual dress: jeans and denim shirt, looked at odds with the smart dinner jacket, the crisp white shirt, and the neat bow tie of the man sitting next to him.

Henderson shook hands with Raymond Jack, Potter's solicitor. When Walters had switched on the recording equipment, they went through a more formal set of introductions, each person present in the room stating their name and role in this interview.

'Sorry to take you away from your dinner, Mr Jack. I hope you don't regret it.'

'They were coming to the speeches, which can be a bit of a bore, but I'd been looking forward to hearing the comedian they'd booked. But,' he said, shrugging his shoulders and looking at his client, 'needs must.'

'Mr Potter, you have been arrested on suspicion of killing Roger Maitland.'

'I didn't kill him. I've told you this before.'

'On the night of Roger Maitland's murder, Saturday 6th May, you said you were at home with your partner, Rosie Caruthers, at your house in Horley.'

'We've been through this; I made a mistake.'

'Please let me finish. When British Airways supplied us with your partner's roster for the night in question, she wasn't at home with you at all, she had flown to Las Vegas.'

'You know all this. She got called away at the last minute. I forgot about it and didn't update my calendar.'

'It's an easy mistake to make, Inspector,' Jack said, 'you must see that?'

'I do, Mr Jack, if only the second explanation he supplied us with, about him being home alone, had been true. What do you know, it's bogus as well.'

'How did you...? I can explain.'

'I'd like to hear your explanation, but I warn you, Mr Potter, if you say you were at your home in Horley with Al Cowan or a woman you picked up in a bar, I'm not buying it. I can prove on that Saturday evening, your house remained empty.'

'I won't ask how you can say that, but I'll take your word for the moment. The reason I'm being cagey about my whereabouts on Saturday night is because I was with a man who doesn't, for reasons I'll make clear in a minute, court publicity or invite the attentions of the police.'

'Who's this?'

'Retired Brigadier Jeffrey Urquhart-Sigmund. He's a former commander of the Parachute Regiment. He served in Northern Ireland during the Troubles, and doesn't court publicity, as Republicans would like to kill him.'

'Even today?'

He nodded.

'Why were you visiting him?'

'Rosie was away and he's an old friend. He kind of took me under his wing in Afghanistan, as he said he admired the work done by my dad and felt as appalled as I, at the way Maitland treated him.'

'Where can we contact this person?'

Potter gave him the address.

'This is where you were, in Hampshire on the 6th May?'

'Yes.'

'You're sure about that?'

'Yes, I am.'

'Why didn't you mention it earlier?'

'For the security issue I mentioned before. The less people who know where he lives, the better. Also, he's an infirm, old man. I didn't want him troubled by visits from your officers.'

'That's something I will decide. You realise how this will go down if he denies seeing you?'

'He won't. Can I go now? I've told you what you wanted to know.'

Henderson ignored him. 'When we searched your house in Horley, we found this.'

Walters passed over a photograph of the bayonet discovered in a box under the bed.

'My, that's a sight for sore eyes.'

'I suspect it's the bayonet you had when you were in Afghanistan.'

'It's the one I've used for the best part of my army service. Saved my life more than once, but I haven't had it out in the open air for years.'

'Do you expect me to believe that? The width of the blade matches the size of the wounds found on Roger Maitland.'

'Yeah, along with thousands of other keepsakes brought back from the Gulf by troops, not to mention all the knives bought in outdoor and kitchen shops and on the internet.'

'Maybe so.'

'You're convinced I killed him, aren't you?' he said, raising his voice. 'No fucking way.' He turned to his brief. 'They can't do this, can they, fit me up for something I didn't do?'

'They won't fit you up, Lucas, I'll make sure they don't. Let's wait for the result of the knife analysis. I'm confident nothing will be on it and you will be exonerated.'

He slunk back in his seat and sulked.

'As Mr Jack said, Mr Potter, your bayonet has been sent off for analysis. If we find the slightest trace of Roger Maitland or Lester Grange's blood, you won't be going anywhere for a very long time. Interview terminated at twenty-forty-nine.'

FIFTY-TWO

Carol Walters turned the key and opened the door to her apartment in Queens Park. She'd arrived later than intended but determined the evening wouldn't be a complete write-off. She took a quick shower, applied makeup then dressed. She'd had something to eat at the office around six when her energy levels were starting to wane so she didn't need to start cooking.

She put all thoughts about Lucas Potter's guilt or otherwise to one side and stepped out of her flat and snapped the door shut.

'Going anywhere nice, Carol? You're looking great.'

She turned to see Greg from upstairs taking his little terrier, Bobby, out for a walk. Only a couple of years older than her, his taste in clothes, music, and films slotted him a generation or two away. This she knew as he'd once asked her out, and with nothing much better to do, she had accepted. It didn't rank as the worst date she had ever embarked on, but still one she had no intention of repeating.

'Thanks. I'm off to the pub with some friends. Maybe go dancing later.'

They walked downstairs together.

'I've got two left feet, me. I watch *Strictly Come Dancing* religiously every year and I think to myself; I could do that. After the final, I make a promise I'll take some dancing lessons, but a few weeks down the line I lose the impetus.'

'With something like dancing, you've just got to get out and don't think too much about it. Join a club, but only think about what you're doing after you've been. Give it a try, see if you still like it.'

'You think?'

She opened the exterior door, pleased to see the evening still light and warm, a harbinger of long summer days to come.

'Failing that,' she continued, 'book yourself a personal dance teacher. It'll build your confidence if later on you want to join a club.'

'Hey, that's not a bad idea, thanks.'

'See you later,' she said, as she headed in the opposite direction.

'Cheers, Carol. Hope you have a great time.'

She wondered if Greg had perhaps misinterpreted what she meant by dancing. Not for her and her friends the foxtrot or the paso doble, but gyrating to dance tracks by the likes of David Guetta and Calvin Harris.

She walked into The Sidewinder bar in Kemptown. With it being a warm evening, her friends had commandeered a table in the beer garden outside, although as they were a noisy bunch, it might have been the decision of the pub manager.

'Bloody hell,' Lena shouted, 'it's Carol!'

Her friends weren't the type for overblown displays of affection when often a nod, or perhaps a gentle hug from a closer friend, would suffice. This time, having had a head start on the booze, judging by all the empties on the table, she received the bear hugs of a long-lost relative.

'You're late, Walters,' Serena said, 'it's detention for you.'

'What, in a pub? I don't mind if I do.'

They laughed as they retook their seats. She found it difficult joining a group with an hour or more advantage on the booze than her. Not just because they were more relaxed and boisterous than she was, but it also raised a number of questions, such as: how to get a drink, had they set up a kitty or were they buying rounds, and what conversations had been hammered to death before her arrival?

'How does a girl get herself a drink around here?' she asked.

'Stick a tenner in the pot,' Elaine said, indicating the beer jug in the middle of the table, 'then call over Delectable Dom.'

'Stick an old bus ticket in there, see if I care,' Elaine said. 'I just want to see Delectable Dom again.'

They all cackled at that one.

'Who's Delectable Dom?' Walters asked.

'She's in for a treat, is she not, girls?' They all laughed.

'How have you been?' Greta beside her asked. 'You weren't working today, were you?'

'I have to admit it, yes.'

'Bloody hell, you're never away from that place. Me, I finish at five-thirty and that's the last time I think about work until the next morning.'

'You'd have a hard job thinking about hair for too long, even for someone who loves what they do as much as you.'

'I suppose you're right. Hey,' she said, nudging her, 'here comes Delectable Dom.'

'Well, hello Dom,' Elaine said, 'have you come to take us away? I mean, take our glasses away.'

'I take it you lot want another round.'

'Yes, we do.'

'Aw, I'm not sure. This is a respectable establishment.'

'We are respectable, we just keep it well hidden. Hey, you have to meet our new arrival. Dom, this is Carol.'

He turned and nodded. 'Hello Carol.'

'Hello Dom.'

The look lingered longer than necessary, but she didn't mind. He was handsome, not in the youthful way of some lads she passed when she came into the pub, but a more mature, rugged appearance. Aged mid- to late-thirties with short hair, a close-cropped black beard and deep brown eyes.

He took the drinks order and departed, leaving the women babbling like love-struck teenagers. Both Greta and Lena were married, while Serena lived with her boyfriend. Only Elaine and Walters were single.

'See what we mean?' Greta said. 'Isn't he a belter?'

'I admit he exudes a certain rustic charm.'

'Rustic charm?' Elaine said. 'You been reading *Pride and Prejudice* again?'

'What happened to Nick?' Greta asked. 'I liked him.'

'He often got called away on business at the last-minute, cancelling dates and leaving me high and dry. I didn't want to live like that.'

'I had a similar experience with a bloke,' Elaine said. 'He sold me the work trips excuse as well, but one night I followed him and spotted him going into this terraced house in Burgess Hill. Turns out, he was already married, which he forgot to tell me about, and he's also got two young kids.'

'Bloody hell, what a bastard. That takes some nerve!' Greta exclaimed.

'Not to mention being a good liar.'

The startled responses were brought to a halt when the drinks arrived. Dom dished out the glasses and again gave Carol a lingering look, this time with a cheery smile. When she'd hit the big 4-oh, she imagined the days of blokes eyeing her up across the floor of a pub or a coffee bar were gone, but maybe hope springs eternal after all.

When Dom left, the conversation continued unabated as they discussed movies, television shows, clothes, work, and husband issues. In situations like this, the five friends out for a drink, those in uneventful marriages looked with envy at the single life. The singletons, on the other hand, couldn't always be bothered to make the effort required every time they went out and often wished for a simpler life.

She volunteered little about her job. The Maitland case was at a delicate phase. One injudicious comment about a suspect might be overheard, or told to someone with connections to the media, and the following morning a barrage of negative press would appear on the radio, television, and social media. Not only would it prejudice the court case against the accused, it could result in her censure, or even her sacking.

When everyone finished their drinks, rather than stay for another round, they decided to move to a pub in the centre of town. The logic being they would be closer to the clubs near the seafront for those who wanted to dance the night away.

They picked up their things and trooped through the bar, calling goodbyes to the staff, and in particular to Delectable Dom. When she walked past, she gave him her best smile which he returned. He leaned over and thrust something into her hand.

She looked at it. A piece of paper and a phone number.

'Call me,' he said.

FIFTY-THREE

For DI Henderson it had been a normal weekend. He had worked all day Saturday and most of Sunday. The only bit of 'leisure activity', an early Sunday morning run along the seafront, and dinner with Kelly in the evening. Now, back to work at the start of the new week, but at least he felt they were on the home straight.

He dealt with dozens of emails and read through some of the piles of paper he had been ignoring these last few weeks. It included reports on the latest developments in DNA technology, details of a reorganisation at Surrey Police, and a report on the expected rise in fentanyl deaths due to a European push by Mexican drug lords. Good information for a murder detective, but difficult to digest and understand the importance of during the intensity of a murder investigation.

At a few minutes past eleven thirty, Walters walked in.

'I won't ask if you've had a nice weekend,' the DI said.

'It wasn't too bad, what was left of it.'

'Oh?'

'The barman at the pub I went to on Saturday night, if you can believe it, gave me his number.'

'And?'

'I called him. We're going out next week.'

'Good for you.'

Henderson untangled the cables of his desk phone and placed it in the middle of the meeting table.

'Is Harry coming?'

'Eh?'

'You know, the guy you work beside with the short hair and cheeky smile? Is he coming? I think your head is still in the pub.'

'He's talking to a bloke from upstairs. Says he's aware of the call, and be along in a minute.'

A few moments later, Harry appeared.

'Morning gov, morning Carol. Sorry I'm late. I've been talking to Davey Franks from the Web Hacking team. He told me Sergeant Ed Robson over at John Street has been suspended from duty for sexual misconduct. It's alleged he's been receiving sexual favours from drug addicts and vulnerable women on his patch.'

'The big bloke with the quiff of black and white hair?' Walters asked.

'Yeah, the very man.'

For a second, Henderson pondered what a black and white quiff looked like, when his desk phone rang. It was a scheduled call from Vicky Neal, so he pressed the 'speaker' button.

'Hello Vicky.'

'Hi gov.'

'I've put you on speaker. Carol and Harry are with me.'

'Hi guys.'

'Hi Vicky.'

Vicky Neal and Sally Graham had travelled to Whitechurch in Hampshire to interview Lucas Potter's alibi, retired Brigadier Jeffrey Urquhart-Sigmund.

'First off,' Henderson asked, 'did you speak to the brigadier?'

'Yeah, we did. Luckily our visit coincided with a woman who comes in twice a week to cook and stick his clothes in the washing machine. She answered the door as she said the brigadier would have ignored it.'

'An obstinate old fellow, is he?'

'No, I would say deaf as a post and very confused. The helper says it's Alzheimer's, but the doctors say they're not sure.'

'It doesn't sound promising.'

'It gets worse. When I asked him about talking to Potter, he says he remembers seeing him, as he has a lot of affection for the young man, as he calls him. The thing is, he isn't clear about when this meeting took place. It could have been six weeks before, or even six months.'

'So, Potter might have been to see him two days after Maitland's murder, or perhaps a couple of weeks before, and the brigadier would be none the wiser?'

'Yes. He couldn't even tell me the day of the week or what he had for breakfast. It means we can't prove his alibi, but we can't disprove it either.'

'Vicky,' Walters asked, 'did his day visitor offer any insights?'

'She only works Mondays and Thursdays, so if Potter had visited out of those times, she wouldn't know anything about it. She doesn't remember him mentioning any other visitors over the last couple of months.'

'Potter's alibi is for the Saturday night,' Walters said. 'Even if he stayed with the brigadier until late evening, say, seven or eight, it would still leave enough time for him to get over to North Chailey and kill Maitland.'

Henderson terminated the call a few minutes later.

'We still don't know Potter's whereabouts on that Saturday night,' Henderson said.

'We need something to prove he's lying,' Harry said, as he got up to leave, 'and for me it means finding DNA traces on his knife. Catch you later, gov.'

Henderson checked his watch: too early for lunch, but he didn't want to sit at his desk yet, he wanted to digest this new information. Instead, he walked over to the staff restaurant for a coffee and perhaps a snack if something grabbed his fancy.

Checking alibis was a routine part of police work, and cons offering up lies and obscuration went with the territory, although it wasn't always the guilty party doing it. Others did it as they didn't want anyone knowing where they were, maybe because they were seeing a lover, committing a criminal act unrelated to the one being investigated, or down the pub when they were supposed to be working or looking after a child.

If Lucas Potter wasn't trying to cover up a murder, what was he doing that was making him continuously lie about his situation? Perhaps accusing him of lying might be putting it a bit strong, but at the very least, making sure his activities and location were obscured from their eyes.

He bought a coffee and a jam doughnut and walked back to his office.

With more time, he would like to find out more about the theft Potter claimed to be investigating the day before Lester Grange's murder. They'd confirmed his visit to the Royal Sussex Hospital the day after the incident he told them about, but it could have been for anything, or perhaps an injury he sustained when stabbing Lester Grange the same night.

Perhaps the theft Potter had been so concerned about wasn't from one of his clients as he claimed, but contraband of his own which he stole or was storing for someone else. If so, this might be the reason why he couldn't furnish a solid alibi for the time of Roger Maitland's murder.

He sat at his desk and sipped the coffee. He took a bite from the jam doughnut, the first since going out with Kelly, an advocate of clean eating. It was wonderful, making him wonder why all the things that were supposed to be bad: chocolate, cream, and jam, tasted so good.

An email arrived from the forensic department, the team analysing the bayonet found at Potter's house. He pushed the coffee and doughnut to one side, clicked on it and started to read.

FIFTY-FOUR

Avalon swooped low over the bare countryside. With its all-seeing eye and heat-seeking detectors it searched relentlessly for any targets. It was Vixen's newest and finest drone to date, equipped with the most sophisticated and lightest tank-busting missile system fitted to any of their drones, made to their own specifications by QinetiQ. It was also cloaked in radar deceiving stealth paint, and fitted with the latest version of their AI.

Adrian Chapman was convinced this would be its final test. If it passed with flying colours, he believed the army were now prepared to put in an order. And what a test they had set up for it. They were at an army shooting ground in Cambridgeshire, and assured by those in attendance no dog walkers, cyclists, or hikers in the last ten years of operation had breached its defences.

This was an important consideration when operating any of their drones in the wild, in particular, one so ruthless and lethal as Avalon. For this part of the test, its attack setting had been moved to 'target all', and while the drone would ignore a pooch, its owner would definitely be in its sights.

The army had allowed some farm animals to wander into the field, twelve cows and twenty-odd sheep, in the hope the animals would meander close to some of the drone's targets, requiring Avalon to distinguish the difference. Some brave troops were scheduled to pop out of a concrete bunker at regular intervals to attract the drone, before popping back inside when they were spotted by it.

The one-and-a-half-hour demonstration went without a hitch, with no loss of animal life and no killing or maiming of any locals. Instead, it attacked as required: an old army Land Rover and a concrete pillbox which appeared to be staffed with two combatants. A pure expression of its power could only be conveyed in the battlefield, in particular when opposing forces were difficult to distinguish from the terrain, military personnel were hard to tell from civilians, and if enemy units were holed up in defensive positions.

'That's some machine you've made, Adrian,' Graham Neve, Head of Flight Procurement at the MOD said. 'With its stealth paint job, it even looks aggressive.'

'They're getting better all the time. The AI is set up in such a way, that if, say, SAS troops are dressed to look like the Mujahedeen or Taliban, they can wear a small detector under their clothes and Avalon won't target them. Avalon can be programmed to target anyone not wearing one.'

They were walking back to the main building where some food and drink would be available.

'It's a brilliant machine. For years we've been planning on a big plains war with Russia. You know the sort of thing, two hundred T90 tanks on one side, two hundred Chieftains and Leopards on the other, with jet fighters dropping bombs where they can.'

Chapman nodded and looked interested, although he had heard this scenario several times before.

'Things have changed since the Second World War. With most of the battles being fought nowadays, and you can think of Yemen, Afghanistan, and to a lesser extent, Ukraine, the deployment of jet fighters and tanks doesn't really work.'

Neve went on in this vein in the time it took to reach the main building and help themselves to some food. Chapman felt hungry, as he had been so nervous about the demo he had eaten nothing all morning. Then, something odd occurred. It had only happened before when Roger had been in the chair, but Neve didn't leave his side, and instead encouraged others from the army and MOD to come and talk to him.

He walked back to his car a few minutes after one o'clock, his mood buoyant. Not only had the MOD promised to submit an order by the end of the week, it seemed at last he had been accepted into their hallowed group. They all spoke to him as an equal, not as before with disdain, believing him to be Roger's bag carrier.

In the hours it took to drive back to Uckfield from Cambridgeshire, he put his other hat on as Development Director and mapped out in his head the steps the team needed to take to ready Avalon for full production. They would not be buying all the tools, equipment, and machines necessary for its manufacture just yet, but putting plans in place so as soon as the order arrived, they could do so.

This was the big one. Roger had placed huge store on Avalon becoming a great success as he believed it would be their inroad into the US market. He'd made no secret he also wanted it to succeed for selfish reasons. If the US Military decided to spend millions on UK drone technology, Vixen would need to set up a sales, distribution, and spare parts network in the US. Roger wanted to run it so he could be closer to his daughter, Katy.

With Roger gone, Chapman would be making the same push, not because he had any desire to live in the US, but he believed Vixen products were superior to anything available elsewhere. Less bullish than Roger, he spent time explaining to the MOD delegation how Avalon had heightened capabilities to determine friend or foe. This had been Chapman's influence on the product's development, as Roger wouldn't have included it unless at the MOD's insistence.

Arriving back at his office in Uckfield, he passed several members of staff, desperate to know how the demonstration had gone. The rest of the team were coming back in a much slower van, so they would hear their version of events when they returned, but what he did say was: 'It went better than I expected. They really liked it and are prepared to place a major order.'

He felt elated when he entered his office, in part by the imminent appearance of a large order, but more by their acceptance of him as a person. So much so, he decided to do something he had been putting off for some time.

Located at the back of the room was a small, secure cabinet, the like of which he imagined to be located in the office of every large defence contractor. As acting Chief Executive, he had the key. He believed it contained sensitive military information, which, up to now, he didn't feel ready or entitled to look at.

He wheeled the cabinet towards him and with his heart beating fast, turned the key.

FIFTY-FIVE

At long last, the final member of the army unit attacked by the wayward Vixen drone had been found. Henderson wanted to interview Kieran Stock as he blamed Vixen for the attack. Although uninjured in the attack, so he didn't need to live close to an army base like some of the others, he had suffered from PTSD.

'How did Houghton react when you told him?' Walters asked from the passenger seat beside him.

'He didn't say anything. Lucas Potter had been his man, and now he isn't.'

'Did you gloat?'

'Did I hell. I've got to work with him, remember?'

'I also had Potter in the frame. With his father's shares, he would be a millionaire now, swanning around the flesh pots of Ibiza rather than eking out a living standing outside dark warehouses for most of the night.'

'He had the motivation, right enough. People have killed for a lot less.'

'Could he have duped our forensic boys?'

'Like how? Cleaned the bayonet with hydrochloric acid or bleach?'

'Something like that.'

'We might have accused him of doing it, if the team hadn't found traces of other blood from the time

Potter had been deployed in a war zone. If using bleach or some other caustic substance to clean it, it would have wiped off everything.'

'I guess, but I still think he's a good fit, and it's possible he used another knife. Couldn't we follow him or put a tracker on his car?'

He shook his head. 'In most cases, we often tread a fine line between gathering evidence and harassment. In this case, it's not something I would be tempted to sanction. As far as Potter is concerned, he's a free man. Houghton thinks he might sue us for wrongful arrest, so how would it look if his brief produced a Sussex Police tracker device in court?'

'Shame, I'm convinced he did it.'

Kieran Stock lived in a terraced house in Staines. Those in the army unit attacked by the drone received compensation from the MOD and Vixen, those injured being given more than those who were not. By the state of the untidy garden and the paint peeling from window frames, either Stock didn't receive much, or he had spent it on wine, women, and song; for sure it wasn't on bricks, mortar, and paint.

Henderson knocked on the door. The door opened a little and part of a face appeared, but only the hair and eyes.

'Yeah? The fuck you want?'

The voice had a hoarse quality, the sound of someone after a lot of shouting at a rock concert or working with noisy machinery.

'We're detectives from Sussex Police. We'd like to talk to you, Kieran.'

'What about?'

'The killing of Roger Maitland.'
'Who?'
'The Chief Executive of Vixen Aviation.'
'Vixen, did you say?'
'Yes.'
'Good riddance to bad rubbish.'
'Can we come in and talk?'
'I'll think about it. Show me some ID.'
They did.
'I don't have anything to say to you.'
'Why not?'
'I don't like visitors and I don't like cops.'
'It won't take long. I wouldn't ask if it wasn't important.'

He appeared to be debating this in his mind for a couple of moments.

'Fuck it!' he said, before flinging the door open with a violent shove.

They walked inside while he stayed back, checking to see if anyone else was out there. Satisfied, he slammed the door shut. The lounge was easy to find, the house being small, everything only a few steps away.

'You're a hard man to track down,' Walters said.

'Keep a low profile, me. Don't want the poxy government or army spying on my business.'

'If you're not working, you can claim benefits, like Universal Credit. It would put some more money in your pocket.'

'I told you. I don't trust the government or any of their agents.'

Disability Allowance seemed more appropriate, Henderson thought, as he seemed incapable of doing any meaningful work. The lounge looked as untidy as the exterior of the house. It wasn't the scattering of old newspapers and magazines, the bane of the old and drug users, but a general malaise from a lack of cleaning: dust on flat surfaces, cup stains on the glass table, smears on the windows distorting the light from outside. Against his better judgement, but in a bid to keep his suspect calm, he cleared a space for himself and Walters on the settee and they sat down.

Stock was slight in frame, a shadow of the bulky soldier in the picture on the mantelpiece, and the grey tracksuit he wore looked a couple of sizes too big. He had jet-black hair, in need of a good wash and trim, and his rugged face was covered in five-day-old stubble. Taking a closer look, Henderson noticed the newspapers and magazines were way out of date, changing his view of an untidy man who kept up with current affairs, to one who couldn't be bothered to throw out his rubbish.

'Kieran, we are here about the death of Roger Maitland.'

'You said before. Somebody killed him, you said.'

'Were you aware of his death before I said it?'

'How could I be? I don't read newspapers and never switch on that bloody thing,' he said nodding at the TV. 'It's full of government propaganda.'

'We've been told you had some strong views about those responsible for the drone attack on your unit in Afghanistan.'

He drifted away for a moment or two, perhaps reliving that day.

'Kieran?'

'Yeah?'

'I said, you have some strong opinions about Vixen.'

'Them and the army are like this,' he said, crossing his fore and middle fingers. 'You scratch my back and I'll scratch yours.'

'Did you receive compensation?'

'Pah. It didn't last long. The board of inquiry was nothing but a cover-up. No way would there be a proper investigation of the attack.'

'Who did you blame for the attack?'

'Vixen. The drone malfunctioned; shot us not the enemy.'

'Do you blame anyone in particular?'

'Yeah, I do. The bloke who made the dodgy drone.'

'Roger Maitland?'

'Maitland?' He thought for a moment. 'Yeah, him and that other bloke ran the company what made the drone. I don't know who killed him, but if I did, I'd tell them they killed the wrong man. They should have gone after the other guy, what's his name?'

'Jerome Potter?'

'Yeah him, Potter. He's the guy what made that bloody drone do what it did. Somebody should have topped him.'

Outside, on the way back to the car, Henderson said, 'I think he's a shadow of the soldier he once was, and even how his comrades remember him.'

'They made him out to be the bolshie type, always disagreeing with his commanding officer, but now he seems afraid to leave the house.'

'Do you think he's capable of killing Roger Maitland and Lester Grange, putting on an act for our benefit?'

'No way is he putting that on. He's not able to look after himself, never mind attack someone else.'

FIFTY-SIX

Wednesday morning Henderson took a seat in Chief Inspector Houghton's office. It wasn't unusual for the man in charge to receive regular updates. After all, Henderson was the Senior Investigating Officer, the person responsible for managing a team of detectives and other officers, and accountable for all aspects of the inquiry. Houghton was the public face of the investigation and the person left carrying the can if it all went belly-up.

The unusual part was the number of formal sit-down meetings like this one, rather than him popping into his office, or the other way round for a quick chat. He put this down to the nature of the publicity surrounding the murder of Roger Maitland and Lester Grange. With the murder of Lily Osborne earlier in the year, newspaper coverage verged on the hysterical, with feature writers asking if the streets were safe for young women.

Roger Maitland was neither young nor female, but a successful businessman with a colourful past. Therefore, media coverage hadn't been the screaming headlines of a front page exclusive. More often the story appeared on page eight or nine, speculation by a former policeman or businessman. In addition, the factual reporting in the financial pages of things happening at Vixen, like a new drone order, never failed to mention it was also the company with two murdered senior executives. With this sort of story popping up every now and then, no one was ever likely to forget it.

'Sorry about the delay, Angus,' Houghton said as he came into his office a minute or so later. 'Yet another one off on sick leave. I thought things were bad during the pandemic, but now we seem to be having another bout of something contagious.'

'All my people are in, and for the moment, looking fit and healthy.'

'How's the Maitland-Grange case going?'

'We interviewed the last of the soldiers who might have held a grudge against Vixen, a guy called Kieran Stock.'

'The army unit attacked by the drone?'

'Yes. He had elected to stay in the army after the attack, but suffered PTSD and was invalided out. I suspect his condition hasn't improved much, despite receiving treatment, and he's living the life of a recluse.'

The CI paused for a moment. 'With no one from the patrol raising their heads above the parapet, and with you releasing Lucas Potter on Monday, you're clean out of suspects.'

'Not quite. We have statements from Maitland's wife, and escorts, stating he liked rough sex, and we understand when he partied with his military contacts, no holds were barred.'

'The assumption being that, flying too high on a mix of booze and drugs, they did something illegal, something so bad our killer is making them pay for their actions?'

'Yes.'

'The problem is, no one will tell you what that is.'

'I don't think they're going to confess they killed an unknown householder when they drunkenly discharged a loaded weapon, or threw one of their pals in the river for a laugh and he drowned. We need to look for an opening, one of them to admit that something untoward happened one night.'

'No, they're not, which means I see this investigation dragging on and on, or us calling a halt and it becoming a cold case.'

'The key thing is finding someone present at the time of the incident or someone who knows more about it. The people we've spoken to so far, are aware of a little but not enough.'

'Follow that through, Angus, but I want some of your team working on Potter.'

'Why?'

'He fits like a glove. With Roger Maitland out of the way, he's now got Adrian Chapman to deal with, who, by all accounts, is a more reasonable man.'

'I agree, but–'

'Angus, we're talking about four hundred million big ones here. Street punks will stab and shoot one another for a couple of grand. What lengths would someone go to grab such a huge prize?'

'I can't disagree with that argument, but we have no evidence to hold him.'

'In addition, he's given us an unsatisfactory alibi, and the bayonet you found could be one of many blades in his collection.'

Henderson didn't see much point in arguing, the Chief's mind was made up.

'Forget his alibi. Seize his electronic gear and shake down his house, his place of work, any other places he goes. Of course, he may have ditched the knife and the clothes he wore for the killings, but we might find something else like a map or a photograph of Maitland or Grange's house.'

'Okay.'

'So, are we good?'

'When we spoke a few days ago, you were concerned he might sue for harassment or wrongful arrest.'

'Let him. I've been talking to Andy Youngman about it. His view is if he's guilty, he won't sue, but if he does, we'll cross-examine him in court with the best barrister we can find. The guilty always let something slip so no way will a judge uphold his case.'

FIFTY-SEVEN

When Henderson announced the CI's decision to pursue Potter at the evening update, many in the team cheered. They were convinced of Potter's guilt, but for others, the news went down like a lead balloon.

'We've all seen him, or at least read the interview transcripts,' Harry Wallop said, 'the case against him is circumstantial. We don't have enough firm evidence.'

'If you'd met his alibi for the Maitland murder,' Neal said, 'retired Brigadier Jeffrey Urquhart-Sigmund, he didn't know the time of day or if he lived in Washington or Wellington.'

'Potter must have been up to something he doesn't want us to find out about,' Sally Graham said. 'Maybe he's visiting a girlfriend or buying stolen goods.'

'In my experience,' Phil Bentley said, 'a lot of security firms sail close to the wind. One I know hires ex-cons, and would you believe, they're used to guard a bonded whisky warehouse.'

'Which is the reason I agree with the chief inspector,' Henderson said, 'when he says to disregard the issues with his alibi. Potter works in a business, as Phil says, which is likely to include some dodgy characters who will do whatever Potter asks them, providing they're paid enough money. We've searched his house so now we'll search his business and take away electronic gear and analyse it.'

'That'll really piss him off,' Walters said.

'We're not in the business to be liked,' he replied. 'With luck, we'll find something tying him to Maitland and Grange, maybe a Google Maps search of North Chailey where Maitland lived, or Lindfield for Lester Grange, or purchases of knives and dark clothing from eBay.'

'We analysed his personal laptop when we searched his house,' Neal said, 'but discovered nothing of consequence on it.'

'True, but I imagine he spends most of his time on his work computer.' He paused for a moment, thinking.

'I don't want the whole team working on this. Vicky, you take charge. You can have Sally and Phil.'

'Right gov.'

'Obtain the search warrants and organise the raid.'

She nodded.

'The rest of you will be researching Roger and Lester's personal life.'

'How do we do that,' Wallop asked, 'when everyone we've spoken to claims they were told little?'

'We're going to do something I've shied away from since the beginning of this investigation, as it seemed like a huge amount of work with no guarantee of payoff. That is, to see if we can identify the military personnel Roger and Lester dealt with. I'm hoping I'm referring to a central core of characters who met them on a regular basis, and not hundreds of faces walking on and off the stage like a bad avant-garde play.'

'It's possible,' Walters said.

'Won't they claim military secrets when we ask them something they don't want to talk about?' Wallop asked.

'They can try, but we have to be smarter than that. We've been told they had boisterous parties, so they can't flannel around. They have to tell us something or we just keep asking.'

Henderson headed back to his office a few minutes later. He'd glanced at the clock in the Detectives' Room as he walked past, seven fifteen in the evening. He would be heading for home as soon as he wrote a couple of things down. He decided he would go back to Vixen in the morning and refuse to leave until he had a half-dozen or a dozen names he could work with.

He didn't think Adrian Chapman would deny his request, he wanted to catch the killer as much as the DI, but did he know enough to help him? Last chance saloon would be Daniel Hill, Manufacturing Director. He had been more or less a confidant of Roger from the early days before Lester came along, although Henderson imagined his recollection might be poor and his information a bit out of date.

He wondered if Houghton's continued, dogged pursuit of Potter was in a bid to save face. The DI imagined Houghton telling Andy Youngman, Assistant Chief Constable, the man with overall responsibility for Serious Crime, Potter was their man.

Reading transcripts of interviews, with the suspect denying murder or expressing disbelief at being accused, could never be a substitute for a seat in the room, as words could not faithfully replicate a suspect's attitude, tone of voice, or the emotions displayed in heated moments. Potter sounded like an innocent man caught in something not of his making, and he wasn't some derelict, desperate for money, but a man running a successful company. Yes, he felt bitter at the way his father had been treated, but he appeared to the DI like someone who had put that sorry business behind him and decided to carry on with the rest of his life.

A trap lay ahead and Henderson had to be careful not to fall into it. If the seizure of Potter's electronic equipment proved he had been casing out Roger Maitland and Lester Grange's homes, the team could be accused of doing a sloppy job at gathering evidence first time round.

The phone rang, breaking his chain of thought.

He picked up the handset and said, 'DI Henderson.'

'Angus, it's Bob at the main desk. There's a man here to speak to you. His name is Adrian Chapman, says he's chief exec of a company called Vixen Aviation.'

FIFTY-EIGHT

Henderson led Adrian Chapman into Interview Room Five. The smart, dark suit suggested he had come straight from work. He also carried a small folder, reinforcing the businessman persona, but wearing the expression of a man being marched to the guillotine.

Henderson came alone, most of the team had gone home, and as Adrian said he wanted to talk, he didn't set up the recording devices.

Once seated and both comfortable, Henderson asked, 'So Adrian, what brings you out at this late hour?'

Chapman clasped his hands in front of him, the way Henderson's primary school teacher in Fort William made his class sit when doing the attendance roll first thing in the morning.

'I don't know how to say this without sounding like a complete wimp, but as it's only you and me here, and as I don't see any lights on the recording equipment, I think I can be candid.'

'You can indeed.'

'There's a small cabinet in Roger's office I had never noticed in all the time I had meetings with him.'

'When I'm in a meeting with my boss, I don't notice much else. I'm too busy trying not to make a fool of myself, and concentrating hard in case he throws a curveball in my direction.'

Chapman smiled, but it looked forced.

'When I first moved into Roger's office, I ignored it. The cabinet has a label on top, "Top Secret – Authorised Personnel Only". I never felt accepted by the people we were selling the products to, and I didn't feel, I don't know what you call it, worthy. Also, I expected I wouldn't appreciate half of what it contained, so I left it until I knew more.'

'It's a reasonable response. The documents might contain genuine military secrets which you perhaps wouldn't understand and couldn't ask anyone about. While with others, they could be so full of acronyms, jargon, and abbreviations, you would need a military dictionary to comprehend.'

'How accurate you are. At what I hoped was the final Avalon demonstration in Cambridgeshire on Monday, I felt at last I'd been accepted by the customer, and as a result of the successful test, we've been promised our biggest order to date.'

'Congratulations. You must be very proud.'

'I am, but not only that, I've since fielded serious enquiries from several EU countries, Scandinavia, and, only today, the US.'

'You're clearly doing something right.'

'The thing is, and my reason for seeing you tonight, is after the Avalon demonstration and buoyed by my newfound status as a friend of the MOD, I opened the cabinet and took a look through its contents.'

'Did it contain the big military secrets you expected?'

'It did, and more. Roger had access to a lot of the MOD's blue-sky thinking; how military strategists think the world will be in ten, twenty, thirty years' time.'

'I suppose this is something they need to do. When you think of the time it takes to design, develop and manufacture jet fighters and aircraft carriers, they can't avoid it.'

'Indeed. Various other documents were aimed specifically at Vixen: reports from the army about developing a remote fighting capability. In civilian speak, this is risking the loss of a drone or a robot in a battlefield and not the death of a soft-organed human.'

'It does sound a bit like *Star Wars*, but it's to be applauded as no one likes to see body bags returning from war zones.'

'You can see it happening already. Several big American jet fighter manufacturers have been demonstrating planes being flown by robots.'

'Interesting.'

'Yes, and people like us at Vixen will be at the forefront.'

'Good luck with that.'

'This isn't what I wanted to talk to you about. At the back of the cabinet I found a file marked "Personal - Keep Out". I opened it and took a look. It contained copies of emails to Roger from an unknown sender.'

'How do you mean, "unknown"?'

'They were sent by someone calling themselves Jo-Jo and originated from an anonymous Hotmail account.'

'Okay.'

'The emails are aggressive and to the point, but the main issue is this Inspector: Roger Maitland was being blackmailed.'

FIFTY-NINE

Walters boarded a London-bound train from Brighton Station. The journey took about an hour so she brought along plenty of reading material. She was on her own this morning as DI Henderson stayed behind to brief the team on the latest development as told to him by Adrian Chapman.

Someone using the handle Jo-Jo had sent an email to Roger Maitland four years ago, describing how Maitland had killed Jo-Jo's mother. The email went on to say the sender knew that Maitland had buried her body in the grounds of the house he occupied in North Chailey. Jo-Jo didn't mention the name of his mother, nor the location of her burial site, but demanded payment for his continued silence.

According to the email, Jo-Jo's mother had died seven years before during a perverted sex game perpetrated by Maitland, involving tying a tight ligature around her neck. Jo-Jo made clear the demand for fifty thousand pounds would be the first of a series of demands arriving at three-monthly intervals. In five years, when the total reached the grand sum of one million pounds, he would consider the debt settled.

Roger had been instructed to make payments using the details contained in a text which he would receive a few minutes after receiving the email. He was told to memorise the details before deleting the text. She supposed the lack of names and the untraceable email account would ensure anyone seeing the email at a later date would be none the wiser as to the blackmailer's identity.

They had pulled Roger's bank account details a few weeks back and had spotted fifty-thousand-pound payments being made quarterly up until a few months before his death. For a man with a large income and significant outgoings, this was one large payment among many.

Nevertheless. they had sent a query to his bank for the name of the recipient, and even though no response had arrived as yet, she was not holding her breath for a positive result. If the blackmailer was smart enough to use an anonymous email account and a burner phone for the text, the account would probably be somewhere untraceable like the Cayman Islands and in the name of a shell company with a couple of obdurate lawyers as directors.

At the beginning of the email exchange, the blackmailer stated that if Roger failed to make a payment, evidence of his guilt would be handed over to the police. Later, the emails became more aggressive, expressing how much Jo-Jo missed talking to and seeing his mother, and threatening that if Roger omitted a payment, he and Lester Grange would be killed. Roger, for reasons unknown, didn't make a payment in April. He was killed early the following month.

Everyone involved in this investigation believed this to be proof positive the emails came from the killer of Maitland and Grange. Even CI Houghton agreed, and instructed Henderson to cease his pursuit of Lucas Potter. The problem now? Identifying the anonymous blackmailer, Jo-Jo.

In trying to find this person, Henderson decided to target four areas. He set up a team to search the acres around Maitland's property with ground-penetrating radar. He tasked the IT group with trying to identify the email sender. Maitland's bank would be asked again to name the beneficiary of the extorted money. Finally, Walters was given the green light to continue her research on the missing escort women.

After finding Louise Gatiss' article in *The Argus* about missing Brighton escorts, Walters had done some research of her own. With so many other promising leads to investigate, it had been filed away as it didn't seem relevant. Her trip today was to talk to the author of the article, who nowadays worked for a different newspaper, located near London Bridge.

They arranged to meet in a café. She spotted Louise easily; tall, slim, with today's *Daily Telegraph* under her arm. They shook hands and Walters walked to the counter to buy coffees. Louise also wanted a chocolate muffin, a strange request, she thought, for a girl who looked wafer thin.

'Here you are,' Walters said, placing two coffees and a muffin on the table. She took the seat opposite and opened her folder, a copy of Louise's article on top. Louise was a pretty girl with a sharp, striking face and dark shiny hair.

'What's your secret?'

'You mean this?' she said, holding up a piece of muffin before sticking it in her mouth.

'Yeah, how do you keep so slim eating one of those? If I ate that, when I walked out of here my skirt would be too tight.'

'Everybody asks, because they tell me I eat like a horse. In reality, it's nothing magical. I walk to the station in the morning which is about a mile from my house. I walk from London Bridge station to my office on the twelfth floor, and when I want to talk to a source, I'm out of the office and walking if I can. In terms of steps, I do over twenty thousand a day, every day.'

'Amazing.'

'You wanted to see me about the missing escort women?'

'Yes.'

'When I wrote the article you have in your hand, I got some promising sightings for a few weeks afterwards. I followed them up but nothing new surfaced. They soon dried up, but what didn't was the abusive messages.'

'What?'

'Misogynistic prats started sending me dick pics, or a picture of a bloke with a rope around his partner's neck, or a mock grave with a dead-looking woman inside.'

'That's terrible. Did you report it?'

'For all the good it did. These guys hide behind multiple IDs. Close one and they pop up in another. I did the only thing I could and changed jobs, and changed all my contact details. It's the best decision I ever made.'

'Have you done any more work on the missing women?'

'I wanted to when I moved here, but my boss said no, she didn't think there was any mileage in it. I had to do it in my spare time.'

'In your article you mentioned Harriet Blackford, Lisa Daley, Barbara Hines and Ana Lomidze. Any more you'd like to add or take away?'

'Yeah, Ana contacted *The Argus*, oh, about four months back. She'd been talking to a friend she hadn't spoken to in a while, who told her about the article. She's alive and well and living back in Georgia.'

'Good to know. Can you tell me anything about the other women?'

She opened her file. 'Lisa was last seen out with a guy in Brighton. The next day, her agency, Shore Media, expected her to report in, but she didn't. Despite phoning her mobile and sending someone around to the flat she rented in the North Laines, she disappeared right off the map.'

'Okay.'

'Harriet and Barbara were both with the *Brighton Tide* agency.'

'Oh, Barbara as well? I didn't realise.'

'Yes. It was those two that started me off with this investigation.'

'Right.'

'*Brighton Tide* take care of their girls better than most. If a client misbehaves, Oli and Dave are sent round to give them a talking to. I've seen them, they're big guys, believe me.'

'What happened to them?'

'Some of the women, against company policy, would hand out their phone numbers to a select group of valued clients. This allowed the client to phone them without *Brighton Tide* knowing, and of course, all the money came to them.'

'But they couldn't depend on Oli and Dave if the situation turned sour.'

'Hence they only gave out their number to a select group of clients.'

'I see.'

'Both Harriet and Barbara were suspected of doing homers. They either did this, and something went wrong between them and the client, or they packed it in and started a new life with all the money they made from their little bit of subterfuge.'

Louise's phone rang. Following a thirty-second conversation, she gathered her things.

'I'm so sorry, Detective Walters, I have to go. I hope what we've discussed helped.'

'It has, thanks.'

'I'm sure glad someone's taking an interest in these women after all this time. I'm confident you won't receive half of the abuse I got, not if you mention you're a cop. Thinking about it now, maybe I should have done the same. See ya.'

SIXTY

The grounds around Oakwood House looked splendid in the late May morning sunshine. Spring sunshine had a unique quality, unsurpassed by the other seasons. It wasn't the blazing fire of summer, or the insipid coolness of winter, but a gradual increase in warmth to disperse the dawn mist and, in time, evaporate overnight condensation.

Henderson would have loved to wake up in this house to meet the sunrise, but not to look upon the two odd-looking men with their strange device as they walked at a slow pace around the garden. He had deployed a ground-penetrating radar team at the first opportunity following the revelations of Adrian Chapman on Wednesday.

However, without specific guidance from Jo-Jo's emails as to the location of the burial site, they would have to cover the whole place – all five acres of it. In addition, once the whole garden had been checked, it would stop speculation from various members of the team, and no doubt from the press after they were briefed, as to whether there were more bodies waiting to be found.

A previous team under Henderson had done the above-ground search of the garden in the days following the discovery of Roger Maitland's body, looking for anything the killer might have dropped, or snagged on a bush or the fence surrounding the property. The ground was a mix of a large area of lawn bordered by woods, consisting in the main of silver birch and beech trees. He'd told the team at the time to spend more time in the woods, following the likely path a would-be killer might have taken.

Also, the woods had been the place where the killer would have lain in wait until all the lights in the house were extinguished. If he had stayed in position for any length of time, the DI reasoned he would have left traces. He might have flattened and broken some bushes and branches, thrown away a cigarette butt, dropped something out of his pocket, or forgotten to retrieve something he'd brought with him: binoculars, torch, food wrapper. Alas, the team found nothing.

Maitland had spent considerable money turning the house into the show home it had become. He'd either renewed the fence at the beginning of the development work and failed to maintain it, or when he bought the property, it was already in situ, as some parts were in much need of repair.

In the place Henderson was standing now, some time ago a few winters back, a tree had fallen on the fence, pushing part of it down. This made it easy for someone from outside to climb in and out. He looked along the limb for threads or fabric, but knew nothing new would be found as his team, for sure, would have looked there.

His phone rang.

'Morning gov,' Walters said, 'how's it going over at the house?'

'Morning Carol. They've done the lawn, and they're now taking a break before they start in the woods. I think it's a more likely place to bury a body.'

'I agree. If he had buried her under the lawn, he would be worried the grass wouldn't grow, or the opposite, an overabundance of growth in one particular spot.'

'In a house as big as this,' he said, 'it's inconceivable Maitland wouldn't have thrown a few garden parties and invited people over for dinner. All it would take is for one of his guests to notice the odd body shape in the grass and tough questions would need answering.'

'Now that would be funny; dark and bleak maybe, but funny nevertheless.'

'How did your London trip go? How are you getting on with finding our missing women?'

'Louise and I had a helpful discussion. I have to say, at first I thought this would be a thankless task as we would be going over the same ground she covered while she worked at *The Argus*. I've since realised she didn't have access to a lot of the systems we do, in particular the PNC.'

'The women have form?'

'Two of them do. For soliciting when they were younger.'

'Good, it gives you something to work with.'

Henderson moved out of the way to allow the team to decide how best to use their machine to cover the woods.

'It does. The reason I called is Houghton's been down a couple of times.'

'Looking for me?'

'No, I don't think so. He's been talking to Phil and Sally about general stuff.'

'You think he feels bad about Potter?'

'I don't doubt it. I'm just glad he didn't make a statement to the newspapers.'

'He wanted to, but I told him to hold off until we had Potter back in custody and the search warrant had been served.'

'A delaying tactic, if ever I saw one.'

'Call it what you like, it saved us a lot of embarrassment.'

She laughed. 'Here's hoping Jo-Jo's emails aren't a hoax.'

'I'm confident they're not. For sure, Maitland had been a big spender with big sums moving in and out of his bank account on a regular basis, but even we noticed fifty grand disappearing every quarter.'

'Yeah, you're right, all we need to do now is–'

'Detective Henderson!'

'I have to go now, Carol. Teri the radar op is calling.'

'I hope it's because they've found something. Talk to you later.'

Henderson put the phone away and went in search of the radar team. He spotted them at the back of a large bramble outgrowth.

'Teri, how do I make my way past the vegetation?' he called. 'I'm sure you didn't walk through it.'

'Over there,' she said, pointing, 'you should see the path.'

He found the path, skirted the brambles and arrived at the small clearing where the team had stopped.

'Have you got something?'

Team Leader Teri Ingham nodded, her face a stoic mask. 'We have a strong reading here.'

'It couldn't be a dead dog or something similar?'

'Maybe, if he kept Great Danes or wolfhounds.'

'I don't think he did. It's a large shape?'

'It sure is.'

Henderson pulled out his phone.

SIXTY-ONE

'Going out for a run, Angus?'

No, I always walk around in tight-fitting bright coloured tops, shorts, and Day-Glo striped trainers.

'Yes, making the most of the fine evening.'

'It's such a lovely evening, right enough,' his elderly neighbour Molly Jefferson said. 'The winter's been so long, and wet too.'

'It has, see you later, Molly,' he said as he set off.

'Bye,' she called. 'Enjoy your run.'

Friday around seven wasn't the best time to run along Brighton seafront. Despite the early hour, some would have had too much to drink over the afternoon and stagger into his path. While others would be so full of the joys, talking loudly to their mates and laughing at anything, to hear him coming up behind. If he came too close, they might all of a sudden stop or step to one side at the wrong moment.

When the ground radar team received their positive reading, the DI had called in an excavation team. He'd stayed on at the site in case they pulled up a dead animal, so his presence would temper the jibes and insults that as a consequence would be flying.

They'd dug down. The grave wasn't shallow, and in ways more understood by pathologists than himself, this had helped to preserve the remains they found. When they'd brushed the soil away, fragments of dress material and the bones of a woman appeared, identified by the small hip radius. More soil was removed and jewellery appeared, tarnished by time and erosion but still identifiable as earrings, a necklace, and a bracelet.

This transformed the work being carried out at Oakwood House from a search into a crime scene. Soon he had the area cordoned off and the pathologist called. Henderson now waited to hear if any DNA could be recovered.

Often in cases like this, a missing person case for example, discovering the DNA wasn't always useful. The missing man or woman might not have fallen foul of the law and so they would not be on the DNA database. In the case of the missing escort women, a couple of them had been arrested for soliciting, so with luck if DNA was recoverable, details would be on the system.

The race was on to identify this woman and identify her they would. If not from DNA, from the work being done by the rest of the team. This became important for a number of reasons.

Once they confirmed her identity, they would start the hunt for her son, Jo-Jo. This wasn't the only reason. It was human nature to have sympathy for a real person, but not for a pile of bare bones. He was mindful this grave might not be the final resting place of Jo-Jo's mother. One, or both of the other missing women could be buried there. In the time it took for the excavation team to arrive with their shovels and Hazmat suits, he'd instructed the ground radar team to comb the rest of the woods. To his relief, no more graves were found.

To try to drown out all thoughts about missing and dead women, Henderson turned up the volume of the music he was listening to, a Spotify playlist, rock music from the 70s and 80s. He'd tried playlists specifically curated for runners and gym enthusiasts, such as Running UK and Cardio, but they were filled with dance tracks by artists he'd never heard of, despite occasional forays listening to Radio 1 and Heart Sussex.

He reached Shoreham, the halfway point of his run, and without stopping, headed back. Times like this made running enjoyable. In spite of the hazards provided by drunken and thoughtless pedestrians, Brighton could still beguile him. Lights switched on in the hotels and bars he passed, laughter drifted up from those wrapped in towels and blankets on the beach, and the sun sank down below a sparkling sea, casting a long orange streak.

Plenty of people were about: strolling, walking dogs, on skateboards, and running. He had to take those relaxing moments when he could, as this weekend would be like the last one, a write-off in terms of leisure time.

His phone rang. He pressed the button on his headphones and slowed to a walk.

'Henderson.'

'Hi gov.'

'Hi Carol. Not out with Delectable Dom?'

'No, he's working tonight.'

'So, every Friday night from now on will be an early one for you?'

'I don't think so. He's only working in the bar until his new job starts.'

'I like him already, a man who can't hang around doing nothing.'

'I would ask if you're sitting down, as the news I'm about to impart might floor you, but I gather from the heavy breathing you're running.'

'Correct, on Brighton seafront.'

'We've found one of the missing escort women.'

'Brilliant. Which one?'

'Lisa Daley.'

'What's her background?'

'She's originally from Leeds and when she went back for a couple of days to visit her mother, she came out of a pub and witnessed a grisly murder. It was a dispute between two drug crews, and pretty horrific, as a couple of guys armed with machetes hacked the victim to death.'

'Gruesome right enough.'

'She recognised one of the attackers as they had gone to the same school. Cut a long story short, she became a key witness at the murder trial. As her appearance in court would make her a target for the drug gang, the West Yorkshire force set her up with a new identity, job, and house, far away from Brighton and Leeds.'

'She's alive and well?'

'That's as much as they would tell me.'

'How did you find her?'

'With great difficulty. When all our systems came up with nothing, we worked the Leeds angle. Vicky used some contacts she has up north.'

'I'll pass on my thanks to her in the morning. With us locating her, will it put her in any danger?'

'It shouldn't. All we know is her original name, Lisa Daley. The detective I spoke to would only confirm a woman of that name joined their Witness Protection Programme, but he wouldn't tell us if we asked, which we didn't, her assumed identity and current location.'

'I'm glad to hear it, and well done. Now only two to go.'

'Yes, and would you believe, they were both escorts at Brighton Tide. Now isn't that a big coincidence, or what?'

SIXTY-TWO

Henderson parked the car at the back of Brighton Crematorium. He walked towards the low, grey building, a noticeable reluctance in his steps. He knew of no detective who enjoyed attending a post-mortem, even for a body that had been in the ground for so long. Traffic had been slow despite leaving his apartment early, but would become busier from now on, not only with Saturday morning shoppers, but day-trippers heading to the coast to enjoy a bout of fine weather.

No matter the warming effect of the sunshine or blue skies outside, walking through the entrance to the mortuary, the ambient temperature dropped. In an ante room, a mortuary assistant helped him into the protective suit and bootees required for looking at dead tissue. He wouldn't be doing that today, with no tissue on weather-dried bones, but nevertheless it paid to be cautious.

He walked into the pathologist's domain. The usual procedures of a typical post-mortem would not be much in evidence with no organs to weigh and inspect for damage. Still, much could be learned as even old bones had many secrets to reveal.

'Hello Grafton, how are you?'

'Hello Angus, I'm well. You?'

'The same.'

'You did well to find her. I understand she was more than a metre down. Most cons think it's enough to cover a body with some soil and a pile of leaves, hoping Mother Nature will do the rest. Hence the reason so many bodies are uncovered by dogs or foxes.'

'The burial took place on private land and in a wood, so the gravedigger, or diggers, weren't overlooked. They could take their time and do a proper job.'

'It certainly helped us. As you can see, her skeleton is more or less intact. The ones covered by leaves are often discovered soon, but sometimes not before a fox or dog has helped themselves to a bit of it.'

Grafton had arranged the bones on one of his wide dissection tables. Where the bones were no longer fused, the pathologist had placed them in the correct anatomical position, to make it clear this had once been a functioning human being.

'First off, but I'm sure with all your experience of PMs, you might have guessed, this is the remains of a woman.'

Henderson nodded. In front of him wasn't a clean-picked skeleton, it would take many more years in the ground for that to happen, but one resembling the mainstay of a million zombie movies: wisps of faded hair, brown skin wizened and the texture of parchment, holes where the eyes had been, and no substance to the frame, as if all the muscles, tendons, organs and fat had been sucked away.

'She's of average height, about five foot seven, so not a large woman. From the analysis we've done of the bones, she has been well nourished, with a diet principally from these islands. I would hazard a guess at Southern England if pushed.'

'Okay.'

'Now, if you look here,' he said pointing at the neck with his steel indicator, 'I would say without fear of contradiction, although with one small proviso, she has been strangled. The proviso is this: her skull is intact, so she received no blow to the head, and her ribs don't have any nicks to indicate a bullet or stab wound. However, I cannot preclude the possibility of a bullet or stab wound going through her body cleanly, hitting vital organs but not striking or nicking the bones.'

'Understood.'

'We can be confident she has been strangled, however, because as you can see, here,' he said, pointing with his little metal pointer, 'these are the hyoid bones.'

Henderson nodded. He knew all about them from other choking and strangulation cases he had investigated.

'They are broken, which is a definite indication of strangulation. With the limited information we have, we would now be into the realms of speculation to determine if this had been caused by a rope, scarf, or leather ligature. In this case, we have been able to recover from around the bones in her neck some tiny fibres of fabric which you can see here,' he said picking up a blown-up photograph. 'We are confident these came from a red silk scarf.'

Henderson made a mental note to go down to North Chailey and look through Roger Maitland's clothes. In Roger's will, his daughter Laura had inherited the house, and was keen to sell it but couldn't do so until Henderson no longer considered it a crime scene. With the discovery of a body in the garden, she would have to sit on her hands for some time yet.

The finding of Exhibit A, Grafton's term, in the garden provided more proof to his argument, so Laura could be resisted for the time being. Roger might have kept the murder weapon, and while it wouldn't do much to help solve this case, it would be another piece of the jigsaw to slot into place.

'Is there enough, I don't know, material for you to extract DNA?'

'I should say so. Some of her teeth are intact, not enough alas, to make a useful dental mould, but sufficient to extract her DNA. It should be available Monday.'

'Excellent.'

'You think she might be on the system?'

'There's a very good chance.'

'I'm glad to hear it. The last important item I think I should draw your attention to, Angus, is this.'

They moved from the area around the throat to the hip. Grafton's pointer honed in on the pelvic bone.

'Look here.'

'I can't see anything.'

'You have to look closely.'

Henderson bent over, getting as close as he dared.

'Can you see those small circular marks there?'

Henderson leaned over. 'Yes.'

'They are called parturition scars. This woman has given birth.'

SIXTY-THREE

Henderson parked the car in The Drive in Hove and walked to the payment machine. Although he baulked at the prices, he liked machines like this one which allowed him to make a contactless payment. Since the pandemic, the cash in his wallet had remained static, as now all his main and incidental expenditures was made on plastic cards.

When he returned to the car, Walters stood looking at something on her phone before tapping out a reply.

'Is it Delectable Dom or someone from the office?'

'You've got to stop calling him that. The poor guy will develop a complex. No, it's Sally asking for suggestions of other places where she can look for the two missing women.'

'Once you've been through all the corporate systems and social media sites, there's not much left.'

He locked the car and they started walking.

'I mean,' he continued, 'we have a list of all the social media, job search, and dating sites; everything we could think of at the time. If they're not there, they could have changed their names or be using an anonymous handle when online.'

'I told her to concentrate on looking at job sites. New ones are popping up all the time and both women are young enough to work.'

'Same with dating sites. Last week I was listening to Planet Rock and they've launched one. When you think about it, it's such a great idea. Right off the bat, if two people decide to go out they have something in common.'

'Yeah, I like it. Plus, it's not like, I dunno, chess or collecting beer mats, there's a whole host of things they can do together: go to a concert of their favourite band, spend the weekend at a festival, or go up to Earl's Court where they often have vinyl album and single sales.'

They turned into Church Road and headed west.

'I like Hove,' Walters continued, 'I think I might move here at some point.'

'It's a slower pace of life than Queen's Park. Less young families and their kids playing in the park, and more of the retired taking a stroll with their little dog along the seafront.'

'You make it sound like Eastbourne or God's waiting room, which I don't think it is. Yes, it's a quieter place to live, but it means I won't see ladies of the night hanging around the park, or find needles in the gutter as I walk to my car.'

They turned down Albany Villas and as the name suggested, the road consisted of two lines of well-cared for white villas and Regency-style apartment blocks, leading down to the sea. One of the villas had been converted into offices, with one side occupied by a company called Pavilion Investments.

They walked up the stairs at the front of the building, opened the door, and faced the receptionist behind the desk. Henderson hoped it didn't show, but he thought the woman looked stunningly gorgeous, and was wasted taking calls and meeting people like them. She could be on television presenting *Love Island*, or if she had brains to compliment the good looks, *Countdown*.

'We have an appointment with Mr Stefanopoulos.'

'And you are?'

'Detectives from Sussex Police.'

'Yes, I have you in.' She picked up the phone. 'He hasn't done anything wrong, has he? He likes to think he sails close to the wind, but I thought it was nothing but bluster.'

'No, he hasn't done anything wrong. This is about another matter.'

She nodded. 'I'll give him a call.'

A few minutes later they were shown into Theo Stefanopoulos' office. They were on the upper floor of the building, with windows overlooking the road, the morning sunshine lighting the large window and the space in front of it. It still retained the aura of the lounge or drawing room of a smart villa, in spite of the oversized desk, a web of wires, and all the electronic kit required to run a number of businesses.

Mr Stefanopoulos looked too young, early thirties, to be occupying such a large and opulent office. The face looked well-groomed, as if he had spent the first hour of the morning having his hair trimmed, his face shaved, and his clothes brushed.

'What can I do for you, Detectives?'

'We understand you own a business called *Brighton Tide*.'

'Which part of the police did you say you were from?'

'Serious Crimes.'

'Is running an escort business considered a serious crime in this country?'

'No, it isn't, but what we're concerned about is this: two women who once worked at *Brighton Tide* have gone missing.'

'No one has gone missing, Detective. The escort business is short-term, one where our longest serving woman has been with us for no more than five years. They become restless after a while and move on and find other employment.'

'If you believe that, have you seen this?' Walters said, passing over *The Argus* article written by Louise Gatiss.

He glanced at it before flicking it back to her a few seconds later. 'Yeah, I read it at the time. Scaremongering, I call it. You do a lot of it in this country.'

'We have genuine concern for two of the women mentioned in that article, Mr Stefanopoulos, both of whom have in the past worked for *Brighton Tide*. Barbara Hines and Harriet Blackford.'

'You don't expect me to know everyone in my organisation and understand what they do from day-to-day? I employ nearly four hundred people across thirty-two businesses.'

'I'm not expecting you to know, what I'm asking is for you to tell *Brighton Tide* to release all the information they have on those two women.'

'They have refused?'

'They have.'

'Why?'

'They say the files contain confidential information.'

'Then I have to respect the judgement of the management.'

'Mr Stefanopoulos, let me remind you, we are engaged in a murder investigation. You may have seen in the weekend's newspapers a team recovering a body from the garden at a house in North Chailey. We believe it could be one of those women.'

'It's you!' he said pointing. 'I saw you talking to that reporter on *South Today*.'

'Yes.'

'Hey, hey, a big media star, right here in my office, but why are you bothering me? I watch crime dramas all the time and I know once you have DNA, everything's sorted.'

'Her details might not be on the DNA database. Even if they are, it will only give us one of the missing women.'

He nodded. 'Yeah, but I still don't want to overrule my managers. It's bad for business.'

Henderson took a deep breath. He didn't want to threaten the man but his obstinate stance left him no choice. 'We seem to have reached an impasse and I feel nothing I can say will change your mind.'

He shook his head. 'No, it won't.'

He looked Stefanopoulos straight in the eye, and said, 'Then you force me to do this. I will go back to the office and obtain a search warrant, and you'd better believe I'll have no trouble obtaining one as this case involves the possible murder of one of your employees. My team will come here, into these offices, and remove every computer they find in this building. They will go through the filing cabinets and take away all the files you have relating to your escort businesses. Now, don't you think that would be bad for business?'

'What a stuck-up arse,' Walters said as they walked up Albany Villas. It's not as if we're talking about current employees of *Brighton Tide*, these women left years ago.'

'I don't know what it is. Maybe in Greece they distrust the police so much they will do anything not to cooperate, but at least he's agreed to tell *Brighton Tide* to release the information. When they do—'

His phone rang.

'Hang on Carol.' He fished it out. 'Henderson.'

'Hello gov.'

'Hi Vicky.'

'The DNA of the body found at North Chailey has come back. She's on the system.'

SIXTY-FOUR

They now knew the identity of the body found in the woods at Oakwood House. Her name was Harriet Blackford, one of the missing escort women first identified by Louise Gatiss. It meant they could concentrate all their efforts on researching her children, of which she had two: Douglas and Mark. One of them had to be Jo-Jo, Roger Maitland's blackmailer.

Houghton had put his Potter fixation behind him, and added his considerable support in the hunt for Maitland's blackmailer. However, Henderson had the feeling he would not let Lucas Potter go, and after this case had been done and dusted, he would want the team to go after him. He couldn't get over Potter's loss of four hundred million pounds which convinced the CI he'd had a hand in the murders somehow.

After lunch, his three sergeants came into the office and sat at the meeting table. Harry was now in charge of the team researching Harriet Blackford, using files sent by *Brighton Tide*. Vicky was doing the same for Mark Blackford, and Carol, Douglas Blackford.

Henderson picked up his file and took a seat beside them.

'Right, I have to say, this part of the investigation feels odd. For once, we're not looking for the family of the victim to tell them we've found their mother, but trying to discover which of the victim's sons killed two Vixen directors. Harry, make a start.'

'Harriet Blackford joined *Brighton Tide* ten years ago. She was in mid-thirties at the time and a good-looking woman. In the three years she worked there, she became one of the company's premium earners.'

'Define premium.'

'Only the top five percent of women in profit terms are given the designation. They're allowed to keep a higher percentage of their earnings and are eligible for a quarterly bonus.'

'It sounds so corporate.'

'I suppose it does. When she disappeared off the map, they were naturally keen to find her, and the steps they took are in the file.'

'Did they talk to Roger Maitland?'

'No they didn't, which makes me think, following on from what Louise Gatiss told Carol, Maitland must have been one of her "homers"; a client she met off the clock.'

'It certainly looks like it.'

'The reason we couldn't unearth much recent stuff on social media or other websites about Harriet, is because she's been dead for over seven years. The *Brighton Tide* stuff will prove more useful when we ramp up the search for Barbara, providing she's not dead too, as the file includes other names she's used in the past.'

'Why do they do that?'

'*Brighton Tide* advises them to make up a few alternative names. These can be given out to clients who insist on knowing. It's to stop harassment and some clients becoming obsessed and stalking them on social media.'

'Sensible, but you're right, it should help us track down Barbara.'

'Anything else?'

He shook his head.

'Thanks, Harry. Vicky, tell us about Mark Blackford.'

'He's twenty-two and works for a parcel delivery service. He's a troubled kid, according to his former headmaster, as he and his brother were brought up by their grandmother who wasn't equipped to deal with a couple of young boys and their grief.'

'Not a good start for anyone in life.'

'The boys in Croydon nick say he's a low-level drug dealer. He's on their radar, but not enough to warrant any action. In their opinion, he takes after his brother.'

'Does he indeed? I think we should move over to you now, Carol.'

'Doug Blackford is a serious, dyed-in-the-wool career criminal. He's young, twenty-seven, but old for his age and runs a million-pound business as the right-hand man of Jason 'Scouse' Wallace. He heads a gang responsible for most of the drugs, prostitution, protection, and people-smuggling rackets south of the river.'

Henderson blew a puff of air towards the ceiling. 'Bloody hell, that's all we need. Our main suspect is a career criminal and close associate of Scouse Wallace.'

'Blackford's been in jail a couple of times, but only in the early days. He's regarded nowadays by the drug squad as more or less untouchable. Any time he's been in custody, witnesses retract statements, evidence is flimsy as he never touches the merchandise himself, and does whatever his expensive solicitor tells him to do, which is to say nothing.'

'What do we know of his movements? He might be a big-time drug dealer, but he's in our sights for two murders.'

'We know loads about him. The drug unit follow him from time to time so we know where he lives, the gym he uses, the coffee shops he prefers, the whole nine yards.'

'Put a surveillance team together, Carol. I want to know his movements over the next three days. We need up-to-date information on his whereabouts.'

'Will do.'

'We'll also need to obtain a warrant to search his house. Where does he live?'

'In Addington.'

'I'll have to clear what I'm planning with the Met, Croydon nick, and now I think about it, the NCA, as he and Scouse are likely to be on their radar as well. What I'm thinking with the house search is we need to find more than a series of anonymous emails; I want solid evidence linking him to Maitland or Grange. If he's as street smart as his background suggests, this might prove hard, but even the smartest criminals are known to make mistakes and keep mementos.'

The sergeants departed ten minutes later. Henderson had a few things to do, the first being to brief Houghton. If a senior cop in London wasn't informed about the surveillance car, the operation to arrest Blackford and the search of his house, they would be screaming down the phone to Youngman or Houghton. The first call his bosses would make would be to Henderson.

The DI would rank the arrest of a high-ranking criminal as being similar to a celebrity or a well-known politician. Newspaper editors loved to report on anyone in the public eye, the higher the fall from grace the better. The fact he would be relatively unknown to the public didn't matter, as their readers all understood hackneyed phrases such as drug lord, baron, kingpin, and narco boss.

Once he had made the requisite phone calls, and with luck, gained the required permissions, the investigation would move into the time he hated. Waiting around for something to happen.

SIXTY-FIVE

For the next two days, Henderson was desperate to do something, but couldn't. Using a combination of surveillance by his team, and information from a previous operation by the Met, they knew Doug Blackford liked to eat out on Thursday nights. Scouse was his regular dining companion and the restaurant would be replete with numerous minders and heavyweights.

It wasn't Henderson's choice to lift him at a restaurant, but due to an increase in tension among South London drug gangs following the shooting of an Albanian drug dealer on Tuesday, Blackford had scrapped many of his well-established routines. Since the start of the week, he hadn't slept at the same location twice, didn't go to his favourite coffee shop, sending a mate instead to fetch his chosen brew, and hadn't been seen around his regular street hangouts. This Thursday night, Henderson's team had followed him to a restaurant not on the Met's list.

When he'd made his calls to the Met and NCA to inform them of the operation, they were full of enthusiasm for him to proceed. They didn't have any confidence in nabbing him on a drugs charge, but they were hopeful a murder one would stick.

Henderson and his team were parked close to the Lugano restaurant in Beckenham. It looked a good spot for a couple of criminals to meet. It was located at a crossroads, and this being a busy part of London, double yellow lines ensured no parking anywhere near the intersection. Therefore, the men inside could be confident no one would be parked outside, ready to ambush the two men as they departed.

'I'd like to be earwigging the conversation they're having,' Henderson said.

'You and the rest of the South London drug squad, I imagine,' Walters said.

'After the death of the Albanian, I imagine they must be discussing what action they should take if the Albanians retaliate and one of their own men is killed.'

'If they do respond, I don't think Scouse and Blackford can afford to sit about and do nothing. By all accounts, the Albanians are a ruthless lot and will trample all over them if they don't meet force with force.'

'From what I understand about Scouse, he's a hardwired psychopath. He's not the type to take it easy and be comfortable with all the millions he's making. He will still go out and stab or shoot one of his dealers if he thinks he's been skimming off the top.'

'Which means sparks will be flying over the next few days.'

'I don't doubt it, but thankfully it's not a problem we will face.'

They sat in silence for a few minutes. The radio sparked up. 'Movement detected inside the restaurant. It looks like our targets are about to leave.'

The Sussex detectives got out of the car and walked towards the restaurant on the same side of the street. Other officers were doing the same from the far side of the crossroads. They were all wearing stab-proof vests with the word 'Police' emblazoned across the chest, so the minders wouldn't mistake them for an Albanian revenge squad.

They knew what Doug Blackford and Scouse looked like thanks to various mug shots taken when they had been arrested in the past. They also had seen more recent pictures supplied by the Met's surveillance team.

No sooner had they reached the restaurant than three identical black BMW X7s pulled up, and parked on the double yellow lines directly outside. The drivers exited their vehicles and opened the rear door for their impending passenger. If they were surprised to find a posse of ten cops standing outside, most of whom were armed, it didn't seem to alarm them.

Two big guys, looking like refugees from a heavyweight boxing gym, were first out of the restaurant, checking the coast was clear and that the transport had arrived. Scouse came out first. A stocky guy, below average height, his black and grey hair combed and gelled back across his scalp, and his rugged and scarred face wearing a trademark scowl.

'What's this, a protection detail to save us from the fucking Albanians? Well, let me tell you, copper, those bastards don't frighten me one bit.'

'This isn't about the Albanians,' Henderson said, 'and it isn't about you.'

A few more minders walked out and this time Doug Blackford was between them.

'Douglas Blackford,' Henderson said. 'I'm arresting you for the murder – hey!'

The minder nearest the DI, a muscled guy about the same height as Henderson but carrying twice his weight, shouldered him, shoving him backwards and causing him to lose his balance. An officer caught him, saving him from hitting the deck, and he watched as the minders surrounded Blackford and quickly shepherded him towards one of the BMWs.

'Stop him!' Henderson shouted as he tried to get to his feet.

The cops couldn't break through the phalanx of bodyguards shielding Blackford, despite the angry calls from officers and the pointing of weapons. Blackford climbed into the car. In seconds, the door slammed shut. The car revved its engine and drove off.

'Back to the vehicles!' Henderson shouted. 'Follow them!'

Henderson and Walters raced back to their pool car. Before the doors were closed, Henderson took off in the direction taken by the three BMWs. He floored the car, a dangerous thing to do in an urban area like Beckenham, but saved in part by the late hour. Nevertheless, he had to be wary of headphone-clad dog walkers or those tottering back from an evening spent in the pub.

'Do you know this area of London?' he asked Walters.

'Nope.'

'Me neither, so I've no idea where we're headed.'

Henderson overtook a slow-moving car. He peered through the windscreen, scanning the road ahead. 'There they are, I can see them.'

The line of BMWs were travelling as fast as they dared, weaving past parked cars, overtaking stopped buses, and ignoring traffic lights and pedestrian crossings.

'Blackford's car left before the others, so he must be in the front car,' Walters said.

On a straight stretch, the car at the back of the BMW group overtook the one in front.

'Did you see that?' she said in astonishment.

'What are they playing at?'

'Trying to confuse us, as the cars are near enough identical in this light.'

Just when he had adjusted to the change, the car at the back of the line braked hard, and the car in the middle, or perhaps the one at the front, made a rapid left turn.

Walters picked up the radio and broadcasted the name of the road it had gone down, hoping one of the patrol cars behind, although they couldn't see any as yet, would follow it.

'I reckon Blackford's still in the front car.'

'Me too.'

A few minutes later the rear car did the same as the previous one, making a sharp left turn. Walters picked up the radio and informed the other cars of the BMW's manoeuvre while Henderson kept following the last car. On a busy section, close to a row of closed shops, he switched on the car's flashing light and siren, and a few moments later, and much to his surprise, the BMW pulled into the side of the road.

Throwing caution to the wind and not caring about them being dangerous criminals, he strode towards the BMW without waiting for any back-up to arrive. When he reached the vehicle, he hauled open the rear door.

Scouse in the back seat took one look at him and laughed, an alien sound from a customary stern and sneering face. 'Fucking had you there, mate. You've just seen the tactics we'll use to outfox the Albanians. Aren't you glad to see it worked?'

SIXTY-SIX

'So, if I can paraphrase, you lost him?'

Houghton stared at Henderson, features stony, hands on hips, his infamous volcanic temper bubbling under the surface, threatening to explode; the morning after the night before. Houghton knew he couldn't say much after his stubborn pursuit of Lucas Potter. This made it 1-1, but Henderson reckoned at 2-1 the game would be over.

'How do you propose to find him?'

'A warrant has been issued for his arrest and all coppers in South London are on the lookout. At least with the trouble the Albanians are expected to cause, he'll be keeping a low profile and won't run the risk of trying to flee the country.'

'For your sake, I hope you're right.'

The chief inspector stomped off without uttering another word.

Henderson had gone over the details of the events in his head before going to bed the previous night, and again at three thirty in the morning. He decided he wouldn't have done anything different. Sure, he could have taken double the number of cops, and so they would have outgunned the minders of Scouse and Blackford in bodies and brute strength. However, if the suspect had come quietly, the DI would have been accused of wasting police resources and being heavy-handed. Not to mention, those additional bodies were not available at the time.

Blackford would be a hard man to track down. Not only because he would be keeping a low profile due to the threat posed by the Albanians, but in his day-to-day career as a drug dealer, he was already mindful of not running into the police or other rival gangs.

Now free from the CI's inquisition and his dismay at the wisecracks he'd receive from the cops he knew in the Met, he collected Walters and walked out to the car park.

'I came by your office when Houghton was there,' Walters said when they were out of earwigging range. 'I took one glance at his face and hurried away as he looked livid.'

'He only sees results, or the lack of them. He doesn't see the planning and execution going into them. Otherwise, he would appreciate last night's lift had about a fifty-fifty chance of succeeding.'

'Yeah, if it had turned violent, there were nine of them, including the BMW drivers, and I reckon most were carrying something. With them being more used to meting out violence than we are, in a stand-off we might have been in trouble.'

They got into the car and Henderson set the satnav for a street in Addington, Croydon. Doug Blackford wasn't staying at his house because of the heightened level of threat, so the forensic team Henderson had sent to his house this morning didn't expect to be disturbed.

The house in Bishop's Walk looked newly-built with its own driveway and gates, situated well away from their neighbours. It looked huge, probably containing five or six bedrooms.

'What age did we say he was, twenty-seven? What's he doing in a place like this? He should be out having fun, not hobnobbing with financiers and television stars.'

'Given his occupation, no one's going to sneak up and surprise him. I imagine there's a fence surrounding the property and judging by the CCTV cameras at the top of the house, strong security.'

'He and his girlfriend and baby must rattle around in all this space.'

'He's got to spend the millions he makes from the drug business somehow.'

'I suppose property is as good a place as any.'

They walked inside the house through the unlocked open door. The symmetrical and traditional shape of the house didn't prepare them for how it had been furnished. Perhaps it came with the house and was fitted by the original builder, but Henderson suspected not, as everything looked new.

It was designed to resemble the interior of a Malibu beach house. Clean white surfaces were everywhere, from the tiled porcelain floor to the largest piece of granite the DI had ever seen as the kitchen worktop. All appliances were top end and the lounge looked out to the swimming pool and garden through gigantic windows.

'This place is stunning,' Walters said. 'I take back what I said in the car. The boy, or his missus, has taste.'

They made their way upstairs to the sounds of the search team rummaging.

'Look at the size of that bath,' Henderson said, as they walked past a bathroom. 'It's in the middle of the room and it's huge. This feels more like a boutique hotel than a house.'

'Hi there,' Geoff Thomas, the team leader said when the DI headed into a spare bedroom. 'I'm not sure if your presence here is a good or bad thing.'

'Why do you say that?'

'We can't seem to gain access to this, I don't know what you'd call it, a secret room. So, it's bad for you to see us struggling, but if you have any ideas how we do it, I'd love to hear them.'

'What makes you think it's a secret room?'

'If you tap any of the upstairs walls, they're solid.' He walked to the wall beside Henderson and rapped his knuckles against it. 'See what I mean?'

'Okay.'

'There's not a bit of chipboard anywhere in this place, not like the box I live in. Now, if you tap here...' he said, tapping the wall where he and another team member, Tony McQueen, were standing. 'Do you hear the change?'

'Yes, it doesn't sound hollow, but different compared to the other wall.'

'Now, if I tap all around,' Thomas said, doing just that, 'I get the shape of a door.'

'I'm with you now. Going by the sophistication of the house, I imagine he has an app on his phone to open it.'

'I thought the same, but I live in hope there's some sort of override around here.'

'I spotted a big control panel downstairs,' Walters said, 'but I thought maybe it had to be for the outside lights and pool.'

'Yeah, we noticed that as well. We thought they were the lights and the wave effect on the pool.'

'I'll go down and check,' Henderson said.

'No, I'll do it. You stay here, sir,' McQueen said. He walked off.

'How's the rest of the house?' Henderson asked Thomas.

'I guess we don't have much to report. It's a big house with only three occupants, so they don't fill all the space. In addition, they've taken away a lot of their stuff, including electronics and cars, as they're sleeping elsewhere on account of the expected Albanian threat.'

They made small talk for a couple of minutes, before Henderson heard a distant whirring. He assumed McQueen had started the waves in the pool, no doubt startling some of the birds he'd noticed gathered around it. Instead, the door outlined by Thomas earlier slowly opened.

SIXTY-SEVEN

The door to the secret room in Doug Blackford's house looked to Henderson like a work of exquisite engineering genius. The outline of the door left no trace on the wall, and the heavy door opened on pneumatics, seated on oiled bearings, meaning it moved with silent precision.

Inside could only be described as a weapons storage room. A back wall, illuminated by an automatic light, housed a variety of guns, knives, knuckledusters and coshes, all neatly displayed on their own mounting. Almost aesthetic in style, it reminded Henderson, for some reason, of his father's tool shed in Fort William, the neat organisation of which had his mother suggesting the poor man suffered from OCD.

'God, look at all the guns and knives,' Walters exclaimed, 'you'd think he commands an army.'

'Have you ever seen pictures of the gun rooms of American collectors on social media or YouTube?'

'No. Have you?'

'Yeah.'

'Why were you looking at something like that?'

'I can't remember, likely it caught my eye when trying to find something else. It might have been a video comparing the six best handguns for sale in the US.'

'Whatever floats your boat, but I can't talk. I often look for makeup tips or how to make a meal with only five ingredients and before I know it, the afternoon's gone.'

'My point is this: maybe these aren't just the weapons of his trade, but he's got some sort of Americana fix. Could be he's trying to replicate the gun rooms of those collectors.'

'It might be the thing to do in Arizona or Texas, but he's broken about a dozen UK laws.'

'I think you're right gov,' Thomas said as he examined the weapons. 'Some of them date from the Second World War.'

Henderson took a look at the knives. Blackford had so many types: stilettos, flick, switchblade, hunting, and in a variety of styles and sizes. Any one of them with the wider blade could be the Maitland and Grange murder weapon. He turned to Thomas.

'Quite a collection,' the DI said.

'What do you want to do with them?'

'I want every item removed and tested.'

'Everything?'

'Yep, every single one.'

'I bet Terry in ballistics will love you.'

'He can take a view on what he examines first. Me, I think some of the older weapons, like the Luger, Webley, and Browning should be tested last, but the modern Glocks and Sigs may well have been used in previous gang shootings.'

'Fair point.'

'For the knives, the wider-bladed knives should be tested first.'

'I'll pass it on. Shall I make a start packing up?'

'Yeah, go on.'

Henderson and Walters walked out of the secret room and back into the bedroom.

'It looks like a guest bedroom,' Henderson said, as they headed for the stairs. 'I don't think anyone sleeping in there would be aware of what lies behind the wall. The door is so well camouflaged.'

She smiled. 'It would just be Blackford's luck to need a gun in a hurry, but he can't reach it as his partner's mother is fast asleep.'

'I'm sure that's not the only place he keeps guns. In fact, I think the secret room might just be for show, his private collection if you like, and the weapons he needs for the day-to-day intimidation of dealers and to shoot rivals might be hidden somewhere else.'

'So, once again we await the results of a forensic analysis and this time, I hope it's a better outcome than we had with Lucas Potter.'

They were outside the house and heading for their car when a strange sound broke the silence. Henderson looked around, and spotted the gates of the property opening. The house stood at the top of a slope and the curve in the driveway meant the DI could only see the upper part of the gates. The new entrant wouldn't see Henderson's car or the forensic team van until they were inside the gates and had negotiated the curve.

'Stay there!' he ordered Walters.

He ran to his car, started the engine and turned it to face the road outside. When the new arrival appeared, a large blue and white Chevrolet, he knew it had to be Blackford. The DI was prepared to ram Blackford's car, but instead he used the space between the car and the wall to squeeze past. He then angled the car so it blocked the driveway.

He dashed out of the car and ran towards the Chevrolet. He had almost reached it when the driver's door opened. Blackford turned, took one look at the rapidly approaching DI, and legged it in the direction of the woods at the back of the house.

He was younger than the DI and fast, but just when it looked as though he would open a large gap between them, Walters ran across his path. He stopped, in two minds what to do. This allowed Henderson to close the gap between them, but before he reached him, Blackford shoved Walters out of the way and ran towards the back of the property.

Passing under the gloom thrown by the trees, Henderson could now see Blackford's target, a tall steel gate built into the back fence. Being security conscious, the DI felt confident it wouldn't be left unlocked. The time he took to open it might be all Henderson needed to close the gap.

About ten metres from the gate, Blackford suddenly veered off to the right. It confused Henderson at first, until Blackford bent down and turned to face him holding the thick limb of a tree. The street punk didn't bother with any cagey side-stepping, sizing up his opponent, instead, he rushed at Henderson. Before he could muster any defence, Blackford smacked the DI over his head with the limb.

If not for the seriousness of the situation, Henderson could have laughed, as he felt little when the limb shattered into hundreds of small pieces; it was rotten to the core. The detective reacted first and threw a punch at Blackford's face. This caught him by surprise, but before he could land another, Blackford came at him, fists flying. One caught Henderson on the side of the head, causing him to stagger back. As he did so, his foot caught a tree root and he fell to the ground. Allowing him no time to get up on his feet, Blackford leapt at him, his fists punching any exposed flesh.

Henderson defended his face and Blackford punched his body. When the DI moved an arm to protect his body, the punk punched his face. His resistance started to weaken and just when he thought he couldn't take any more, the battering stopped.

Henderson lay there in a bed of leaves and broken branches, trying to summon the energy to get up and see where he had gone.

'Are you all right, gov?'

He rolled over and pushed himself into a sitting position. Everything ached: his ribs, stomach, chest, face. To his surprise, Blackford had not disappeared through the open gate as he'd expected. Instead, Walters was on his back in the process of cuffing him.

'What the hell happened?'

'I saw him giving you a belting, so kicked him in the side of the head with one of these.'

She indicated her shoes: a thick heel, square shape with a flat point.

'For sure,' he said, 'way more effective than one of my punches.'

'He's out cold. Unfortunately, we might have to wait a while until he wakes up.'

SIXTY-EIGHT

CI Houghton breezed into Henderson's office, a broad grin across his face.

'Congratulations Angus, I knew you would nab him!'

He shook the DI's hand with some vigour. Thank goodness, for a moment he thought the CI might come in for a hug. Not only did he feel sore after his brush with Doug Blackford, but this was his boss, a man who no doubt had been bad-mouthing the DI all the time Blackford ran free.

'How are you feeling?'

'Better. Downing a couple of Ibuprofen helped.'

'Once you've seen him, get off home. Have a bath and an early night.'

'Will do.'

'What do you think made him return to the house?'

'He said they'd forgotten to pack his partner's eczema cream, but he was spinning us a story.'

'Oh?'

'Yeah, he later let slip they're planning a hit on the Albanians who had suddenly come into a whole lot of new weapons. I reckon his return trip was to pick up bigger and better armaments.'

'I assume you've got enough to hold him until forensics come through?'

'No problem. Even if all the guns turn up clean, the possession of an arsenal of weapons alone will give him some serious jail time.'

'Indeed, it will. To add to his pain, you could always add some affray and traffic charges for Thursday night.'

Henderson nodded, but knew he wouldn't go there. The transgressions of parking on double yellow lines and speeding in a thirty-mile-an-hour limit paled into insignificance against the ownership of a deadly arsenal and committing murder.

'I'm about to make a statement to the press about his arrest.'

'Do you think that's wise?'

'I do. What's the problem?'

'I'm only just on my way to interview him and it's likely he'll refuse to speak to me. In which case, we will need time to gather evidence in order to build a stronger case against him.'

'I hear what you're saying, and most of the time I would agree with you. However, this is an important case and the media hounds are buzzing. Not only are we removing the murderer of two Vixen directors, we are also taking down a major drug dealer in South London. Have you any idea how this will go down at the Met? They will be having parties and our names will be prominent.'

'Even still, I think it's too early.'

'Worry not Angus,' he said putting a hand on his shoulder. 'I'm confident you'll have the whole thing wrapped up, maybe not tonight, but within the next few days.'

He strode off.

Henderson called Walters and they headed over to the Interview Suite.

'You're moving a bit better. I told you those pills would help.'

'Yeah, thanks. Houghton says he's going to announce Blackford's arrest to the press.'

'That's a bit premature, don't you think?'

'I'd be happy with something a tad more circumspect; *a suspect has been arrested, or, someone is helping us with enquiries*, but he's going to say a murderer and major drug dealer has been arrested, and mention Blackford by name.'

'I agree, it's way too early.'

'Especially as Blackford is all set to deny everything or say nothing at all.'

They walked into Interview Room Four at six thirty. Henderson had a preference for evening interviews. It wasn't because he didn't have much of a home life to return to, but often a suspect would be more relaxed, and any evidence gathered in the day would be in their possession.

Sitting beside a calm and confident Doug Blackford, a top London lawyer, Charles Winterton-Smythe, 'Charlie' to Blackford. He had made a name for himself fighting David and Goliath cases: a woman seeking compensation from a polluting multinational, a rape victim suing the Met for mishandling her case.

Winning these court encounters not only garnered huge publicity for his firm, Winterton-Chase, it gave them an enormous payday. Almost as a side line, he represented members of Scouse's crew, a man he'd first met when he'd secured a twenty-grand pay-out for the South London gangster for wrongful arrest.

When the electronic recording equipment had been switched on, Henderson took a good look at the young man across from him. Unlike the DI, with a bruised face and who found certain sitting positions uncomfortable, the suspect's features were unmarked. Pity.

'Mr Blackford, I'm showing you a picture of a woman that I'm sure will be familiar to you.'

Walters passed a photograph over to him.

'For the tape, this is a picture of Mr Blackford's mother, Harriet.'

'What the fuck are you bringing her up for?'

'You're upsetting my client Inspector. I suggest you show purpose.'

'If you will allow me to continue, you will understand this case is all about Mr Blackford's mother. Mr Blackford,' Henderson said, looking at the accused, 'as you would have seen if you had picked up a newspaper recently, your mother's remains were found in the garden of a house in North Chailey in Sussex last week.'

'Inspector! I must protest in the strongest possible terms. This is no way to announce to my client you have discovered the body of his mother. Have you no compassion?'

'Your client was well aware his mother was buried in that garden, so don't preach to me about compassion.'

'How could I? I've no idea where fucking North Chailey is, for Chrissakes.'

'You knew because you sent those emails to Roger Maitland, Chief Executive of Vixen Aviation.'

Walters passed over a copy of several emails sent to Mr Maitland, setting up the blackmail and the blackmailer's subsequent threats. The defendant and his brief had already seen all the emails, as copies had been handed to Winterton-Smythe before this meeting. Therefore, the brief's shock at the DI revealing the burial place of Blackford's mother was purely for theatrical effect.

'In the email, you not only accuse Roger Maitland of killing your mother, you tell him you know she's buried in the grounds of his house.'

'Somebody else sent those. You've no proof I did it.'

'Then why did you not express surprise when you saw them? If someone else sent them, then I would expect you to be shocked that they knew so much about your mother's death.'

He shrugged. 'No comment.'

'I have no doubt you sent them. In the first email you use the words, 'my mother' and 'buried in the garden'. We found a body in the garden of Oakwood House and through the wonders of DNA, have established she is your mother. You might not believe the facts, Mr Blackford, but a jury will have no such problem.'

'Pah.'

'It wasn't you?'

'No fucking way.'

'If not you, perhaps it must have been your brother.'

It had the effect Henderson anticipated, but more so. Blackford's blank expression changed into a snarl, his index figure pointing and jabbing. 'You keep my fucking brother out of this.'

Winterton-Smythe, realising a line had been crossed, whispered something to his client before calling for a recess.

Henderson and Walters walked down the corridor to the coffee machine, joining a small queue spilling out of the observation room.

'You've got him, gov,' Phil Bentley said. 'No way can he deny it.'

'The emails are hard evidence, for sure, even without knowing the identity of the sender, but my concern is it only ties him to the blackmail. Despite a threat to kill Maitland if he reneged on the deal, I think the idea of actually killing him would be a step too far for any jury.'

'Did you see his face though, when you mentioned his brother?' Sally Graham said. 'I think the comment touched a nerve.'

Henderson nodded. 'I agree.' It had been a deliberate comment as he knew from information they had about him how protective he was of his twenty-three-year old younger sibling, Mark. Doug had provided him with a place to live and a car, but like a lot of young men who were given the trappings of wealth too soon, and without having done the hard graft required to earn it, it sent him more off the rails. If he continued his drug-dealing ways, he would be in jail at the same time as his brother.

A major omission from the observation room was Sean Houghton. At this moment, he was regaling all the journos and TV crews in the conference room with details of their big snatch.

Fifteen minutes later, Henderson and Walters were still standing in the corridor drinking coffee, while those in the observation room had returned to their posts. As Henderson went to chuck both cups into the recycling bin, and considered popping over to the conference room to find out what Houghton had been telling the waiting media pack, Winterton-Smythe appeared and called them back inside.

Once seated, Blackford's lawyer put on his jury face, clasped his hands together, and faced Henderson.

'After careful thought, my client has admitted sending the emails. He found out about his mother's death from one of her colleagues at *Brighton Tide*, the agency she worked for, and decided to extort money from Roger Maitland so he wouldn't forget what he'd done. While he admits extorting money, he denies being involved in his murder in the strongest possible terms.'

SIXTY-NINE

Henderson dumped his belongings in his office. Without waking up his computer, he headed over to the staff canteen. The previous night, he went home early and had a bath as Sean Houghton suggested, but not the early night. He spent it instead in the company of Grafton Rawlings.

They were doing fine, necking a few beers and putting the world to rights, until someone suggested opening the whisky. Grafton, professional and business-like in the realms of his domain, the Brighton Mortuary, a grim vocation by anyone's standards, could be a humorous and engaging individual when not dissecting bodies with a sharp knife.

During a major investigation, Henderson made a point of not reading newspapers, although when he went into his local corner shop for a coffee, he often stopped to read the headlines of those on the rack. Grafton told him many knives had been out for the DI's blood at his supposed mishandling of this case. His critics however, had melted into the background, like sun alighting on a patch of snow following Doug Blackford's arrest. Now the feature writers treated the DI as the new flavour of the month.

He didn't much feel like breakfast this morning as his stomach wouldn't have liked it, but he had to eat something now or the hangover would morph into a nauseating headache. While debating the merits of a bacon roll versus one with egg or sausage, a hand alighted on his shoulder. He turned.

'Oh, hi Gerry, how are you?'

'Good Angus, you?'

'A bit dodgy if I'm being honest.'

'Working too hard or drinking too much?'

'The latter.'

Henderson and Gerry Hobbs had worked together in Serious Crime. Following his promotion to DI, Hobbs now worked in the drugs unit. Henderson selected a bacon roll and a large cup of tea and both men headed over to a vacant table close to the window.

'For some reason, Gerry,' Henderson said as they sat down, 'I always seem to bump into you in the canteen.'

'It's no mystery. It's when you need time to think or have a hangover so you want a break and some sustenance. I've just experienced the morning from hell in the Hobbs household, so much so, breakfast was taken off the menu.'

Henderson enquired about Hobbs' wife, Catalina, and his twin children, Milly and Aleshia. Hobbs responded with a little less enthusiasm than normal, perhaps a feature of his disturbed morning.

'Angus, do you realise what a bloody hero you've become in the circles I move in?'

He bit into the roll; it tasted delicious. He hoped his delicate stomach appreciated it. 'What?'

'Yeah, beyond arresting him for murder, I think you've no idea who Doug Blackford really is, and what he's involved in.'

'You're right.'

'He's a senior member of the Clapham Crew, the outfit run by Jason Wallace, Scouse to his mates. I gather the two of you have met.'

'How could I forget?' The cartoon cackle, a poor excuse for a laugh, which sounded when Henderson had opened the door of the decoy BMW, thinking he had cornered Doug Blackford. For the first time in a while, he'd been tempted to plant a fist into a suspect's sneering face.

'The Clapham Crew turns over, we think, about two million a month.'

'Whoa, I had no idea they were so big.'

'Drugs are their big thing, but they've dabbled in guns, prostitution, and supplying slave labour to work in restaurant kitchens and nail bars. Over the last year in South London, they've been responsible for at least five murders and about twenty stabbings and maimings.'

'Serious stuff.'

'You bet, but the term "right-hand man" doesn't do Blackford justice. For Scouse and Blackford, think chairman and chief executive. Blackford runs the show while Scouse visits the drug capitals of the world looking for better deals and more ingenious ways of importing the product.'

'So, with him gone from the stage...'

'You think you can hold him?'

'Without doubt. I've got him already on an extortion charge, plus in his house we discovered a room full of guns and knives.'

'Firearms offences as well? Excellent. His incarceration will certainly create a vacuum Scouse will find difficult to fill, but hell, I work in Sussex. For the moment at least, it's not my problem.'

Henderson walked back to his office, his stomach a little calmer. He didn't know if it was due to talking to his old mate, or having some sustenance, but whatever it might be, it worked. He pushed open the double doors leading to his floor to be greeted by the sight of Walters rushing towards him.

'What is it? A fire, or a bomb alert? I didn't hear an alarm?'

'No, there's no fire. The forensic report on one of Blackford's knives has come through.'

'Only one? What do they say about it?'

'Take a look and see.'

He walked with Walters into his office and woke up his pc. Among the various missives about Diversity Workshops, Unconscious Bias training courses, and invites to a new bridge club, he spotted an email from the forensics lab.

He opened it and read the wording of the email before looking at the attached photographs. The lab had been given over twenty knives to examine, and as per the DI's instructions, they dealt with the broad-bladed knives first. One knife in particular drew their attention, as it looked to be well used and the blade razor sharp. This one they inspected first.

He scrolled down to the annotated photographs. First, a picture of the knife. It looked to be a hunting knife, perhaps American in origin, with a large carbon-fibre style handle offering a firm grip, and a strong, wide blade, serrated on one edge. True to the previous description, the handle had been worn with several chips, and the blade marked and pitted.

Successive photographs displayed blown-up sections of the knife which had been subjected to a number of techniques, more often than not containing the word, 'spectroscopy', which Henderson could barely pronounce, never mind explain to someone else. He punched the air in triumph when he saw the words: *a blood stain trace has been identified as belonging to Lester Grange.*

SEVENTY

'Angus, what's going on?' CI Houghton asked.

'How do you mean?' Henderson said, as he switched the phone handset to his other hand in case he needed to note something down.

'I'm receiving a host of complaints from various departments. They're not getting their results from forensics. It seems the entire team are all working for you.'

He laughed. 'When we raided Doug Blackford's house, we discovered a large arsenal of guns and knives, yes?'

'I remember.'

'Some of the guns we found were for show only, and a few, even the experts agree, might be dangerous to load with ammunition and fire. This includes a couple of guns from the First World War, and one or two pieces of East European kit.'

'I didn't realise.'

'The cache wasn't only to terrorise rival gangs in South London or to start a war, it marks him out as a collector.'

'If so, there should be less guns and knives to analyse than you first thought.'

'For sure, but Lester Grange's blood has been found on a knife.'

'Brilliant! You've got the sod for murder, fair and square. Charge him.'

'Don't worry, I will, but not yet. I need the rest of the knives examined. The one used to kill Roger Maitland is bound to be there.'

'I admit, it would be weird charging Blackford only with Lester Grange's murder, when we know the two men were friends and Roger Maitland was central to whatever the two men were involved in.'

'I agree, therefore I would appreciate if you can hold off those other departments looking to use forensic expertise for the time being, so we can put this case to bed.'

'I'll see what I can do.'

Henderson returned the handset to its cradle.

He checked his emails. He'd receive an email from forensics only if a weapon had traces of blood or was flagged on the system as having been used in a previous crime. If the weapon came out clean, unused, or unable to be used, he would be sent nothing, but a summary of all their findings would be issued at the end of the process. So far, he'd received three emails. One about the knife with traces of Lester Grange's blood, and two about guns used in previous crimes.

The shootings had taken place in South London almost a year back and involved the Clapham Crew clashing with a growing outfit from nearby Streatham. Once Blackford had been charged with everything on the DI's plate, he would turn him over to detectives from the Met who would no doubt be pleased to find some of their unsolved crimes coming off their list.

Around five thirty, he received the summary from forensics, proof that all weapons in Blackford's arsenal had been analysed. He called the lab and complimented them for doing a sterling job at such short notice. After all, it wasn't every day they were handed a large haul like this one. He wanted to ask if they were positive about Roger Maitland's blood not being on any of the knives, but he knew not to ask, if they'd found anything, they would have told him.

He called Walters into his office and after a brief discussion, they both walked over to the Interview Suite.

'It sounds like drug departments all over the south east will start celebrating the minute Doug Blackford is charged with something serious,' Walters said, 'and yet the folks in Serious Crime have long faces.'

'I hate it when a case leaves a loose end, giving us no choice but to live with it. In this one, not having the killer of Roger Maitland is bigger than a loose end, and I don't feel I can, nor do I want to, ignore it. If Doug won't tell us, we'll go after his brother.'

'That one is a dead-end I'm afraid.'

'Eh?'

'I've just found out, Mark Blackford has been on remand for the last six weeks for the attempted murder of a man after a drunken pub brawl.'

'A chip off the old block it sounds.'

Doug Blackford looked a little contrite as he sat beside his brief not uttering a word. Charles Winterton-Smythe looked once again the epitome of legal-sartorial elegance. He wore a different expensive three-piece suit and tie from last time, and his hair, brushed back and gelled, didn't have an errant strand out of place.

'Good evening, Mr Blackford,' Henderson said.

No response.

'You've now admitted sending those emails to Roger Maitland, but why the handle Jo-Jo?'

'When I was young, gran had a dog called Jordan. I couldn't say it, so I called him Jo-Jo. It sort of stuck in my head.'

'Thanks for clearing that up. Mr Winterton-Smythe, I assume you've had a chance to consider the forensic analysis and ballistics report sent to you?'

'Yes, but it doesn't make good reading, Inspector,' Winterton-Smythe said.

'No, it does not. I don't propose to deal with the gun possession issues here. Once we're finished in Sussex, I'll hand you over, Mr Blackford, to the Metropolitan Police and it's up to them how they handle it.'

Blackford's brief nodded.

'Now, if I can turn to the knife analysis.'

Walters placed a photograph of the knife on the table.

'This knife,' Henderson said, 'was found in a room in your house, Mr Blackford. I would call it a secret room as it wasn't obvious when first spotted how to get into it.'

Blackford whispered something to Winterton-Smythe, which Henderson imagined would be along the lines of: *Can he do this? Can he break into my house when I'm not there and take away my stuff?*

'I will be examining the search warrant in some detail, Inspector,' Winterton-Smythe said. 'I will check to ensure all 'i's are dotted and every 't' is crossed. If I find the slightest item out of place, I will apply to the court to have the document struck off and for your search of Mr Blackford's house declared non-admissible.'

'This is your prerogative, Mr Winterton-Smythe.'

A friend in the Met had called the DI and warned him of the tactics Winterton-Smythe would deploy. When faced with a smack-down murder charge like this one, the lawyer would set up a team in his office to examine every document issued by the police: the evidence, details on the charge sheet, the way the accused had been treated. They were searching for the tiniest error, misinformation, or loophole. If anything caught their eye, Winterton-Smythe would then apply to the court and have the item dismissed, a move often resulting in a prosecution collapsing.

Unfortunately, Henderson's friend had called him late in the day, after the first interview with Blackford had taken place, and they were too far down the line to change much. He had to hope everything they had done to date was in order and all procedures had been followed.

'As we found this knife, Mr Blackford, in your house, I assume you are not going to deny it belongs to you?'

'I've been looking after it for a mate.'

Henderson laughed, more for effect because what he said wasn't funny. 'Your poor excuses won't wash. It was discovered in your house, it has your fingerprints on the handle, and when analysed in some detail...'

'Passing to Mr Blackford blown-up pictures of the knife's blade,' Walters said.

'...we found traces of blood belonging to Lester Grange, Distribution Director at Vixen Aviation. Can you explain this, Mr Blackford?'

'I told you, it's not my knife.'

'And I'm telling you, I don't believe you. Mr Winterton-Smythe, I suggest you talk to your client and persuade him to see sense. This evidence is irrefutable: he's going down for this murder.'

'Am I fuck!' Blackford shouted.

'You killed Lester Grange, clear as day!' the DI said, raising his voice in turn. 'I also hope to prove you killed Roger Maitland.'

Blackford half-stood, leaning over the desk, his face contorted and snarling, his finger pointing at the DI's face. This is what rogue dealers and rival gangs in South London would face, not the pious expression of Blackford the choirboy, sitting in front of him in his expensive cashmere V-neck and loafers.

'Maitland deserved to die. The fucker strangled my mother in one of his perverted sex games, and Maitland's bag-carrier, Grange, helped him bury the body.'

Whoa. This was news to Henderson. In two simple sentences he had provided the link they had been missing all along between Roger Maitland and Lester Grange.

'Doug. Keep calm, don't say anything else,' Winterton-Smythe cautioned, for the first time sounding flustered.

'He got carved up good and proper. I wanted to do it, I have to tell you, but someone else wanted it more. Grange might have been a foot soldier, but he deserved what came to him as well.' Blackford slumped back in his seat.

SEVENTY-ONE

After the interview with Doug Blackford, Henderson returned to his office. Walters headed back to the Detectives' Room, leaving him with time to think. They'd got Blackford for the killing of Lester Grange, as no jury would believe his story about him being given the knife by a friend, but what about the death of Roger Maitland? He was the lynchpin. If Blackford blamed anyone for the death of his mother, it would be him. Hadn't he done so in Jo-Jo's angry emails?

Blackford didn't do it: *Someone else wanted it more,* he said. When he uttered those words, for some reason, the name Lucas Potter popped into the DI's head. For the life of him, he could not see a possible connection between a decorated former member of the Royal Artillery, now a security company owner, and a South London drug dealer.

He pulled up the Blackford and Potter files and placed them side by side. He opened both and leafed through the contents, hoping a connection would reveal itself. Had Potter's company done a security job for Blackford? Could Potter be a drug dealer working for Blackford on the fly? Was Potter's partner related to Blackford's? Did they attend the same gym, club, or school?

He believed the answer to all those questions was 'no'. Not only did the two men move in different circles, Potter, at thirty-seven and ten years older than Blackford, was a generation away.

Henderson woke his computer to provide some distraction, take his mind away for a few minutes and see if new connections could be made. An email had arrived from the forensics team. They were either working late or the servers were a bit slow this evening. It was about ten past seven and they did most of their work during office hours.

It included an inventory of every item uncovered in Blackford's man cave, and out of curiosity and the need to find inspiration somewhere, Henderson decided to have a good look through. The guns were an eclectic mix: Austrian, Slavic, American, and Russian. Many were old, but some were new and currently in use by police forces around Europe. The knives were an assortment of flick knives with a variety of mechanisms, stilettos, various hunting knives, and several bayonets.

In cupboards underneath the main display, places the detectives had only given a cursory look, the search team had found medals, belt webbing, scabbards, and ammunition, a whole cornucopia of accessories available to soldiers. They all had been listed and photographed.

Scrolling through, one striking item caught his eye. It looked like an ornamental belt with a big fancy buckle, perhaps only used during ceremonial occasions. Taking a closer look, he spotted an inscription: *Ubique*, and below, *Quo Fas Et Gloria Decunt*. Curious, he keyed the Latin words into

Google and nearly fell out of his chair at what came back: the motto of the Royal Artillery.

Henderson searched through the rest of the inventory, now with a better idea of what he was looking for, and discovered several more items from the Royal Artillery regiment. He then found one bearing the name, 'Lucas Potter, Sergeant.'

He sat for a second or two digesting this, before rushing into the Detective's Room. He waited for Walters to finish her call, which she did seconds later.

'What's the panic?'

'Lucas Potter and Doug Blackford know one another.'

'What? How?'

'I'll explain in the car. Instruct someone to call Crawley and have them send cars to Potter's home and place of business. They are to arrest him on sight. I'll tell Houghton what's going on.'

Within ten minutes, they were in the car heading north, the first time Henderson felt able to speak after all the rushing around.

'You remember the secret room in Blackford's house?'

'Yep.'

'In the cupboards at the bottom, the search team found a load of Royal Artillery memorabilia.'

'Lucas Potter's regiment?'

'Not only that, some items included Potter's name.'

Her face screwed up in concentration. 'For heaven's sake, what would be the chances if Blackford wasn't a drug dealer, but a genuine collector?'

'That's what I thought.'

'Putting on a defence brief's hat for a second, maybe he bought them, I don't know, on eBay, at an auction, or from one of those army surplus places?'

'In the normal course of an investigation, I would be forced to agree with you, but what are the chances it would be two people with strong connections to Vixen? Not only that, they both hated Roger Maitland with a passion, and in Blackford's case, Lester Grange as well.'

She thought for a moment. 'There's no way round it, I can't see any holes. They have to be close buddies.'

The car fell quiet for a couple of minutes, only the sound of Heart Sussex playing low in the background.

'If Potter killed Maitland, and Blackford killed Grange,' she said, 'it makes sense in a perverted sort of way.'

'How?'

'Blackford hated them both, but Potter only hated Maitland. He didn't have any beef that we know about with Lester Grange.'

'It's a good point.'

Henderson's phone rang.

'Henderson,' he said into the microphone above the windscreen.

'Gov,' Vicky Neal said, 'I've had Crawley on the phone. They've been to Potter's house, no sight of him. When they went to Potter Security, he wasn't there either. When one of the coppers looked through his office, he spotted old airline baggage tags in the bin, as if they had been ripped from a suitcase. Are you with me?'

'For sure. He brings a bag or suitcase into the office on his way to somewhere, and spots some old baggage tags on the handle, most likely his recent trip to Florida. He rips them off and chucks them in the bin.'

'That's what I'm thinking. When they presented this to Al Cowan, he clammed up. On the threat of being arrested for withholding vital information, he told them Potter had gone to Gatwick, on his way to South America.'

SEVENTY-TWO

Henderson knew CI Houghton's statement to the press announcing Blackford's arrest would cause trouble. When Lucas Potter became aware his partner in crime, Doug Blackford, a man he'd likely presumed untouchable, had been arrested, Potter realised the time was right for him to skedaddle.

Not for him the problems of the rest of us, deciding where to go, how to afford it, and if his partner could come out and join him. The DI at one time had been friendly with a BA stewardess and she'd told him about the discounted flights available to airline employees, and being long-haul, Rosie would know the main cities of the American continent pretty well. Potter could hide out in his preferred destination, somewhere like Rio de Janeiro or Lima, and a couple of times a month Rosie could head out there to meet him.

Henderson thought of something and before they arrived at Gatwick Airport, he phoned Vicky. He got her to put Lucas Potter's details up on the PNC as a suspect wanted for murder, and to make sure it flashed across to Immigration computers. This way, if they couldn't catch up with him in time, he hoped Potter's passport would be refused when checked by Passport Control, and airport security would be called.

They ran into the terminal building and up towards Security. Henderson explained to the shift supervisor, Dave, what they were doing, and to his credit, he realised the seriousness of the situation and accompanied them airside. They half-ran through the twisty avenue of perfume, chocolate, booze, and gift shops before reaching the main departure boards.

'The only South American flight on the board in the next couple of hours is Buenos Aires,' Dave said looking up. 'Gate 27. It's boarding in about five minutes. This way.'

Having Dave there was really helpful. Henderson could have picked out the flight without too much bother, but finding the gate through the throngs of hundreds of passengers would have taken him more time. They hurried towards the gate, their progress hampered by recalcitrant children, a four-body obstruction strung across their path pulling suitcases, an eight-person flight crew for an airline he didn't recognise, and the big beeping buggies of the airport's assistance team.

When they approached Gate 27, their run slowed to a walk. The gate waiting area was glass-walled and anyone inside would be able to see them walk past. Potter knew what he and Walters looked like, but he didn't know Dave. Henderson placed him closest to the glass. However, Dave wasn't a tall man and someone taking a closer look at the little posse would see Henderson towering over.

Before being exposed by the glass, Henderson decided they would walk briskly and not look into the room. Once they were standing beside the desk at the front, they would be in full view of the room and positioned to block any escape attempt.

They moved inside the seating area at Gate 27 and stood at the ground staff member's desk, scanning the faces, but he couldn't spot Potter anywhere. On the point of asking Dave to double-check the departures board, a male passenger removed the orange Beats headphones from his head, and said, 'You looking for someone?'

'Yes, we are. A man aged late thirties with untidy sandy-coloured hair.'

'A guy like that ducked out the door a minute or so before you arrived.'

'Thanks,' Henderson said. He dashed the same way, Walters and Dave in his wake.

He took the stairs three at a time and on reaching the bottom, felt a cold breeze on his face and spotted an open door. He looked out and saw Potter running across the tarmac.

Henderson ran after him. In all his time as a detective, he knew many in the force who would give the content of their wallets to run across an airport tarmac, but not him. It was safer than most suspect pursuits, as he could be sure Potter would not be carrying any weapons, but more dangerous in other ways. Aircraft, trucks, vans, and cars were all moving, and to the uninitiated, in a seemingly random manner.

Henderson went out running as often as the job allowed, and it became clear in less than a minute that Potter didn't share his passion. If Potter made regular trips to the gym, it must have been to keep his muscles in trim, as his cardio wasn't up to scratch. Just when the DI almost reached touching distance, he suddenly veered to the left and dashed inside a large hanger.

It took Henderson a second or two to adjust to the gloom of the hanger after the dazzling sunshine outside. It looked to be a gigantic garage for all the unusually-shaped vehicles and equipment running around the airport: squat, heavy trucks for towing planes, snow ploughs, and cantilevered steps allowing passengers to reach ground level from the high doors in an aircraft's fuselage.

He turned when he heard a noise and saw Walters and Dave. 'Stand here at the door,' he said, 'and make sure he doesn't escape. Okay?'

They both nodded.

'Carol, alert the airport cops as to what's going on down here and have a couple of them come over to assist.'

'Will do.'

Henderson walked into the garage.

Even though the average UK cop didn't routinely carry a gun, those in airports did, the officers working at Gatwick supplied by Sussex Police. Henderson knew Potter wouldn't be armed, but if he resisted arrest, the pushing of an H&K carbine into his face would seal the deal.

A thought crossed his mind. Potter, wearing his Potter Security hat, had access to many parts of the airport. What if he had concealed a weapon in the garage, anticipating this very eventuality? Henderson didn't believe Potter possessed such a keen level of foresight, but he needed to be wary nonetheless.

The arrangement of parked equipment seemed orderly: neat lines with wide gaps in between. He walked up one such gap and would do the same with the other two.

Peering through a maze of mechanical arms and levers, he spotted movement.

'Potter. You're being stupid. We have armed police outside. You can't escape.'

'Who says I want to escape, but I tell you, Henderson, if they try to shoot me, I'm taking you with me.'

All the time they had been talking, Henderson was making his way up the passage towards the next gap, and so, it seemed, was Potter. When they reached the gap, Henderson could see why Potter didn't try to run or hide. In his hand he held a long metal bar.

He came at Henderson, the bar held over his head ready for a two-handed swing. When it came, Henderson sidestepped out of the way, the heavy bar clanging on the stone floor creating small sparks.

Henderson backed into a shelving storage unit and before he could look for a weapon of his own, Potter approached and took another swing. This time, the bar struck the shelf above the DI's head, leaving a large dent.

Henderson jumped to the side, and decided to make a run for it just as Potter lifted the bar again, a bit slower this time, the bar's weight and vibration starting to hinder him. In what seemed like slow motion, the DI spotted that the shelving unit where he had been standing was swaying. Before Potter could react, several boxes lying on an upper shelf fell and struck him on the head and shoulder. He dropped unconscious to the floor.

SEVENTY-THREE

Henderson could count on the fingers of one hand the times he'd wanted to read about himself in a newspaper. Often, the coverage was critical or downright vindictive. This time he made an exception.

The pictures accompanying many of the articles, probably taken by one of the ground staff at the airport, or a passenger who had sneaked downstairs to witness the incident, looked dramatic. They showed Henderson and a handcuffed Lucas Potter, while all around were sited enormous planes, fuel tankers, pushback tugs, and at the back, a fire crew.

For sure it had excited his colleagues at Malling House, and those at Brighton Police Station. All morning his phone had beeped with a succession of texts, phone calls, and emails from envious officers. He knew many of them coveted airport duty as they saw it as glamorous and exciting, but he hadn't quite realised the depth of feeling.

Potter had been kept in hospital overnight on Monday for observation and possible concussion, and to treat the cuts and abrasions, the result of boxes of alternators and fuel pumps falling on his head. Doctors cleared him to be released into police custody the following morning, and at this moment he was warming a seat in the Interview Suite.

Meanwhile, Sean Houghton was walking around like a cat with two tails. Hadn't he told everyone Lucas Potter was guilty?

His phone rang.

'Hi there Inspector Henderson, it's Geoff. I'm over at Potter Security in Crawley. I think you should sit down for this one.'

'I am.'

'In a filing cabinet, and not filed under "knife" or "murder weapon" or anything stupid like that, but lying underneath the files, we found a broad-bladed knife.'

Henderson sat up. 'Well done, Geoff. Does it have a serrated edge on one side?'

'It does.'

In the forensic report, Grafton had expanded his description of the blade used to kill Roger Maitland to include a serration to one side. It was a common feature on many such knives, but nevertheless the finding interested him.

'Get it down to the lab as soon as. I need to know if traces of Roger Maitland's blood are on it.'

'I will, but I anticipate a problem.'

'Which is?'

'Your popularity with the lab is at an all-time low after you gave them all of Doug Blackford's weapon stash to analyse.'

He laughed. 'Assure them this is the last. I won't bother them again, not until the next time at any rate.'

Geoff laughed. 'I'll see what I can do.'

He gathered his papers together, collected Walters from the Detectives' Room and walked towards the Interview Suite.

'What's the strategy?' she asked.

'We try to establish the relationship between him and Blackford; see if we can destroy his confidence in his criminal friend.'

With the administrative tasks complete, Henderson took a good look at Lucas Potter. His face bore many scratches and bruises, and according to the doctor, so did his elbows and knees. This time his brief, Raymond Jack, wore a more appropriate outfit, a suit and tie.

'How are you feeling Lucas?'

'Fine.'

'No painful injuries?'

He scoffed. 'This is nothing. An IED went off with me standing by, and again when an ammo dump exploded. I had worse injuries then.'

'I'm sure. What made you run?'

'What?'

'What's the attraction of Buenos Aires?'

'Me running? No, I wasn't. I wanted to go out there to see Rosie.'

'I don't believe you. According to our information, she's in Orlando.'

Walters passed to Lucas and his brief a copy of Rosie's flight roster. BA were now more responsive as Sally Graham had developed a good relationship with her counterpart at the airline.

'How do you...? Ah fuck it. I don't see why I shouldn't tell you. I needed to get away from you lot.'

'This is because you saw your mate, Doug Blackford, is now in custody helping us with our enquiries.'

'Don't make me laugh. A guy like that won't tell you diddly squat.'

'What makes you say that? Do you know him?'

'No, I don't. Never heard of him before I read a story in a newspaper.'

'Lucas you're not a good liar. How can you be sure he wouldn't rat on you if you don't know him?'

'He's a criminal, I sort of assumed that's what they're all like.'

'Don't take me for a fool. When we searched Blackford's house, we found a load of military memorabilia. Some of it inscribed with the name of your regiment, and other pieces with your name on them.'

Walters passed over photographs of the items. The shocked look on Potter's face spoke volumes.

'You gave him the gear, maybe for his collection, either because you wanted to stay on his good side, or because you needed him to do something for you.'

'Nah, you're wide of the mark.'

'No? Then tell me how it is.'

He said nothing.

'C'mon Lucas, it's obvious to me the two of you know one another.'

He gave a long sigh. Henderson expected another, *Ah, fuck it. I don't see why I shouldn't tell you,* but he didn't get it. 'He got in touch with me when he found out about my connection with Vixen. We got talking and he said he liked military stuff, so I gave him some of mine.'

'That's not all, is it?'

'What do you mean?'

'We've been in contact with your old regiment. It seems they've a problem with weapons going missing. Ring any bells?'

He shook his head.

'Some of the guns in Doug Blackford's collection are British Army issue.' He looked at Potter for confirmation, but an impassive face stared back. 'However, it'll take some time to verify where they came from. Were you selling guns to Blackford?'

'Hell no. He's a serious criminal, for God's sake. Why would I?'

'Why does anyone? For money, for the power. I think you sold guns to him, and maybe you found there's a market out there, so you stole some more.'

'You do not have any evidence to support those outrageous allegations, Inspector,' Raymond Jack said. 'You are doing nothing but fishing.'

'I'm simply putting the pieces of the jigsaw down on the table and hoping Mr Potter will supply the missing ones.'

'Fat chance,' Potter said.

'You said earlier, Lucas, Doug got in touch with you because of your connection with Vixen.'

'Yeah.'

'What's the connection?'

Like a lightbulb being switched on, Potter all of a sudden realised he had just given the DI a golden ticket, allowing him to connect the two men. He went into an immediate and frantic confab with his brief, and it didn't come as a surprise when Jack requested a short recess. Henderson and Walters retired to the coffee machine in the corridor outside.

SEVENTY-FOUR

'I think we're on the home straight,' Walters said. She took a sip from the sickly looking brew that had just poured out of the coffee machine and winced at the sour taste.

'I'm not so confident. If he clams up and offers nothing, we'll have to wait for the analysis of the knife.'

'He's admitted some things, which gives us greater insight into what had been going on.'

'Yeah, for sure, the Potter-Blackford link is a good one, but there's more to tell on the guns, I suspect.'

'It isn't such a big leap, don't you think, for Blackford to suggest: you kill one and I'll do the other?'

'I've been thinking about that. Blackford is a right nasty sort and I think when the ransom payments stopped, he initially decided to kill Maitland and Grange on his own.'

'But he says he didn't.'

'No. He gave Maitland to someone else who wanted it more. That's what he said. I'm convinced he meant Potter.'

'If it wasn't him, who else? No one we've come across has the same level of grudge.'

'There's Doug's brother, but he's locked up, you said. If Potter doesn't come up with anything useful, we might have to look again at Mark, find out if he was released on bail or the charges dropped.'

'Will do.'

A head appeared from the interview room doorway. 'Shall we continue?' Raymond Jack said.

The detectives threw their empty cups into the recycling bin and made their way down the corridor.

'We established in the first part of the interview,' Henderson said when they resumed, 'that you, Lucas, are a good friend of Doug Blackford.'

'I wouldn't say a good friend.'

'What would you say?'

'An acquaintance.'

'A man who you occasionally did some business with?'

'Yeah, he took an interest in my security business, asked if we did personal security, but I told him we didn't.'

'When we searched your offices, Lucas, we found this in a filing cabinet.'

Walters passed over a photograph of the knife discovered by Geoff.

'Fucking hell!' he exploded as he jumped out of his seat. 'Al was supposed to ditch it!'

'Lucas, be quiet!' his brief hissed.

'How can I be quiet? This will fucking hang me!'

Henderson let Potter's anger continue, but Raymond Jack soon brought him back to his senses and he returned to his seat.

'We haven't yet analysed this knife, Mr Potter, but by the sound of it, we'll find traces of Roger Maitland on it.'

'How do you know it won't be Lester Grange?'

'Because Doug Blackford told us.'

There are few times in life when a single sentence makes a significant impact on the receiver. It occurs most frequently, Henderson suspected, in a medical context, when a patient is informed their pain or shortness of breath is caused by something more sinister. This was one such time. Potter's face visibly fell when hearing his comrade in crime had revealed their big secret.

Henderson waited, it felt like minutes, for Potter to respond. No way would he or Walters say anything to break the tension.

'When he first contacted me about Vixen,' Potter said, staring at a point on the wall behind Henderson's head, 'he told me Maitland had murdered his mother.'

'How did that make you feel?'

'Angry, really fucking angry. This is a guy my father worked with; a man he trusted. We got talking and you're right, Doug liked guns and stuff so I gave him some of my stuff. One day he says to me, *I want to kill Maitland and Grange.* I said, *go ahead mate, I'll not stop you or say anything.* Then he said, *what if you do one and I do the other?*'

'How did you react?'

'I could hardly say to him I'm not doing it because I've never killed anyone before, as it would be a lie. I thought about it for no more than a few minutes and said, *why the hell not?* But listen, I didn't do it for the money as all the papers are saying, or for them to hand back Dad's shares or anything. You have to understand this.'

'I do.'

'I did it for revenge. Cold, bloody revenge. I hated Maitland for the way he treated Dad and for killing Doug's mother. I did the world a favour getting rid of an odious individual.'

Henderson and Walters left the interview room ten minutes later.

She blew out a puff of air. 'Boy, was that intense.'

'I think he realised he'd been backed into a corner with no way out. When he believed Blackford had cracked, although we know he didn't, it all spilled out.'

'It'll make for an interesting trial. The defence will paint Maitland in the blackest of terms and suggest both men were provoked. A trial more about emotion than money, I think.'

'I'm sure they will,' he said, 'but Blackford's blackmailing of Maitland will counter that sentiment to some degree.'

'I'm surprised you didn't mention it to Potter.'

'I intended to, if he continued to deny knowing Blackford, or if he still thought of him as the noble criminal, out to avenge a wrong done to him.'

'It does dent his halo somewhat.'

'I think this calls for a celebration tonight. Ask Phil to organise something; I haven't had a decent drink in ages.'

SEVENTY-FIVE

'Another pint, gov?'

Henderson held up his near-empty glass. 'Thanks, Phil, I don't mind if I do.'

For a change, the team had selected a pub in Kemptown for their celebratory drink which gave Henderson a short walk back to his apartment. Therefore, he didn't need to be mindful about how much he drank as he wasn't driving home, and as additional security, he had arranged to take the following day off.

'Potter surprised everybody,' Sally Graham said.

'You think?'

'Those little hints you dropped about Doug Blackford giving him up must have helped change his mind.'

'I'm not so sure. Doug Blackford is a serious criminal and I'm quite convinced Potter thought he wouldn't give anyone up.'

'Nevertheless, when the chips were down, he didn't hold back.'

'You're right, and I've been wondering about that. Did he know the knife we found in his office would have Roger Maitland's blood on it? If he did, he had nothing to lose by telling all.'

'We haven't had it back from forensics yet, have we?'

He laughed. 'My reputation's shot in that department. It'll take weeks.' He finished the beer in his glass. 'You see, I'd assumed Potter killed Maitland for being the main barrier to him and his mother getting what had been denied, Jerome's shares in Vixen. With Maitland out of the way, he could work on Adrian Chapman and in the end, he may have given them something.'

'I thought so too.'

'Thinking about it now, any award of shares in Vixen would have gone to his mother, not to Lucas, and as we all know, the two of them don't get on.'

'Of course.'

'I believe him when he says he didn't do it for the money, or getting the shares back. They weren't a consideration at all. He killed Roger Maitland because he hated the way his father had been humiliated. It wasn't about money or compensation; it's nothing more complicated than cold-blooded revenge.'

'A pint of Sussex Best for you, gov, and a G&T for the lovely Sally.'

'Thanks Phil.'

'Thanks.'

'I can't get my head around the gap,' Graham said, 'you know, the time between Jerome losing his job and Maitland being murdered.'

'A couple of things were involved. Lucas was still in the army when his father was fired from Vixen, but more important was the blackmail racket Blackford executed with Maitland. He planned it to run for five years, extracting a million, but when Maitland stopped paying, Blackford then decided to kill him.'

'Do we know why he stopped paying?'

'He wasn't short of cash, if anything he'd become richer than the year before. My guess is he felt emboldened, thinking he could counter any threat, perhaps because of his contacts in the military.'

He took a sip from his pint. The second, or third, in this case, never tasted as good as the first, but he enjoyed it nevertheless.

'I don't think they met as Potter said they did,' Henderson continued, 'Blackford contacting him about their shared interest in Vixen. I bet it was over an arms deal, Potter selling guns to Blackford's lot, the Clapham Crew. He and Blackford got talking and realised they had something else in common. When Maitland stopped paying the blackmail money, Blackford then contacted Potter and told him if he wanted to kill Maitland, he would help him.'

'The choice of knives rather than guns is a strange one. They had plenty, as both men bought and sold the things, and Blackford even had his own private collection.'

'I think Blackford wanted Maitland and Grange to die slowly and in pain, and he persuaded Potter to go along with it. Also, guns leave irrefutable evidence not only at the scene, but on clothes and hands. Knives, if cleaned in bleach, or something similarly caustic, leave no such traces.'

'Lucky for us Blackford's knife wasn't cleaned too thoroughly.'

'And I think it'll be the same for Potter's. There's a good dose of arrogance in both men, perhaps thinking no one would make the connection between them and Maitland and Grange, leaving them in the clear.'

'Did anyone find out what happened to Barbara Hines?'

'In every case there's always one loose end. In this instance, I think this is it.'

The End

About the Author

Iain Cameron grew up in Glasgow and moved to Brighton in the early eighties. He has worked as a management accountant, business consultant and a nursery goods retailer. He is now a full-time writer and lives in a village outside Horsham in West Sussex with his wife and a lively Collie dog.

Flying too High is the twelfth book to feature DI Angus Henderson, the Scottish cop at Sussex Police.

For more information about books and the author:
Visit the website at: www.iain-cameron.com
Follow him on twitter: @iainsbooks
Follow him on facebook @iaincameronauthor

Also by Iain Cameron

DI Angus Henderson Crime Novels

One Last Lesson
A popular university student is found dead on a rural golf course. DI Angus Henderson hasn't a clue as the killer did a thorough job. That is, until he discovers she was once a model on an adult web site run by two of her tutors.

Driving into Darkness
A gang of car thieves are smashing down doors and stealing expensive cars. Their violence is escalating and the DI is fearful they will soon kill someone. They do, but is it cover for something else?

Fear the Silence
A missing woman is not what DI Henderson needs right now. She is none other than Kelly Langton, the former glamour model 'Kelly,' and now an astute businesswoman, so the tabloid press are baying for a result. Her husband stands accused, but then another woman goes missing.

Hunting for Crows
A man's body is recovered from the swollen River Arun, drowned in a vain attempt to save his dog. The story interests DI Henderson as the man was once a member of a rock band he liked. When another former band member dies, exercising in his home gym, the DI can no longer ignore the coincidence.

Red Red Wine
A ruthless gang of wine counterfeiters have already killed one man and will stop at nothing to protect a lucrative trade making them millions. Henderson suspects Daniel Perry, a London gangster, is behind the gang. He is cautioned to tread carefully, but no one warned him to safeguard those closest to him.

Night of Fire
A body is discovered burned to death, the victim a member of a Lewes bonfire society. Henderson suspects another society is behind it, and with Bonfire Night approaching, he fears it will provide cover for another heinous act. It does, but not one he was expecting.

Girls on Film
A photographer is abducted from her rural studio. DI Henderson finds several witnesses, but no motive. He's convinced the answer lies in the photographer's busy lifestyle: previous boyfriends, environmental campaigning or in the photographs she took. Problem is, her back catalogue runs into millions.

Black Quarry Farm
Holidaying in a rented house at a beautiful vineyard, an innocent couple are shot to death in their beds. Suspicions falls on workers at the vineyard, including the owner, who counts several serious villains as friends.

Blood Marked Pages
A Brighton-based crime author is found stabbed to death in his home - a burglary gone wrong, or a reader taking exception to one of his books? Items scattered over the lounge suggest the killer was looking for something - but what?

Dying for Justice

A defence lawyer is found stabbed to death in his office. DI Henderson realises his late-night appearance wasn't to further the case of a needy client, but to sleep off a heavy night's boozing. Was his murder collateral damage during a burglary, or the work of a disappointed client desperate for revenge?

Pictures of Lily

A single bullet wound to the head killed Lily Osborne. Henderson is puzzled, as her ordinary lifestyle is at odds with her brutal slaying. Is it a case of mistaken identity, or was Lily keeping a secret the DI has yet to discover?

The Essential DI Henderson Box Set – Books 1-4

The Essential DI Henderson Box Set2 – Books 5-8

Matt Flynn Thrillers

The Pulsar Files

Matt Flynn of the Homeland Security Agency, is hunting the sudden UK appearance of a Serbian hitman. The only incident that might interest a top-notch sniper is a hot-air balloon crash in Oxford. It killed five people, including three members of the same family.

Deadly Intent

A dissident terrorist group are hell-bent on starting civil war in Ireland. Alarm bells sound when it's discovered they have purchased a large consignment of weapons from Syrian rebels. Matt Flynn and Rosie Fox of HSA are ordered to stop them.

No Time to Lose

Matt is hunting the kidnappers of David Burke, a senior MI5 man. He attacks and disables a Turkish terrorist group but then another man goes missing, this time a senior detective. Matt knows both victims and soon realises the connection is a voice from the past that won't let go.

Sharma & Jackson Crime Thrillers

Eyes on You

Two men try to abduct Norwich businessman, Sean Morgan in Paris. After spending a night on the cold streets, the police take him back to his hotel. There, a gunman is waiting. Norwich police are treating him as a missing person, but is Sean really innocent or is he harbouring a dangerous secret?

All books are available from Amazon

A Small Request

If you have read any of my books, I would be grateful if you could please leave a review on Amazon. It's the best way for you to voice your opinion about something you loved, liked or hated, and it helps other readers to make an informed purchase decision.

Printed in Great Britain
by Amazon